BIRD ON A BLADE

A SLASHER ROMANCE

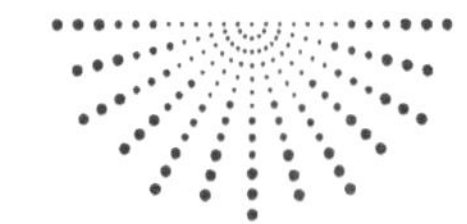

ROSE BITTERLY

Thanks so much for picking up *Bird on a Blade!* This is a dark horror romance featuring a morally black hero. It's also heavily inspired by the slasher movies of the '80s and '90s.

As you might expect, it contains some potentially upsetting subject matter.

Because a certain online bookseller has a history of removing books with comprehensive content warnings, I have opted to put the full, detailed list of both triggers and sexual content notes on my website, which you can access at rosebitterly.com/content-notes or via the QR code below:

Once you're on the site, just click or tap on the book's title to expand the full list of warnings.

However, there are a few triggers that I did want to list here:

- Graphic depictions of sex and violence. Please see the website link for more details.
- Domestic assault (occurs in flashback; NOT between MCs)
- Non-graphic depiction of SA (NOT between MCs)
- Discussion of anorexia and disordered eating behaviors
- Fatphobia (NOT from MMC), including some internalized fatphobia from the FMC

If you have any questions or would like further clarification, don't hesitate to contact me via the form on my website.

-Rose Bitterly

PROLOGUE

SAWYER

August nights are the first gasp of summer's death. There's a chill that creeps into them like in a drafty old house; you can feel the leaves curling into themselves, the green starting to burn away. If you're really lucky, a fog rises up from the valley, cobwebbing the forest.

I think that's why I've always found August the sweetest time for killing.

I slide through the silent camp, heavy boots thudding softly against the grass. Three of them are dead already. I hunt the fourth now, a boy with shorn hair and big muscles. I've no doubt he'll put up a fight, but it'll be mostly bluster.

A crack of movement from my left. I turn in time to see a pale blur shoot out of one of the cabins. It's him. He pants as he runs, arms pumping like a track star. He doesn't see me.

He's heading for the dining hall, probably assuming he can call for help there. He can't; I already saw to that. Cut the landlines. Smashed the CB radio and all their cell phones. If he thinks he can get to a phone, then they aren't communicating with each other, like the cruel, stupid children that they are.

I let him think he's safe. I let him slam, panicked, into the dining hall. Then I walk slowly through the shadows, clutching my Bowie knife at my side, the blade wiped clean of blood. I like the way it catches the moonlight, flashing cataracts of terror into their faces right before they die.

He barred the dining hall door, half-heartedly. I consider creeping around the back. It's a big building; it has three entrances and at least one of them I doubt this stupid boy knows anything about. But it's late. I want to be done by sunrise.

So I shove the door open with a clatter, stacked chairs flying and splintering against the old linoleum. The light is on, sallow and buzzing. Footsteps echo from the kitchen. I go there, slow and deliberate, squeezing my fingers more tightly around the knife handle. He's panicked; I can hear his breathing even though he's not running. A low, keening whimper that makes me smile.

I shove through the swinging kitchen doors, and there he is, crouched next to the big industrial refrigerator, a pale glowing rectangle in one hand.

A cell phone. My heart rate spikes. I thought I had destroyed all of them—

Not hers.

How does this worm have her cell phone? Did she leave it in here? I hadn't sought it out when I was destroying the others—I'd left it for her. A gift, I guess. I knew it was a loose end, of course, but I had planned to work quickly.

"He's here!" the boy shrieks. A voice spills out of the other end of the phone, tinny and distant. "He's—"

I swing my knife and spear the phone, setting aside the quiver of regret. It's just a phone.

The boy scrambles away, too panicked to move properly. His feet tangle underneath him, and he falls on his ass, face lifted to me, features twisted in fear.

Maybe he isn't going to put up a fight, after all.

I grab him by the hem of his shirt, HEAD START FITNESS CAMP emblazoned across his chest, and then slam him up against the wall. He howls and kicks uselessly at me, face red with terror. I study him for a minute. It's always an odd moment, seeing them up close for the first time after weeks of watching from the woods. It solidifies them. Makes them real.

"No," he begs, a few fat tears streaking over his cheeks. "You don't have to do this. You don't—"

I slide the knife into his side, positioning it just beneath his ribs, and then jerk it sideways so that a hot, pleasant waterfall of blood and viscera splatters across my chest. He twitches in my grip, one last gasp of life that I breathe into my lungs. My body shudders with pleasure, and I let him fall like old meat.

There's a long stretch of silence.

And then I hear it. Soft, sweet whimpering.

Her.

My heart twists with excitement, knowing that she's seen all I've done for her. I turn slowly, trying not to betray that excitement, and find her standing in the doorway of the kitchen, one hand on the frame as if she can barely hold herself up. This is the closest I've ever been to her since I first saw her through the dappled light of the trees.

She stares at me, eyes wide as saucers, plush body trembling. Blood stains the shirt stretched across her ample chest, and I startle at that, I'll admit—it means she helped one of my victims, maybe provided them comfort as they lay dying. But why, when they've been so unrelentingly cruel to her for the last two months?

I step toward her, and she doesn't move except to part her lips slightly, her terrified gaze drinking me. I wear my mask, the mask that at this point is a second skin. I consider taking it off, showing her who I am, but something stays my hand. Her fear, maybe. I don't particularly want her to be afraid.

I take another step, half-expecting her to bolt like the feral cats that live around my house high up on the mountain. But she doesn't, and that makes my heart flutter weirdly and my stomach knot up. Like maybe she's not as untouchable as I thought. Like maybe I'll be able to reach out and run my fingers over her thick black hair and smooth, satiny skin.

Another step. She whimpers, then slaps her hand over her mouth. Her eyes gleam with tears, and I realize she's dropped her gaze down to my Bowie knife, which I hold unthreateningly at my side, even as it drips blood across the tile.

"Shh," I say, as if I'm talking to the cats. Her eyes, somehow, go a little wider. "Don't be afraid."

She whimpers again, that low keening sound that makes the skin on the back of my neck prickle. Her fear is delicious to me. I won't deny it.

Okay, so maybe I do want her a little afraid after all.

I keep moving toward her, talking in that same quiet voice I use on the cats. "You're safe," I tell her. "You don't have to worry. They can't hurt you anymore."

With that last sentence, something changes in her expression. A flash of confusion.

"I took care of them for you," I say, just as I realize I'm close enough to touch her. Her eyes keep dropping down to my knife. Does she really think I'm going to kill her?

So I slam my knife in the wall beside her head, the blade thrumming. She jumps and screams but makes no move for it.

And then I encircle her in my arms, hardly believing myself.

She stiffens, her breath fast and panicky. I can feel the wild, frantic thudding of her heart. But she doesn't push me away. She doesn't try to grab the knife.

I knew we were meant for each other.

I pull her into me, delirious at her closeness. Her fear has a wildness to it, like the scent of pine needles, and I breathe her in through my mask, cupping my hand against the back of her head.

Her hair is as soft as I had imagined.

"Don't worry," I whisper against her. "Don't be scared. They can't hurt you anymore. I won't let them hurt you ever again."

She makes a sound like a sob, a kind of wet choking. I gently pull her around so that she can look out at the dining room and not at the body of the boy who tormented her the most. I was there when he screamed at her that she was lazy and fat and stupid as she begged him for a rest. I watched him taunt her with food when she was hungry. I heard the terrible things he said about her, laughing with the others, what a waste it was that her body has the lushness I find so appealing.

I relish that lushness now. That softness.

"Don't worry," I tell her. I keep saying it, over and over, wanting her to believe me. "He can't hurt you now. I took care of him for you."

And then something magical happens.

She hugs me back.

She hugs me back.

She lifts her arms, slow and hesitant, and wraps them around my waist, barely touching me. When she sobs again, I realize she's crying, a wet spot forming on my shoulder.

"Shh," I say, and her body shakes against mine. I pull her a little closer. I wonder if she feels my cock. It's painfully hard from the killing, and from her.

Would she let me do that to her? Lie her down on the cold and bloody floor and fuck her? I don't want to push my luck, even if every nerve in my body is screaming at me to do it, to slice her blood-streaked clothes away with my knife and kiss and bite at the soft flesh of her breasts until she's moaning instead of crying.

No. No, I don't want to risk her bolting like one of the cats and me having to chase her through the woods. Too much can hurt her out there, especially in the dark.

Still, restraint is hard for me, and I clutch a handful of her hair and then kiss her head through the mask. She gasps but doesn't let go, and I think that Mama was wrong, that people like us can find Heaven because this is it, right here, the girl I've watched all summer gasping in my arms, her breasts pressed against my chest, her body hot and soft and yielding.

It's as perfect as late summer.

It's so perfect that I don't hear the dining hall door scrape open, I don't hear the footsteps on the linoleum. I don't hear anything until I hear the hammer of a gun clicking into place—

And then a bullet tears through my brain.

CHAPTER ONE

EDIE

FIFTEEN YEARS LATER

I kill my car's engine and sit, hands resting on the steering wheel, staring out at the camp through the windshield. The past fifteen years have certainly taken their toll. The dining hall is gone, of course. The paint on the buildings is faded and peeling off in long strips, and there are boards hammered over all the windows save for the counselors' cabin, the only part of the camp that's been in use since that night.

When you get overwhelmed, Dr. Valunzuela always says, *deep breaths. Clear your thoughts.*

I'm not exactly overwhelmed right now, but I do it anyway.

Four deep breaths.

Empty my head.

Listen to my body.

I pull the keys out of the ignition and step out of the car. It feels good to move after four hours on the road, winding through the Appalachian Mountains without stopping so I could just get here and know if I'd made the right choice, booking a two-month-long stay at the site of the infamous Fat Camp Killing Spree, as the website had so helpfully categorized this particular short-term rental.

God, I hate that fucking name.

It's September, and the air is cool and breezy. The camp's more peaceful than I've ever known it—certainly more peaceful than it was the last time I was here, covered in Sawyer Caldwell's blood and brain matter while cops and EMTs and tenacious locals swarmed around in the pinkish dawnlight.

I shove the memory aside, something that became second nature years ago when the Fat Camp Killing Spree was still the worst thing that had ever happened to me.

I pull out my suitcase—sparsely packed with a few essentials I bought before I fled the Bay Area—and drag it up to the counselors' cabin. I've never actually been in here, despite being a regular at this place back when it was still Head Start Fitness Camp and not just *that fat camp where a bunch of people died*. The keypad works like the instructions said it would, and when I push into the cabin, I'm pleasantly surprised by how clean and neat it is. An overstuffed couch in the common area. A big flat-screen TV. Pots and pans in the kitchen. A Keurig machine on the counter. I'll need to go into town for groceries.

The only thing that ruins the decor are the framed newspaper articles on the wall about the murders. The one in the kitchen even has a picture of me, my school picture, eighteen-year-old Edie smiling like she doesn't hate herself next to a big black headline screaming, FOUR DEAD, ONE SURVIVOR IN BRUTAL SLAYINGS.

I take it off the wall and slide it in the gap between the counter and the refrigerator.

Only one person who knows who I am knows that I'm here: my best friend Charlotte, who helped me with the preparations in those frantic hours after my husband—ex-husband?—Scott nearly killed me. I'd been planning to leave for good, and he found out.

When I told her where I wanted to go, she had been driving me into San Francisco so I could buy a car in cash, the sun just starting to stain the sky with a rosé sunrise. My left eye was swollen completely shut, instead of partially shut, like it is now. My voice still rasped from where he nearly crushed my trachea.

Charlotte's mouth dropped open and she hissed, "Are you fucking insane?"

But I only shrugged. "It's the last place he'll ever look for me."

"Until it's all over the fucking Internet that Edie Astor's back at the site of the murders!"

I stared out at the blur of a highway. My entire body ached—that's what I remember most. "I'll use a different name," I said numbly. "It's been fifteen years. No one in town's going to recognize me."

"What's the real reason?"

"I told you. It's the last place Scott will look for me." Because he had known all the places to look for me in California. Sent his PIs trailing me to my therapy appointments, my shopping trips. I couldn't go anywhere without Scott watching me.

But I knew, even then, he wouldn't find me in Virginia.

"Besides—" I turned toward her. She was squeezing the steering wheel, eyes fixed on the road, worry lines creasing in her brow. "I need the reminder of what I'm capable of surviving."

I think that was what did it. She nodded and sank back into the car seat. Six hours later, I was driving south down I-5, through the desert. Alone.

I hadn't lied to Charlotte. All the memories of that night, all the blood, the screaming—

the killer

—it feels so far away now. Something terrible happened to me, yes, but I walked away from it. I'd been face to face with the now-infamous killer Sawyer Caldwell himself and survived without so much as a bruise.

Not that I ever, ever told anyone what that encounter had really been like. Not even Charlotte.

I have bruises now, though, even four days later. All over my wrists, ringing around my neck. The swelling in my eye has gone down enough that I can see out of it, at least, but I'll need to wear sunglasses in town. They'll hide the cut on my cheek, too, from where Scott's ring sliced me open.

I saw Sawyer Caldwell's knife dripping with blood, but it was my husband's wedding ring that actually cut me.

Four deep breaths. I count them in my head. When I'm done, I text Charlotte to let her know I've arrived, and then I wheel my suitcase into the hallway and pick the largest of the bedrooms, the head counselor's room. It would have belonged to Lindsay Kirtle fifteen years ago, but she hadn't been there that night.

That's the thing about the infamous fat camp killings. They didn't technically happen at a fat camp.

It's a piece of trivia that pedants love, the sort of thing they'll trot out when they need a trick question at a trivia content. *Name the camp where the Fat Camp Killings took place* and someone who read the Wikipedia entry two years ago after listening to a podcast will shout, "Head Start Fitness Camp!" and then the emcee will shake their head ruefully and say, "I'm sorry, but *technically* Head Start Fitness Camp was closed for the season."

And that is true. The camp was closed for the year, but five of us were still on the campgrounds because my mother paid the camp owner $10,000 for the cruelest counselors to work with me, one-on-one, for an entire week after the camp closed. A last-ditch effort to make me thin before I went off to Stanford and embarrassed her for being fat.

That's why Lindsay Kirtle wasn't there the night of the killings, or Maggie, the swimming instructor who snuck us joints after hours. Or Vic, the Yoga guy who told us how beautiful we all were after his sessions. My mother didn't want anyone who'd tell me I was beautiful. She wanted me to be humiliated. She probably thought she might finally kickstart me into an eating disorder—which, admittedly, did happen, in a roundabout way.

Four deep breaths.

I need to get groceries.

The thought of getting back in my car makes me vaguely queasy after the long drive from the last hotel, and Altarida, the nearest town, is only about a thirty-minute walk on the little hiking trail that winds away from camp. I won't be able to bring much back with me, but I can fill up my backpack to get me covered for tonight.

I have to resist the voice, quieter now but still there, that tells me not to go at all, to just skip dinner and breakfast, it's no big deal, just intermittent fasting, right?

I grab my backpack and stalk outside. My phone dings.

CHARLOTTE

Thank God. Scott still hasn't reached out to me at all. I think you're in the clear.

I doubt that very much, but it's still a nice thought.

The sunlight is warm and dappled with streaks of green from the fluttering trees. I find the hiking trail easily, even though the sign's been knocked over and tall grass creeps around it. The trail itself isn't terrible. I wonder if someone's maintained it. The camp's owner, maybe.

The forest settles around me. It's too late in the year for the cicadas, and it feels quiet without them, even though there are other familiar sounds, like the faint hum of grasshoppers and twittering bird song. When I was at Head Start—the actual camp, not my mom's $10,000 torture session—we used to walk to town every Sunday and spend the day buzzing between the little shops on Main Street. There was a comic book store for a while and a candy shop we'd sneak into when the counselors weren't paying attention. One of those touristy five and dimes. It's surprisingly easy to let those happier memories wash over me.

But then I hear a snap in the woods, a broken branch, and my heart jitters up in my chest. *Just a squirrel,* I tell myself. Still, I glance at the densely woven trees, half-expecting to see a flash of pale mask.

He's dead. He is dead. I saw him die. He was holding me when he died. I saw his body afterward, the mask shattered and half his head gone, a red spongy cavity where his brain should have been. I'd thrown up, retching and choking while Deputy Crosier, the one who'd been on patrol outside the camp and gotten there so quickly, just stared at the body, hands shaking.

Sawyer Caldwell is dead.

But two officers had still come to visit me the day after the murders. I was back home in Arlington by then. They sat down in the formal living room and looked at me and told me they were posting an officer outside the house for the time being, because Sawyer Caldwell's body had disappeared.

I push on down the trail. I know Sawyer Caldwell isn't in the woods. It's just a squirrel I heard. Just some animal stepping on a decayed branch.

And what threat is Sawyer Caldwell to me now, anyway?

It's Scott I have to worry about. My husband, still. Technically.

But he won't find me here, either. I'm alone. I'm safe. I'm registered under the name Hayley Lace.

I've got two months to figure out what I'm going to do next.

So I keep walking through the woods, fingers curled around the straps of my backpack. I got this far. I won't be undone by noises in the forest.

CHAPTER TWO

SAWYER

Fifteen years in the dirt.

It's been nearly a week and I'm still reeling from it, truth be told. Fifteen goddamn years. I knew the first few times would take longer; Mama and Ambrose had both warned me about that. They said that the first few times take a while, and then each time after that it gets a little shorter and it's easy going for a while and you don't mind dying. Then, eventually, it gets longer again, not months or years but decades. Centuries. But I won't have to be worry about that for a long, long time.

Still. Fifteen years.

Everything's changed. My house is gone, nothing but the foundation and the fireplace, which means they took all my stuff, too. The various knives I'd accumulated. My machete. My bones! I'd collected so many, severing them from their bodies and burying them in the backyard with a little plastic flag so the worms could do all the hard work of cleaning off the meat and all I had to do was polish them up.

I don't even have the Bowie knife I used to kill those hateful counselors since it was still jammed in the wall when I got shot.

The camp is different, too. That was the second place I went when I woke up four days ago, after the house. It's all boarded up and overgrown now, save for one cabin. No trace of the dining hall, either; they must have torn it down, too. That, more than the house, makes me sad.

Because for the whole fifteen years that I was in the ground, healing from the gunshot, I thought about her. Her frightened, wide eyes and soft creamy flesh. The damp salt of her tears. Her scent. When all I could smell was dirt and rot I'd think about that scent, piney and sweet, and I'd be back in the dining hall and she'd be in my arms and it'd be perfect again, the closest thing to Heaven my people will ever see.

That first day after I revived, I just wandered around the camp 'cause it was empty and abandoned and I needed to recollect my memories. All I'd held on to in the dirt was her, Edie Astor, and it got me through the worst of things, but I needed to think more clearly now that I was out in the open. Now that I was alive again. At that point, I didn't even know how long it'd been.

The human scent on the camp was faint, like humans come around occasionally but hadn't been there for a little while, so it surprised me when I found that one of the cabins didn't look all broken down like the others. It had a fresh coat of paint and the grass around it was cut short, not overgrown like the rest of the camp. The front door had a digital lock on it, but I was able to jimmy in through the back window.

It was nice inside, decorated and all, but it didn't smell like someone lived there. My people, we can sniff out humans, and my senses were heightened from coming alive again. Everything was new and fresh and working properly, and this place reminded me of the scents in a motel, where no one stays long enough for things to linger. There were other signs, too, like how there were pots and pans in the kitchen but no food, and how the closets were empty. It was kind of like how the camp used to be, although I didn't know why it was just this one cabin and not all of them.

I decided not to worry about it. I took a long hot steamy

shower and stroked my cock for the first time in what felt like decades, groaning as I shot my load down the drain, thinking about Edie the whole time. Then I got out and dried off and walked around the cabin naked, flinging open closet doors until I finally found some clean clothes folded up in the attic storage, jeans and a T-shirt that were a little too big for me. I kept my original boots 'cause they hadn't decayed like the rest of my clothes had.

Then I realized the big black mirror on the wall was the TV, one of those fancy flatscreens, and it took me some time to figure out how it all worked because it was hooked up to the Internet instead of having the staticky old stations I used to watch. That was also when I learned how long it had been because there was a date in the corner, and when I saw it I felt like I'd been shot again.

Fifteen fucking years.

Since then, I've focused on getting my wits about me and doing all the things Mama taught me. Went out to the spot in the woods where I'd buried my false IDs and the big coffee can of cash and my spare knife. Seeing that put me in the mind to kill, but I knew I had to get situated first.

Out here in southwest Virginia, there are lots of old abandoned houses if you know where to look, although what I eventually found wasn't a house at all but an old church, one of those tidy white ones with the steeple and all. I like it well enough. There's a little apartment in the back where the pastor would have lived, and I've been fixing it up the past few days, cleaning it real good because I don't want to feel like I'm in the dirt again. It's got well water, too, so I've got running water even if I don't have electricity. Eventually, I'm going to walk into Altarida and use the cash I buried to buy a pickup track and a generator and maybe some pantry food to go along with the venison I've been eating since I woke up. But I know I'm gonna need to kill someone before I do that. Being around humans with these heightened senses, smelling their blood and hearing their pulses—if I don't get a real kill first, who knows what I'll do in town?

But then something happens that changes my plans.

I smell it when I'm working in the church's overgrown graveyard, clearing away the sticker burrs growing around the gravestones. A sudden, hot flush of human blood.

I rise up from my crouch, sniffing the air. It's cool and breezy and the human blood scent is strong, which means they're nearby. My fingers flex at my side, and I turn, trying to place it.

Smells like it's coming from the camp.

I've got my knife on me, like always, and I creep out of the churchyard and into the woods. The camp's about a ten-minute walk, not far at all. Too close, Mama'd probably say, but the church is dilapidated and wild, set off from the hiking trails. I move through the trees, following the trail of blood. It pulses in my chest, singing out to me, and I ease the knife out of its holster to feel the weight of it in my hand. It's not as good as my Bowie knife, but the blade is sharp like moonlight. It'll get the job done.

When I reach the edge of the camp, I stick to the shadows, surveying the property. A sleek silver car is parked in front of the fixed-up cabin. I tuck myself into the trees, watching. Waiting. It feels good to be on the hunt again, the real hunt. Stalking deer for food isn't the same.

Something in the air shifts. The blood is on the move. A second later, the door swings open—

And I smell it. Pine and honeysuckle. The scent that kept me sane during the fifteen years I was in the ground. The scent of Heaven.

She's here.

Edie Astor steps out into the sunlight, and it's like the first time I saw her, fifteen years and one death ago. My body thrums. The air gets all tight and choking. I want to stare at her like a painting, want to learn all the ways her body can move. I want to pull her into me, consume her bite by bite until we're all tangled together and you can't tell me from her.

What I don't want to do is to kill her, even though it kind of feels the way it does when I see someone I want to kill, my nerves getting all jangly like Christmas lights. But she's just so beautiful, so pristine. It makes me want to protect her, I think. The perfect prey, too perfect even to kill.

She steps into the sunlight and stops, fingers curled around the straps of her backpack, her face tilted toward the sky. She looks older, of course, but I like it, the way her face seems more in focus somehow. Her hair is longer, falling in thick black curls around her shoulders. But she has that same lush body, all that softness I want to grab and squeeze and lick and bite.

Her shoulders hitch, and she turns toward the woods. That's when I see it.

She has a black eye and mottled bruises around her neck.

Both are probably a few days old, given the way they curdle at the edges a little. But I know what both of them mean.

Blood pounds in my ears. Who did this to her? Are they here? No, I only sense her blood. She's alone.

Is that why she's here? To escape whoever hurt her?

The dreamy floating feeling I get whenever I see her flushes away, replaced by a blinding, iridescent rage. As soon as I find out who did this to her, I'm going to cut them limb from limb and paint my body in their blood.

Just like I did fifteen years ago.

She walks past the silver car, and I realize she's going to the hiking trail that leads into Altarida. My rage quiets a little, calmed at the thought of being able to watch her for the next half hour. Just the two of us, alone in the forest. A Hunter and his perfect prey.

I melt into the trees and braid through the shadows, never letting her leave my sight.

CHAPTER THREE

EDIE

Altarida has barely changed in fifteen years. When the hiking trail spits me out of the woods and into the little weed-choked back lot behind the Altarida General Store, I have a weird, dizzying moment where I feel like I'm eighteen again, in those weeks before the murders. Before Sawyer Caldwell became the first pivot in my life, that clear demarcation of Before and After.

Four deep breaths. I suck them down, eyes closed. God, Altarida even *smells* the same, like barbecue smoke and diesel and forest mulch.

The breathing helps. I'm not eighteen. I'm thirty-three. I'm an adult woman, even if my life is currently in shambles.

I stride across the courtyard, happy to be off the hiking trail. It was a nice walk, but I still couldn't shake the feeling that someone was watching me from the trees. Charlotte would tell me it's a sign that I shouldn't be here, back in this place. She wanted me to go to New York, said she had some friends there who could take me in—but I was afraid that would be too easy for Scott to find. He'll hire the best PIs he can to track me down. Not because he *cares* about me, but because it embarrasses him, me leaving. I haven't even thought about how I'm going to file for divorce. Maybe I won't. Maybe I'll just stay here, buy a house as Hayley Lace, and live out my days in Altarida.

That, I think, is the real reason I feel like someone's watching me. Even now, I can feel it, as I step out of the courtyard and onto Main Street. Because even with all the steps I took to hide my tracks—fake names, buying a new car in cash and driving here cross-country instead of flying, never touching my credit card and bank accounts again except for the secret one Scott has no way of knowing about—I'm still afraid he's going to find me.

Find me. Beat me. Choke me. Drag me back to our mansion by the Pacific and lock the fucking food cabinets so I can't continue my recovery.

All so he doesn't get *embarrassed.*

The old anger flushes hot in my face. It's not even anger at him. It's anger at myself, for being taken in by him five years ago, all those pretty promises he made while his bashful nerdy tech guy persona hid the reality of a psychopath.

Hell, at least Sawyer Caldwell didn't pretend to be anything he wasn't. According to the police, he'd been living in an old farmhouse at the top of the mountain full of human remains. There's a red flag who doesn't try to patchwork over it with green.

I pull my sunglasses on now that I'm on Main Street and tug up my collar—not there's really anyone here to see me. No one comes up to the mountains in September. Too early for the fall leaves; too late for summer camping. Still, the stores are open. I duck into Altarida General, breathing in the scent of nostalgia. It looks like I remembered, sunny and dusty. The rows of soup cans and packages of gravy and boxed mac-and-cheese always look faded here, even though they're the same at any grocery store.

The produce section also leaves a lot to be desired. Some limp celery and carrots, a few bags of salad mix. Two years ago I would have clucked my tongue over it even though it could have been a full-on farmer's market of bounty and I'd still have only bought the celery to squeeze into juice.

I grab a bag of salad and pick up some dressing to go with it without even hesitating. In fact, I'm over in the canned goods aisle when I realize what I did, and my chest gets warm and I remind myself to text Charlotte to tell her that I still haven't relapsed. It was tough on the road, too easy to just skip meals instead of stopping at some gas station McDonald's. I'd start to feel that lightness in my thoughts, hazy and seductive. But Charlotte, bless her, texted me at meal times, chiding me to eat. I listened, most of the time.

Here, though, it doesn't feel so hard. I buy some nuts and sharp cheddar cheese and canned lentil soup to go with the salad. Instant oatmeal for breakfast. I'll have to drive to a real grocery store tomorrow.

"So what brings you to Altarida?" the cashier asks as he keys in each of the items.

I feel a moment of pure panic before I remember the story Charlotte suggested: "I'm an artist," I say, which is not true of me but is true of her. "I needed to get away for a while to work on my art."

The cashier smirks a little. "Staying at the old campgrounds?"

I sigh. "It was the only rental I could find around here."

"Hey, I ain't judging. It's a nice property. Just a shame about what happened is all." The register rings, and he gives me my total. I pay him. Cash.

"You should check out the bookstore," he tells me as I shove the food into my backpack. "Just opened up. It's artsy, you know."

A bookstore? Altarida's coming up in the world. "Where is it?"

"Two blocks down."

I thank him and step out of Altarida General and consider my options. There's no real reason for me to go back to the cabin just yet. It's not so hot that my food'll spoil. So I decide to check out the bookstore. Clear my thoughts. Ground myself here, in

Virginia, instead of letting my mind fly back to California and Scott and the night I left.

The breeze toys with my hair as I walk down the street, my backpack heavy on my shoulders. Everything's quiet and still, the street empty, but I still feel like someone's watching me. More than once I glance over my shoulder, the street dim behind my sunglasses, and expect to see some out-of-place man down the block and across the street. Any PI Scott hires won't ever really fit in here in Altarida; he'll have a slickness about him, a glossiness. He'll be too used to dealing with the ultra-wealthy.

But every time I turn around, there's no one, ill-suited or otherwise.

Still, I quicken my pace, muscles tight. My footsteps click against the sidewalk and I strain, listening for an echo, but there's nothing. Just a sense of unease, a prickling on the back of my neck like someone's watching me.

Maybe Charlotte's right. Maybe it is Altarida.

It's a relief when I get to the bookstore, the storefront window painted in pretty, swirling font: SWEET TIDINGS BOOK-SHOP. It's not just a bookstore; it's a bakery, too, with a big cartoon cupcake emblazoned across the glass.

My chest tightens, seeing that. But only a little.

I duck inside, bell chiming overhead. The cashier looks up and smiles; she looks like a college student, oversized glasses and a streak of pink in her hair. "Welcome to Sweet Tidings!" she calls out by rote. I smile at her as I move deeper into the store. It's split in half; books on one side, cupcakes on the other. I can smell them, the butter and sugar, and it makes the back of my jaw ache even as my chest squeezes tighter. A cold, raspy voice in the back of my head calculates calories and carbs, and I think of Charlotte and the weekly milk tea dates we started a year ago, and all the progress I've made.

I'm two years into recovery. I will not be frightened by a cupcake.

Still, I stick to the bookstore side, at least at first. Hardly anyone's in here. An old grey-haired woman browses through the romance section. The door chimes, and a man about my age comes in and immediately starts flipping through the latest #1 bestseller. He's the sort of man I remember always seeing in Altarida when I was younger: thin but wiry, a tangle of tousled dark hair, faint stubble across his jawline. He looks like he works with his hands for a living, which I'll admit appeals to me, after Scott and his lush corner office and his artificially-crafted muscles.

The man glances up at me and I jerk my gaze away, cheeks blooming. Had I seriously been staring at him like a schoolgirl with a crush? I'm not even in the headspace to deal with men right now.

Embarrassed, I duck out of the bookstore portion and into the bakery. The lights are brighter here, like I'm stepping onto a stage. The bakery shelves are lined with decadent, frothy cupcakes that hardly look like food. There are two men in here, too, standing with their arms crossed as the girl behind the counter drops cupcakes into a white box.

I walk up to the counter and study the cupcakes on display. MONTHLY SPECIAL! reads a delicate hand-painted sign. SWEET APPLE CARDAMOM WITH HOUSE-MADE CARMEL SYRUP! The cupcake itself looks like a dream, like the golden sunlight that cracks across a late autumn afternoon. I desperately want to buy one, but the voice is still there in my head: *You can't eat that, you disgusting fatty, what's wrong with you? We're talking 1500 calories minimum. You should be sticking to 500 calories for a single DAY I mean look at you, you disgusting fucking pig. Look how fucking fat you've gotten. Look how—*

A snicker echoes across the bakery. I freeze up, glancing over at the men, who are smirking at me. There's a mirror behind them and I see myself, four sizes bigger than I'd been at the height of my anorexia and still a monstrous size 8.

One of the men snickers again, mutters something to his friend. Both of them keep looking at me.

I swear I hear the word *huge*.

I whirl around, my face burning. Bestseller Guy is a few paces behind me, and he jerks his gaze away too, like he's in on the joke. I feel like a fool for finding him attractive, for finding *any* man attractive. And suddenly I'm a teenager again, lying exhausted on my belly in the middle of a muddy patch at Head Start, sobbing while Blake or Michelle or one of the other asshole counselors screams at me to get up and fucking *move*.

I bolt out of the bookstore, grateful I'm wearing sunglasses so no one in this shitty town can see the tears streaming down my cheeks.

CHAPTER FOUR

SAWYER

My body courses with electricity, every nerve firing at once. I want to kill so bad it feels like a physical ache. There are six humans in this store (five humans and *her*) and I can sense every single one of their heartbeats, pounding arrhythmically in my head.

I never should have come into town.

But I couldn't stop myself. Because Edie's here. Because when she stepped out of the woods, I didn't want to let her go. I wanted to keep stalking my perfect prey.

Now I'm surrounded by actual prey, and I'm losing my fucking mind.

She buzzes around the books, eyes glancing furtively around behind her sunglasses. I pretend to read the book I'm holding, but really I'm trying to cut through the rackety noise of human heartbeats to follow her—her scent and her body's lovely symphony, pulsing blood and soft panty breaths and a kind of quiet rushing sound like the lake lapping against its stone shore.

But it's like listening to music when you're driving down the highway with the window rolled down. The other humans are too fucking loud. Especially the two men in the bakery, talking to each other about some girl they both want to rail. Their laughter scrapes against my skin. Their idiotic chatter makes me want to stalk in there, grab them both by the back of their necks, and slam their heads against the pristine glass displays until everything, the cupcakes and the girl behind the counter and the glossy white tiles, are covered in blood.

But then I feel her, my perfect prey. She's watching me from behind her oversized sunglasses, and for a moment, I almost feel calm.

Then I look at her. I can't help it. I want to see her seeing me.

She startles, jerks her gaze away. I like it, that flush of panic. It gives my cock a little rise in my jeans.

Not as much of a rise as killing those two idiots in the bakery would, though.

She ducks away, slipping toward the cupcakes. I watch her over the edge of the book, considering what to do next. It was stupid of me to come into town, but I got rewarded for it with a glance from her, even though I wasn't able to see those pretty dark eyes.

One of which is nearly swollen shut.

My anger surges again. My bloodlust. I drift closer to the bakery, closer to my perfect prey but also the two idiots, snickering and joking with each other. I imagine that the man who hurt her was like one of those assholes, smirking and smug. Someone too stupid to see the treasure in front of him.

The lights are brighter in the bakery, which I don't like. It makes it feel harder to hide. My perfect prey is looking at the display, and for a moment, I let myself admire her, the lush swell of her hips, her strong shoulders. There is a semi-circle of unbruised skin at the base of her neck, beneath the place she's swept her black hair up into a knot and above the neckline of her thin shirt.

I want to sink my teeth into it and taste her blood.

But then I hear something that shatters that warm dreamy

feeling I get when I think about her, when I see her. The men waiting in the bakery.

They're fucking talking about her.

"Look at that," one of them says, and my skin gets tight over my bones. "They're always flitting around here, huh? The huge ones."

And the other one *laughs,* and that sends the blood surging up into my head, sounding like the ocean. Everything goes burnt at the edges. My knife presses into my side and I'm going to use it to shatter everything in this place, to turn everything red.

I take one step forward—

And so does she.

She nearly runs into me. Stops herself just in time, gaze jerking up. We're close enough that I see her eyes beneath the lens of the sunglasses.

She's crying.

She *heard.*

She pushes past me, the moment lost. For half a second, I consider following her, but she's not my prey right now. Not anymore.

Still, something about her tears focuses me. I don't need to kill the other humans here, the old woman and the two cashiers. It would be stupid, anyway. I can hear Mama chiding me already: *Don't draw attention to yourself, Sawyer. Kill smart.* She doesn't approve of bloodbaths. Says they're stupid. They are stupid, considering the last one got me killed.

I calm the rage. I'll follow the two men, kill them someplace private.

While I wait for them to leave, I go over to the display that Edie had been looking at. A cupcake too pretty to eat, just like she's too pretty to kill.

The counter girl calls out a name and hands over a big white box to the bigger of the men, the one trying to impress a woman. I turn sharply and go outside through the bookstore, listening behind me for heavy-soled footsteps. Back before I died, I always kept a pack of cigarettes and a lighter in my pocket so I could fiddle with them, eyes down and face hidden while I waited for a victim. I don't have that now, so I try to press back against the wall, squinting at the boarded-up old storefront across the way. My perfect prey is gone, which is good—no distractions. I'll look in on her when I'm done.

I might even bring her a gift or two.

It takes them five minutes to leave the shop, the two assholes. They don't notice me. You'd be surprised how little people notice predators.

No, they just breeze past me, still laughing and assholing. I watch them through the fringe of my lashes as they climb into a big blue pickup truck, which is more perfect than I could have hoped for. I was prepared to hotwire one of the old junkers parked on the street, but this is even better, because I move quick as lightning to pull myself into the pickup bed as they roar away. Hunters like me, we can move so soft we can become invisible if we like.

And, like I said, you'd be surprised how little people notice predators.

I flatten myself down on the truck bed, let the engine rumble up through my bones. My knife sears at my side, and I finger the blade, my skin itchy and hot. I'm ready for the release, that gush of hot red blood. Ready for the screams and the begging. Ready to breathe in their last gurgling breath. I need this. It'll calm me so I can focus my attention back on Edie.

The truck pulls out of town, flying down a bumpy country road lined with trees. Already I can feel my next steps forming in my mind. They probably won't look back here, so I can go slow, slide myself out, watch them for a bit before launching my attack. But even if they do, my body's quick and strong after reforming in the dirt. Quicker and stronger than either of them.

We slow; the truck turns. Gravel crunches under the tires and tree branches zip up overhead, concealing the blue sky. My heart thuds with anticipation.

Almost time.

The truck stops. The engine turns off. The doors open, and the men's voices spill out. More grating laughter. They're talking about a football game from three days ago. Mindless chatter. They do not look in the truck bed but instead walk away, voices fading.

I slide the knife out of its sheath and rise up, slow and careful. The truck is parked in front of a run-down little house, and the men are just stepping through the front door, letting it slam shut on its hinges.

My blood is up, raging like a thunderstorm. I can taste copper in the back of my mouth, my jaws aching with an old and primordial hunger. Hunter's hunger, that's what Mama calls it. Jaxon and Ambrose, the closest thing to friends I have, call it the void.

I walk across the yard, sliding through the dappled shadows. The house seems to yawn open for me. I can hear them inside, shuffling around like rats. Laughing. More of that awful, aggravating laughter.

Silencing it is going to be so fucking satisfying.

I go in through the front door because they didn't bother to lock it. Doing this without my old mask feels a little odd, like I'm naked, but I'm so hungry for a kill it's gonna be quick. They won't even see my face.

I find them in the living room.

They don't notice me. They're sitting on the couch, drinking beer, talking and talking and laughing and laughing. The TV's on, some action movie, the volume turned up high even though they aren't watching the stupid thing. For a minute, I just watch them, taking deep slow breaths. I always liked this part, these moments before the blood, when everything's normal for them and my body's on the verge of exploding.

And then I attack.

It is quick, just like I expected. I kill the one on the left first, lunging up to him and slamming my blade into the side of his neck, cutting through all the fat blood vessels there, which I can feel like drumbeats on the air. It cuts him off mid-word, and there's a two-second gap before the other realizes what's happening. He turns toward us just as I pull out the knife, spraying more blood, and then he screams, scrambling to his feet, fumbling around at his jeans for what I can only assume is a gun, even though he's not wearing a holster.

"What the fuck?" he shouts. It's the one who said that terrible thing about my perfect prey, and I slam my blade into his belly so he won't die right away like his friend. He shrieks again and falls backward against the glass coffee table, which shatters with his weight, glass flying everywhere like diamonds. He stares up at me, mouth opening and closing, eyes wide.

I let him see my face after all. He recognizes me from the bakery, a little furrow of confusion between his eyes.

I crouch over him and breathe in deep, inhaling the salty, coppery tang of blood. It all happened so quickly that I didn't have a moment to feel the release, but I feel it now, like a calming current rushing through my blood. My first kill in fifteen years.

"Who—" he gurgles, but doesn't finish the question. Maybe he decides it's not important. "W-why?"

I just look at him, not speaking. There's no answer to that question that he could understand. I marked him and his friend because of what he said about Edie, it's true, but that's not the *why*. That's a human *why,* and my *whys* are different.

I'm a Hunter. I hunt. I cull. I wash my hands in blood because that's what the universe has chosen for me.

"Why?" he asks again, crying this time, tears turning his eyes to glass.

I grab at his hair. He lets out a terrified whimper of fear, which surges adrenaline through my entire system. My cock strains against my jeans, and the pressure's gonna make me come quick. But that's not the important part. Not really.

I press my knife to his throat. He gasps with terror.

Then I dig in with it, slow and careful. Blood beads up like a string of rubies. I cut and I cut. Cut through skin and muscle and snapping tendons until I reach the fragile notches of his spine. Then I wrench through those, too. His blood splatters hotly across my face, and I lick it off my lips as I work.

I feel it when he dies, a shudder in the air. I breathe it in. Come in my jeans, a quick explosion of pleasure. An afterthought.

And then I keep cutting until he's free.

CHAPTER FIVE

EDIE

have u eaten?

I stare down at Charlotte's text, my hands shaking. No, I have not eaten. I brought my groceries home and put them away instead of hurling them out into the woods like I wanted, and I think that should count for something.

My phone dings again.

CHARLOTTE

don't make me call u

I sigh, slide the phone away, and cradle my head in my hands. I keep replaying the scene from the bakery in my head. The two redneck assholes sniggering in the corner, whispering where I can't quite hear even though a lifetime of being an East Coast socialite's fat daughter has primed me to know the signs. I keep hearing it, the word *huge*, over and over. I fucking hate that word. Scott always used it.

Those pictures of you when you were a kid—damn, you were huge, weren't you? So much hotter now.

33

Should you be eating that? We don't want you getting huge.

The fuck is that psychiatrist telling you? Doesn't she care you're getting huge?

My phone rings, cutting through my thoughts. Charlotte's face is on the screen, made up with weird makeup from some art gallery opening or another. She uploaded the picture herself years ago.

I know damn well if I reject the call she's just going to keep calling back. I answer with a sigh.

"You better be eating the best fucking meal of your life," she says as soon as I answer, her photo replaced by the video chat of her sitting on her little patio, the wind blowing her hair into her face.

"Wow, not even a hello," I say dryly. "And you know that kind of thing isn't exactly helpful."

She rolls her eyes. "Whatever. I know you didn't eat. Why not?"

Of course she knows. Charlotte's the reason I even went into recovery. I confessed to her one night, drunk on vodka and water, how miserable I was, how much I hated myself, how every day I yearned for food I was too terrified to eat. How I wanted to be like her—confident in a fat body.

The next day, she dragged me to see Dr. Valunzuela. I was still hungover from the night before, but Dr. Valunzuela in her tidy beige office used the word *anorexia* to describe everything I was going through, and it was like the whole world brightened.

It wasn't normal, the hunger, the calorie counting, the obsession. It wasn't *healthy*.

Of course, Scott didn't agree.

"What's going on?" Charlotte's question jerks me out of my reverie. She chews on a boba tea straw. "It's nearly three o'clock there. Why haven't you eaten?"

I twist a loose lock of hair around my finger and stare at the blank TV across from where I sit on the couch. The curtains are pushed open, too, and I can see the thick woods that crowd around the camp.

"I forgot," I say.

"Don't fucking lie to me!" Charlotte clucks beneath her breath. "Do I need to fly out there? What's the closest airport?"

"You don't need to fly out here," I say, even though part of me wants her to. "You *can't*. You know Scott's probably watching you."

"Fuck him," she growls, but she doesn't push it. Scott has the kind of money that means he can hire the kind of people who will notice if Charlotte hops on a plane to Virginia. The two of us have been over this a dozen times already. "Forget Scott," she says. "What do you have to eat? Tell me there's something."

I cart the phone over to the kitchen and show her the groceries on the counter. "There you go." I spin the phone back around and slump down at the table. "Something happened at the store. I—" I look past the phone and out through the windows. "I don't want to talk about it."

"You don't have to talk about it. But you need to eat something. I'm staying on the call with you 'til you do."

I smile. I figured she would. We've been through this before.

"Edie? I'm about to order a pizza to your fucking cabin."

"I don't think anything'll deliver out here." I force myself off the chair and back into the kitchen. I worried, a little, that staying here would remind me of Camp Head Start, but everything looks so different, so polished, that it's just not an issue. "But I'll make some of this lentil soup I bought."

"Then let's hear that can opener."

I prop Charlotte up on the coffee pot so she can watch me clanking around as I pull out a soup pan. The can opener's manual, but I open the soup in front of the phone to satisfy her.

"Point me at the stove," she says. "I want to see you cooking."

"You're the worst," I tell her, but really I mean the opposite.

She just laughs, her voice catching on the wind blowing through her apartment courtyard.

It takes about five minutes for the soup to heat up, for me to pour it into one of the pretty ceramic bowls and sit down at the little table next to the picture window. And honestly, with Charlotte on the phone? It's not hard for me to eat. Not as hard as I expected, anyway. Once I smell the lentils and the cumin, the back of my throat waters, and I admit to myself just how hungry I am. I spent so long ignoring that sensation that I fall into the habit sometimes, even two years later.

I don't think about the two assholes at the store. I don't think about the store at all.

"So how's the cabin?" Charlotte asks me when she's satisfied I'm actually eating. "How's that whole—" She waves her hands around. "Situation?"

I know she means being back at Camp Head Start. I answer honestly. "It's fine. The dining hall's gone. It looks—it just looks different." I sip at my soup, trying to relish the flavor. "I even took the old hiking trail into town earlier."

Charlotte knows about some of what I went through at Camp Head Start, pre-Sawyer Caldwell. The brutal runs where Blake would withhold water if I didn't increase my time to his liking. The hour-long "death marches" through the forest—Gavin's name for them, not mine. They were proud of it, how well they tortured me. All on 800 calories a day, per my mother's instructions.

A kind of white spot appears behind my vision. I push out all thoughts of Camp Head Start. I don't want to start thinking about Sawyer Caldwell.

"How was that?" Charlotte asks. "The walk?"

"Fine." I don't tell her how my skin prickled like someone was watching me. Then she probably *would* fly out here from California. And as much as I might like some company, I know that's a dangerous idea. "I'm fine, really."

I stir my soup around and take another bite. Now that I've

started eating, it really isn't so bad. It's just that initial hurdle. It's just fighting that bitch of a voice that still lurks in the back of my head.

"That's good. I haven't heard from Scott. You know that makes me nervous."

I don't say anything.

"It's been, what, five days since you left? And he hasn't even pretended to come around asking about you?"

"He knows you helped me." The thought gives me a tight knot in my chest. Scott always hated Charlotte. Called her a "bad influence" on me, as if I'm a child. My starting recovery just cemented that, because Charlotte was the one who got me there and so Scott blamed her for my weight gain—the only aspect of my recovery he gave a shit about. "You need to be careful," I add after taking another bite of soup.

"Scott's not going to do shit to me," Charlotte says, tossing her perfectly-teased brown hair over one shoulder. "He might have someone tailing me, though. I'm not sure. You know, to see if I can lead them to you?"

I frown, even though I had expected this. "Which is why you can't come out here and check on me every time I'm late having lunch."

"Yeah, yeah."

Charlotte stays on the line with me while I finish my meal, a holdover from when I first started recovery and something that always gives me a little comfort, having her there to cheerlead me even if I really don't need it anymore. By the time we hang up, the encounter in Altarida feels small and insignificant. I've been through so much worse than rednecks heckling me in a cupcake shop.

With lunch finished and Charlotte back to whatever she's doing in California, I collapse on the bed I chose for myself. I hadn't let myself realize how fucking exhausted I am from all the travel of the last few days—buying a new car, driving cross-country at a breakneck pace, trying to get ahead of Scott well before he could realize what I'd done. He knows now. I've no doubt someone's tailing Charlotte.

Still, I feel confident that they'll never find me here. Scott will never expect me to come back to Camp Head Start, the site of the worst day of my life.

Second worst day of my life, I think groggily. Because the worst happened not even a week ago, when Scott slammed his fist into me and over, making me scream and bleed on his 1000 thread count Egyptian cotton sheets.

"Fat bitch!" he screamed, punctuating each hit, until the words just dissolved into meaningless syllables. Then he tightened his fingers around my throat until my vision blinked out.

I sink down into my bed here in the cabin. The mattress is cheaper and less comfortable than the mattress at Scott's mansion. Not home. Not for me. Not anymore.

Somehow in all those dark thoughts, I fall asleep. I only knew this because I jerk awake later, and although the light is still on in my room, the windows are dark. Night's fallen.

I sit up, groggy and bleary-eyed. I feel like something woke me up, jarred me out of the dreamless sleep that travel gets you. For a moment, I sit, listening. The cabin is quiet and still. Too cold for the AC, not cold enough for the heater. I don't even have the fan going.

Then I hear it. A soft, distant *thump*.

All the sleepiness drains out of me. I fling myself off the bed and grab my phone and swipe it open. The clock says 8 PM, and there's nothing else, no messages or phone calls. I've got Scott's number blocked, of course, but that wouldn't stop him if he really wanted to get ahold of me. There's nothing from Charlotte, either. Or my parents, whom I'm sure have heard from Scott that I've gone missing.

I put it on silent and slip out of the bedroom, into the hallway. I listen for a moment.

Silence.

I take a deep breath. Remind myself that I'm in the mountains now, not the city, and the sounds are different. It could have been an animal. Nuts falling on the roof. A burst of wind—

Someone knocks on the cabin's front door.

That sound is unmistakable. Three sharp raps. I freeze, panic surging into my throat.

Scott. He's found me.

I look at my phone, expecting to see it lighting up in my hand with some unknown number. But it's dark and silent.

I scurry into the living room, grab my purse, slip on my shoes. If this is Scott or one of the PIs he's almost certainly hired, then I need to run. I need to get in my car and drive until I know I'm not being followed. Then I can decide what to do next. Hire a lawyer. File a restraining order. *Something.*

I stare at the front door, my chest tight. I know I can't do anything until I see who's on the other side.

"Hello?" I call out, my voice trembling. I sidle up to the door and press my ear against the slick wood. It's quiet. "Who's there?"

No answer.

Maybe it's nothing. Maybe it's just the cabin host coming to check on me. Maybe there's a problem with the cabin, and they need to let me know

Then why aren't they answering?

"Hello?" I call out again, pulling my purse up against my body. I slowly unlatch the front door, body braced to run when someone pushes inside.

Nothing happens.

I breathe out, long and slow, and pull the door open. Every single nerve is burning.

No one's there.

I blink out at the dirt-covered driveway, the boarded-up cabins. The woods beyond them, shrouded in silvery darkness. But I *swore* I heard knocking—

Then I glance down.

Then I see it.

Blood on the cement porch, dark in the moonlight. And a severed head, the face twisted in a perpetual scream, the eyes wide with fear—

Staring right at me.

CHAPTER SIX

EDIE

My first thought, as panicky as a rabbit, is that the head looks so realistic. My second thought is that it looks realistic because it's real.

Then I react. I leap over the head and race across the packed dirt, my heart feeling like it's going to pound out of my chest. For a moment, I've fallen back in time fifteen years. I'm eighteen years old and I'm racing across the balmy August night to see if Blake was able to call the police.

Then I slam into my car. No. This is a joke, a cruel and vicious joke. Maybe the head *isn't* real. But someone put it there. Someone who wants me frightened.

I have to get out of here.

I fumble in my purse for my keys, fingers slipping over every stupid thing I've ever put in there—a tube of chapstick, a bottle of hand lotion. Did I leave them in the cabin? No, I feel them buried at the bottom and wrench them out, slamming my thumb frantically down on the unlock button. The car headlights flash, and I grab the handle and—

A gloved hand wraps neatly around my mouth.

I scream, legs flailing, as my attacker pulls me away from my car. My purse crashes to the ground, spilling tampons and lotion bottles everywhere.

My keys gleam in the dirt.

"Don't scream," says a soft masculine voice.

I fight back against him, digging my arms into his thin arm. But the muscles there flex against me with a hidden strength. He drags me up against him, my back pressed against a firm, solid chest. Then he walks backward, pulling me step by step away from the car.

I scream into his glove again, tears blurring my vision.

"Shhh," he says, his mouth close to my ear, his breath warm. "Don't be afraid."

Lightning bolts through me.

I'm eighteen again, but I'm not running. I'm standing in front of Sawyer Caldwell, clutching a flimsy steak knife, and he tells me *Don't be afraid* from behind his filthy, bloodstained mask.

The world seems to pull apart, and I'm not sure that Scott is responsible for this.

"Who are you?" I ask, although he presses my mouth so tightly it comes out as inarticulate muffles. The question tastes like the leather of his gloves.

He doesn't answer except to pull me up to the front porch. I twist away from the head.

It's real. I'm certain of it now.

"He deserved it," the man says calmly. God, he even has the same accent as Sawyer Caldwell, that faint Virginia drawl. "What he said about you."

My nerves light up again.

Don't be scared. They can't hurt you anymore. I won't let them hurt you ever again.

But Sawyer Caldwell is dead. I was in his fucking arms when he died.

The man heaves me into the cabin, his hand still wrapped around my mouth. I hear the door click shut. The lock turn.

Then his mouth is on my ear again.

"I'm gonna let you go." His fingers curl slightly against the bones of my face. "And I don't want you screaming. Do you understand?"

I don't say anything. He sighs.

"I just want to talk to you, but I can't do that if you're screaming."

Then he draws his hand away, slowly. For some reason, I don't scream. Just like how I didn't even try to attack Sawyer Caldwell that night fifteen years ago.

I do, however, turn around, bracing myself for another blood-stained mask.

Instead, I find the guy from the bookstore. The one reading the bestseller.

He looks at me, dark eyes burning. He's dressed like all the men who live around here, grey flannel and dark jeans. Heavy work boots. Was this what he wore this afternoon? I can't remember. I'm too panicky, too breathless.

"Do you remember me?" His eyes feel like mouths, swallowing me whole.

"Y-yes." I take a step back, and he matches it, slow and preda-tory. I have no doubt if I try to run, he'll tackle me. "You w-were at that b-bookstore. In town."

But he frowns, shakes his head. A curl of dark brown hair falls across his forehead. "No," he says. "No, I mean—" He gestures toward the windows. To the camp.

To the place where the dining hall had been.

This time, it's my turn to shake my head. "This isn't fucking funny," I tell him, curling my hands into fists. I've got nothing. Not my keys, not my phone. The kitchen, and its rack full of knives, is too far away. "I don't know who you think I am, but—"

"Your name is Edie." Something about the way he says my name feels almost... reverential. A prayer.

My head swoons.

"I don't know what you're talking about," I shoot back, a beat too late. "My name's—" Fuck, I've forgotten the fake name Charlotte and I came up.

But at the same time, I don't think this man has anything to do with Scott.

He grins. It's almost handsome, although there's a sharpness to it that makes me suck in my breath. "I know who you are, Edie," he says. "I haven't stopped thinking about you for fifteen years."

Blood pounds in my ears. The man tilts his head a little, and it's so much like fucking Sawyer Caldwell, just without the mask, that for a moment, I think I'm going to pass out.

"No." I shake my head, say it again more firmly. "No. Sawyer Caldwell is dead. I was there when he died. I was—"

I stop, faltering. Because he's shaking his head now, his burning dark eyes never leaving mine. "Can't die," he says. "Didn't die. Just went into the ground for a bit."

Then he reaches out his hand, palm down, stretching it towards me like he expects me to jerk away.

"Stop this!" I shout, wrenching away from him.

He lifts his gaze, eyes big and weirdly puppy-dog-like, and curls his fingers back to his chest.

"I don't know what bullshit fucking podcast you listened to, but Sawyer Caldwell is *dead*."

Except there were those two officers at my parents' house in Arlington.

Don't want to worry you... body disappeared...we've got a detail on the house...

"I ain't dead."

"You aren't Sawyer Caldwell."

He tilts his head again, studying me, brow furrowed a little. I wait for him to give me that cruel grin again. For him to reveal he's been filming this whole thing as some kind of bloodthirsty social media prank.

Instead, he takes a cautious step forward, eyes burrowing into me. "You had their blood on your shirt," he says softly. "They treated you something awful and you still gave 'em comfort, didn't you? I always remembered that."

I go still. "Lucky guess," I snarl. Or try to. It comes out like a whimper.

The man smiles a little, like he's amused by my attempt to be intimidating.

"What else can I tell you to prove it?" Another step. I'm frozen in place, just like I was that night fifteen years ago. A real-life final girl, the podcasts called me, but I wasn't a final girl. I didn't fight.

He spared me.

"How about this?" He stops, his eyes never leaving mine. They're as deep and black as the swimming hole two miles from the camp where I used to swim laps between orange buoys. "I'd just killed the last of them. The one with the muscles."

Blake Foster. You could know that from reading the Wikipedia page. I don't say anything.

"I heard you," he says softly. "That scared little whimper."

I will myself not to make that sound now.

The man takes another step toward me. "I told you not to be afraid." He has this faraway look in his eyes, like he really is remembering, and that scares me more than anything.

At least, until he says what he says next.

"You let me hold you."

Every atom of air in my body flushes out of me. I swoon, staring at him, this handsome, terrifying man with his dark curling hair.

Because I never told anyone that. After Deputy Crosier shot Sawyer Caldwell, he assumed that Caldwell had been strangling me, and I never denied it. I looked Crosier in the eye and told him that was exactly what had happened, and no one ever questioned it.

"Who are you?" I whisper, backing away.

The man immediately clears the space between us, pressing me up against the wall, his wiry arms caging my body. His eyes bore into me. This close, I can see they aren't really black, but a dark, chocolate brown, flecked with scatters of gold.

"I told you," he murmurs, and I can feel the warmth of his breath. "I'm Sawyer Caldwell."

"No!" I shout, and I try to worm away from him, ducking beneath his arm. He moves fast as a snake, twining that arm loosely around my chest, pressing my back up against him. It's not exactly threatening. It feels like the embrace Sawyer Caldwell gave me right before he died.

"Sawyer Caldwell is dead," I shriek, digging my hands into his arm, trying to pry him free. But he's strong. Stronger than he looks.

"I'm not dead, Edie." He presses his mouth against my ear. "And you didn't let me finish."

I freeze, heart hammering. He draws me closer, one arm across the top of my chest, the other winding around my waist. When he pulls me up against him, I swear I feel the ridge of his cock pressing against my ass.

"Don't," I whisper, tears limning along my lashes.

"Don't what?" He nuzzles my neck, takes a deep breath in as if he's smelling me. He keeps his arms around me as he peels off one of his gloves and tosses it to the ground. "Don't tell you about what happened that night?"

As he takes off his other glove, I stare straight ahead, at the empty wall, the curtains drawn tight over the windows, the black TV screen.

Don't say it don't say it don't say it—

"You hugged me." His voice has that sense of reverence to it. "I held you, and you held me back, and I knew you were grateful for what I did for you."

Tears stream over my cheeks, and I tremble against him, his

thin, strong body. It *feels* like Sawyer Caldwell's body, that's what terrifies me the most. Because of course I fucking remember it. Wrapping my arms around his shoulders. Clinging to him, sobbing, terrified. That bizarre, horrifying fragment of comfort he offered me—

No one knows that. It's the only true secret in my entire life. I never even told Charlotte, and I tell her everything.

I knew you were grateful for what I did for you.

"No!" I scream, and with a burst of strength, I erupt away from him. I spent years battling my survivor's guilt. I starved myself because of it, punishing myself for being the only one left standing even though I was fat and ugly and unathletic and—

The man grabs me again, quick as a cat, and yanks me up to him, pinning me to him, his mouth forming spots of warmth on my neck as he speaks.

"It's me, Edie," he whispers.

"H-how?" I sob. "Deputy Crozier fucking shot you! I was covered in your fucking blood! I picked your brain out of my fucking hair!"

The man sighs, nuzzles against me. "Good lord," he murmurs, his hand drifting down over the swell of my belly. "That's a pretty thought."

Hearing that sends something jolting through me. I don't know if it's revulsion or desire.

But then his hand slides between my legs, his palm rubbing over the crotch of my jeans, and I have my answer.

It's desire.

"To answer your question," he says, his touch soft and almost hesitant. "I ain't exactly human. I can't die, like I said."

"That's ridiculous," I whisper.

"Ridiculous or not, it's true."

He's still touching my pussy, rubbing the heel of his hand against my clit, over my jeans. I know I should try to stop him.

But, to my shame, it feels good.

He guides me across the living room, still stroking my pussy. I go with him, not fighting, just stumbling backward with him, because it feels so fucking good, how he's touching me, one hand on my cunt and the other squeezed around my bicep.

"Are you really Sawyer Caldwell?" The question comes out in a gasp. But I already know the answer, don't I? There are two impossibilities here. I saw him die. And I told no one what he did in those moments before his death.

And yet here he is, the only other person who could know the truth.

There's no denying what happened fifteen years ago. I'll never forget what Sawyer Caldwell felt like as I clung to him. I'll never forget what he said to me.

I squeeze my eyes shut as the man—as Sawyer—pulls me down onto the sofa, arranging me so that he pins me against him as his hand undoes the button on my jeans.

"Yes," he mutters, finally answering the question. His voice is strained. Focused. "I dragged myself into the ground to heal."

"No one heals from that," I whisper.

"Hunters can. I can."

He slides his hand into my jeans to stroke me over my panties. Why aren't I stopping him?

Why am I listening to this?

Why do I *believe* him?

Because no one could know what he did that night. NO ONE.

"Damn, Edie," he says, snapping me back to the present. "You sure are wet for me, aren't you?"

There's genuine surprise in his voice, and hearing him say that, confirming it, makes me moan. He laughs like he's delighted and then slides his finger under my panties, and I feel him for the first time, skin on skin.

It's been so long since someone else has touched me that I can't bear to push him away. Instead, I moan again, louder, as his fingers rub slow, lazy circles on my clit.

"I never thought I'd be so lucky," he says softly. "That you'd be here. That I'd get to make you come."

His words flood heat through my chest, and I shouldn't be feeling this. Not about him. I close my eyes and try to pretend it's someone else touching me, someone who isn't a resurrected killer. But no matter who I picture, whatever handsome actor I try to craft out of the aether, he's replaced with Sawyer Caldwell fifteen years ago, soaked in blood and wearing a mask.

"Stop," I say weakly. Not so much to him. To myself. For liking this.

He just laughs. "Not until you come," he says. "Though I'll be honest, I don't know if I'll be able to stop myself from doing it again."

I moan at that, my hips rolling against his hand of their own accord. I've never come twice in a row.

So why do I feel like Sawyer Caldwell might be the one to make me do it?

He shifts a little, slides his hand deeper into my panties. One of his fingers slips inside my pussy, and I gasp as he curls it against my inner wall. His thumb still works my clit.

This man knows what he's doing.

"How..." I gasp the question out, my pleasure mounting. "How are... you really... really Sawyer Caldwell?"

In response, he slides another finger inside me. My legs fall open, trying to accommodate him. It's like my body reacts to him one way, my brain another.

"I know you recognize me," he murmurs, slowing his strokes. Teasing me.

He's right. I do.

I squirm against him, pressing down on his hand. My jeans slide down my hips, revealing a stripe of my soft, pale flesh.

"You're dead," I whimper, burying my face against his chest. "I saw it. You died."

"Told you. I can't die."

He does something, hooks his fingers against me in a particular way, and I let out a low, guttural scream, bucking my body against him. Sawyer chuckles.

"That's it," he says. "That's it. You're close, aren't you?"

"You're *dead*," I say, as if repeating it will make it true.

"Then you're about to cream yourself on a dead man's fingers." He leans down and brushes his lips against my ear. "I can't tell you how many times I thought about this while I was recovering in the ground. I've wanted you from the first time I saw you in those tight little shorts." He's working me faster now, and the heat is building. Still, I pull away a little to look up at him.

Why is Sawyer Caldwell so goddamn handsome?

I try to focus as best as I can. I can't handle this nonsense about him being in the ground, how he healed. So I focus on the other thing thing he said. "How long..." I gasp. "How long were you watching me? At the camp?"

His fingers stroke rhythmically against me, and I match that rhythm with my hips until I'm doing most of the work, wantonly riding his hand.

"Long enough to see them treat you like shit," he says. "Long enough to know you'd be worth killing for."

And to my horror, that's when my orgasm slams through me. I come at the idea of him killing my four tormenters. I gasp and thrash against him, half wishing I could stop the cascade so I can tell myself it isn't the idea of death and murder that finally sent the pleasure surging up through my body.

Even though, if I'm being honest with myself, this isn't the first time.

Sawyer doesn't stop touching me, his fingers drawing out more and more contractions in the muscles of my pelvis. I slump against him, gasping for breath, until finally, the aftershocks fade. He stops his stroking, but doesn't take his hand away from my pussy, just keeps it there, cupping me gently.

I don't move. I *can't* move. A sense of self-loathing creeps in. How could I come at that? At their deaths?

They tortured you.

They hated you.

They deserved it.

I take a deep, shuddery breath and shift against Sawyer. He makes no move to stop me until I try to sit up, at which point he releases my pussy and grips my hips with both hands, pressing me into the couch.

I look up at him through the tangled net of my hair.

He stares down at me, his eyes dark and hungry. But also... faintly astonished, like he finds this whole scenario as unbelievable as I do.

"Now what?" The question comes out barely a whisper. If he really is Sawyer Caldwell, I have to remind myself, it's very possible that I'm going to die.

But he doesn't attack me. He doesn't move for a knife.

Instead, he tugs on my jeans, pulling them down to my thighs.

"Get these things off," he says. "I've been waiting fifteen years for a taste of your cunt."

CHAPTER SEVEN

SAWYER

I've always liked making women come. It's the next best thing to killing them, really, the way their breath gets fast and shuddery and their bodies go limp and they just lose sight of everything. Except you get to do it over and over again to the same woman.

When I was younger, Mama decided it was time for me to learn Hunter ways. She figured I'd want to kill the way she does, which is to stalk a man and cut his throat while they're in bed together. So she brought me some girls to practice on. But I couldn't bring myself to kill them. They didn't do nothing to me but make me feel good, showing me all the fun you can have with a living human body. I wanted to kill people who deserved it.

So Mama stopped bringing me girls, but I sought them out myself. That was how I learned about making them come. A couple of them taught me everything I needed to know, and I got addicted to it, feeling their pussy muscles clenching around my cock, their clits throbbing against my tongue.

That's what's happening now. My perfect prey is coming for me, grinding her pussy up against my face, and it's exactly like I imagined all those times when I was in the dirt.

When I brought her the head, that little token of my affection, I never thought it would actually lead to this. I *hoped* it would. But hope usually doesn't mean much.

Usually.

"Oh my god," she pants, the syllables matching the movement of her thrusts. "Oh my god, oh my god, oh my god."

I keep licking her until she stills, her thick gorgeous thighs trembling on either side of my head. Only then do I let myself look up at her. I replace my mouth with my fingers, keeping my touch gentle.

"I'm done," she gasps, hands flailing. She's sprawled back on the couch, her shirt hiked up to just beneath her tits. "You can stop."

"No," I say, dotting some kisses against the dark thatch of her pubic hair, breathing in the scent of her arousal. A little musky, a little sweet. Reminds me of the woods around the camp. I didn't think this would really happen, but now that I'm here, I'm not letting go.

"No?" It comes out a squeak, and she picks up her head to gape at me. "You can't—It's too much—"

"No," I say again, and then I move up over her stomach, nuzzling her soft flesh. I keep one hand on her pussy, stroking it softly. I expect her to fight back, the way she did when I dragged her into the cabin, but she doesn't, just sputters out questions at me.

"Why?" she says. I like how she's still trying to catch her breath. "Why are you... doing this?"

I stop my trail of kisses just beneath her shirt hem and look up at her. She looks a bit like how she did the night I killed her tormentors—eyes wide, hair a mess, cheeks flushed pink. All that's missing is blood splattered across her full chest, a thought that makes my cock throb.

"I told you." I push up her shirt until I spot her bra. To my delight, it's lacy and transparent and I can see the dark moons of her areolas through the fabric. "I've been waiting fifteen years for it."

I pull away from her pussy so I can pull her up to sitting and reach around to get rid of this bra. She moves with me, loose and pliable, even though she keeps arguing.

"I still don't understand how it's you." Her eyes glimmer. "Or why me. Why you didn't—" She swallows and I know she was going to say, *kill me*. I'm glad she doesn't ask so I don't have to try and explain. Mostly because I don't know how to put it into words. I just want to focus on her right now.

I snap the hooks of her bra and throw it away. Her tits are fucking gorgeous. Big and soft and trembling, and I think about the first time I saw her. She was running, jogging down one of the narrow trails in the woods. One of the pieces of shit I killed two months later had been yelling at her to go faster, but I managed to tune him out by focusing on the way her tits bounced inside her shirt. It wasn't the only thing that drew me to her, but goddamn it if it wasn't one of them.

"Are you really Sawyer Caldwell?" she asks for what feels like the hundredth time.

I look up at her. She gazes back at me, eyes big and searching, like she still doesn't believe it. In a way, it's fair; I had my mask on that night. She never saw my face. And there aren't any pictures of me to be printed in the newspapers and the like—Mama insisted.

I stroke her cheek with the back of my hand. She jolts a little, like a frightened rabbit, but doesn't pull away. "There were only two of us in that dining hall," I tell her. "I told you what I remembered. What happened between us."

She's shaking, and I know she knows it's me, deep down. We shared something that night, and I knew about it. A good girl like her, someone who's not a killer, she wouldn't have told anyone. Can't argue with any of it.

I reach down between her legs and tease her clit again.

"Fuuuuuck," she gasps, flopping back on the oversized couch cushions. I take that as an invitation to pull one of her nipples into my mouth. It's a perfect little pebble on my tongue, and I suck gently on it, then pull more and more of her tit into my mouth, as much of it as I can.

She groans, a sound that sets all my nerves on fire. I slide two fingers inside her soaking wet cunt and stroke, moving around until the tenor of her moans changes, grows deeper and darker.

"Stop," she mumbles. "It's too much. Stop."

I switch over to her other breast, massaging the first one with my free hand. She seems to melt beneath me, and then she's making noises but not actually saying anything, just kind of grunting and keening and panting.

Like I said, it's almost as good as killing. With her, it's better, because it means she stays with me.

"You're gonna come for me again." I speak into the mound of her breasts, breathing in the salty-sweet scent of her sweat. It's like caramel apples. Like tree sap in the spring. "Three times. Do you understand?"

"I can't," she gasps, which is a lie, because I can already feel it building up in her, the way her pussy's fluttering around my fingers.

"You can." I lift my head so I can look at her. She's leaned back on the couch again, her eyes squeezed shut. "You're almost there, baby."

It slips out, calling her *baby*, but her lips part when I say it and she lets out this small helpless noise that almost makes me come in my jeans.

I work her a little harder, quickening the rhythm of my strokes. Her body goes rigid beneath me, and I'm tired of waiting so I slide my thumb over her clit, giving it a nice firm press. That does it. She completely dissolves, moaning and thrashing. I press into her, keeping her still so I can keep coaxing the orgasm out of her.

"That's it," I breathe, slowing my strokes just a little. "That's it, baby. Keep coming for me."

"I c-can't," she gasps. I pull my fingers out of her and just rub my thumb around her clit. It flutters like a dying pulse. She keens, a sound that's half pain and half pleasure, and I don't know if I'll ever be able to stop touching her. Not if she's going to make sounds like that.

Still, when she sinks back against the couch, gasping and flushed, I lighten my touch a little. I wish we were on a bed or the floor, some place where I could stretch out beside her, one hand between her legs and the other tucked under her neck like a pillow. Instead, we're in this weird tangle, me half-sitting on her as I work her pussy. It's making my arm tired.

"You have to s-stop," she says, voice shuddering. "Please. That, um, the h-head—" The word comes out strangled, like she doesn't quite want to say it. "Shouldn't you move it?"

The question's so unexpected from her, naked and legs spread and soft body sheened with sweat, that I laugh. "Is that what you're thinking about right now?"

To illustrate my point, I slide a finger back into her pussy.

She gasps, her eyes going wide. "No! I just—What if someone sees it—You need to st—"

"I'm not going to stop." I lean over her, brush her cheeks with my lips. She doesn't pull away from me, the way my victims will when I move in to kill them. "And no one's gonna see the head. No one comes out here."

I slide another finger into her, slow and easy. She quakes beneath me, making more of those little pleasure-pain noises. God, I could listen to them all day.

"Besides." I move my mouth over to her ear, then kiss the side of her throat so I can feel her pulse beating furiously beneath her skin. When I speak, I speak to that pulse, to that wildly pumping blood. "The head was a gift for you."

She stiffens then, clamps her thighs shut against my hand. I just laugh and sit up so I can see her confused, frightened expression.

"Gift?" she whispers.

"Mmhmm." I pull my hand away and gently pry her thighs apart. She fights me, her quad muscles flexing beneath her skin. I like that, her strong, shapely legs. I like the idea of chasing her through the woods and then fucking her instead of killing her.

I look up at her. "You didn't recognize him, did you?"

Something shifts in her face. That recognition she'd been missing. Understanding. And then, the best of all: dark lust. It passes over her features like a cloud moving over the sun. It's only for a second, but I see it.

She liked her gift.

"You can't leave that here," she says in a small, terrified voice.

When I reach between her legs, she doesn't try to close them.

"I won't," I tell her, keeping my voice soft and low as I run my fingers up and down her slit, relishing the silky petals of her cunt. "I'll take it someplace safe for you, though."

She whimpers at that, and although her voice is still afraid, I feel a surge of heat from her clit. "There we are," I mutter. "Let's get you one more orgasm."

"That's not going to happen." She looks at me, lifting her shoulders. Her pupils drown out her honey-colored eyes, making them look nearly as dark as mine.

I grin, accepting the challenge.

"Then try to get away."

She stares at me for a long moment with her lust-drowned eyes and then says, "What?"

I slip my fingers out of her pussy and press the heel of my palm against it instead. Her lips part and I see a flash of her tongue and imagine sliding my cock into her mouth, a pretty thought that I set aside. Too risky.

"You can try to get away," I repeat, kneading her cunt a little. She's overstimulated. I can see it in her flushed skin, her hooded expression. And I can feel it too, the wet spot spreading out on the sofa. "Make a run for it." I lean down over her, drop my voice a little. "Make me catch you."

For a moment, she only stares at me, breasts rising and falling as I rub between her legs.

Then she scrambles away. I fall back, watching to see what she does. If she wants to escape, really escape, she'll go for her clothes first. Maybe the door, since her purse and keys are still lying in the dirt outside.

She does neither. Instead, she ducks into the kitchen, all opened up on the other side of the room, and snatches a knife out of the knife stand.

Then she whirls around to face me, the blade catching the bright fluorescent bulbs overhead until it gleams like the sun.

CHAPTER EIGHT

SAWYER

It's the *hottest* fucking thing I've ever seen in my life. My perfect prey, my Edie, trying to act the predator?

It takes every ounce of willpower not to bolt across the room, bend her over the counter, and bury my cock into that sopping, overstimulated pussy.

I don't do it, though. Not tonight. My blood's up from my earlier kill, and I don't want to get rough with her. Don't want to kill her on accident.

I do, however, want to devour one more orgasm out of her before I leave.

So I stand up and amble across the living room. She stares at me, clutching the knife so tightly her knuckles whiten. Her hair is tousled and mussed from where she dropped back against the couch, the curls all twisted together. Looks the way it did fifteen years ago.

"I told you," I say, coming around the counter. "I can't die."

She backs up against the counter, knife raised. I'm not looking at that, though. I'm looking at her. Her thick, voluptuous body, the way her waist curves in just above the wide flare of her hips and swell of her belly. Those long muscular legs. I want them wrapped around my shoulders.

"You told me to run for it." Her voice shakes a little.

"So why didn't you?"

I close the space between us with Hunter speed, moving so fast she cries out when I close my fingers around her wrist. The knife flashes as I spiderwalk my fingers up to hers and peel them open to take the blade away from her. Her lips open and close, but she doesn't answer. Doesn't have an answer, I'd reckon.

I slide the knife into my belt. I could use another.

"Well?" I press closer to her, drop my hand to squeeze her breast. Can't help myself.

"I'm n-naked," she whispers.

I nuzzle against her neck, breathing in the scent of her sweat. It's mostly sweet, kind of floral like the woods in springtime. But she's scared, too, enough to undercut the sweetness with a rich, dark spice. I lick her before I respond, tasting the salt.

"Clothes are right there."

"You w-wouldn't l-let me—" She gasps as I bite gently against her skin, showing enough restraint that I surprise myself. I start kissing downward while she stutters out her response. "You w-wouldn't let me g-get dressed—"

"No." I speak against the top swell of her tits, then slide my nose down the valley between them, moving over her belly. "But not for the reason you're thinking."

I don't actually know what she's thinking. Probably that I want to kill her. But that's the last thing I want to do.

I drop down to kneel in front of her and prop one leg on my shoulder. Her fear makes her pliable. Or maybe it's her desire. I can smell that too, hot and musky, as I settle myself between her legs and run my tongue along her slit with a long, delicious lick.

She screams, but there's no fear in it. Not a single drop.

I press my tongue up into her cunt, plunging it in and out of her. I want to suck on her clit, but I know I need to go slow if I want to get a fourth orgasm. And I *want* that fourth orgasm. I want to hear her begging me to stop, that it's too much. I want her trembling and quaking against my mouth. I want her to die in that way that means I won't lose her forever.

"Why?" she says weakly. "Why do you keep…"

She doesn't finish her question, and I don't bother to answer her. I just lick her faster, lapping up every drop of her wetness, one hand braced against the thigh flung over my shoulder. My cock throbs, and I know if I don't take care of it, I'm going to be too tempted to fuck her. So, as I eat her, slow and teasing, I pull my dick out, moaning a little when the cool air of the cabin hits my burning skin.

My perfect prey moans too, her hips rocking against my face. It's involuntary; she accompanies each buck with a panty, "It's too much. It's too much."

But she doesn't ask me to stop.

I stroke myself as I move away from her sweet, fluttering pussy and up to her clit. As soon as my lips brush against it, she jolts and cries out with a choking sob. It's the most beautiful fucking sound in the world, and I squeeze my cock tighter, quicken my strokes, and strum her clit with my tongue.

She goes wild, whole body thrashing, her fingers tugging so hard on my hair that it hurts a little, which just pushes me closer to my own release. "Please," she keens. "It's too much. I can't—Oh my fucking god."

When I hear the tremor of tears in her voice, my lust surges up in me, as hot and thick as blood. I wrap my lips around her hard, throbbing clit and suck, tongue flicking over that perfect little nub. She moans with pleasure, but she's crying, too, whimpering and gasping, and it's the crying that pushes me over the edge. My balls tighten up against my cock and then my orgasm tears through me, pulsing and bright. I groan against her cunt as hot cum erupts through my fingers and splatters on the kitchen tile.

"I can't," she's still gasping, still rocking against me, her voice still ragged with tears. "It's too much. I can't. I—"

She comes. After four times I know what her body feels like when she does, the way her entire pussy contracts and her thick, strong legs start shaking. She screams, arching her spine against the counter, her hand yanking so hard on my hair that I sigh at the pain. I lick her through it, the way I did the first time, relishing every sobbing moan. Only when she sags down do I pull away, giving her some peace.

I'm not sure if she even notices. She slumps against the counter, legs splayed and shaking, her gaze fixed on the ceiling. I stand up, tuck myself back inside my jeans, wipe the cum off my fingers. Then I step closer to her and put a hand on her thigh.

She jolts at my touch and looks up at me. Tears streak over her face, glistening like jewels. "I can't take it anymore," she tells me, her desperation clear. "If you're going to kill me, just fucking kill me."

I lean over her, drinking in how fucking perfect she looks: her pale skin flushed red, her eyes glassy with tears, her hair wild. I did that to her. I did all that to her, and she's still alive for me to do it again.

"I'm not going to kill you."

She blinks at me, her lower lip trembling. The desperation softens into confusion, and I cup her face to run my thumb over her tear-dampened cheeks. In the bright kitchen lights, I can see the mottled bruises around her eye and throat more clearly. Over on the couch, the light was dim, and they had been less noticeable.

I lean over her and kiss her cheek. Or intend to; I can't stop myself from licking her tears away. The saltiness reminds me of blood.

She stiffens beneath me. But she doesn't try to pull away.

"Why are you doing this?" she whispers.

I pull away from her. Smooth my hand over her hair. "Because I've been dreaming of it for fifteen fucking years."

Her eyes widen, and I scoop my hand behind her head and pull her up so that she's standing. She stares at me, shaking her head a little. I half-expect her to go for the knife in my belt but she doesn't, and that just makes my heart get all tight and strange in my chest.

I run my fingers over the dark skin beneath her eye. She jerks away. Looks away, too.

"Who did this?" I ask, then drop my hand to trail along her throat. "And this?"

Something seems to wash through her. It's kind of like fear, but not fear of me. I can tell that much. My muscles tense. I'm worried she won't tell me, because I need to know. And if she won't tell me, I'll have to find a way to get it out of her.

But then she answers. "My hus—my ex-husband."

Fire surges in my chest. "Your husband did this to you? Did he hit you?"

"Yeah." She crosses her arms over her chest, hiding her gorgeous tits from me. But then she peers up through the tangle of her hair, kind of shy, and I like that better. "Yeah, he hit me. And worse."

Worse. I know what those bruises around her throat mean. Anger simmers inside me.

"Why?" I ask, and it comes out all wrong, kind of accusatory. Her eyes darken.

"I mean, what was his reason?" I hate how I stumble over my words. Eating her out is easier than talking to her. "Not what did you do. I know you didn't do anything."

Something in her face softens like she understands what I'm asking. "I don't—" She takes a deep breath. "Because I wouldn't do what he wanted. And because he knew I was going to leave him." She squeezes her arms more tightly around herself. "That's why I'm here. I was planning to leave him, but when he did this, when he—" She stops herself. "I had to get out. So I came here. The last place he would look for me."

Her eyes meet mine, and I don't understand much, but I understand that *I'm* the reason he wouldn't come looking for her here, because of what I did for her.

"I would never do something like that to you," I say, nodding at her eye, at the dark bruises around her throat.

She stares at me like she isn't sure how to respond.

When I came in here after she found the head, I just wanted to make sure she wouldn't call the cops. But being so close to her, smelling her, I couldn't stop myself. Especially when she didn't even try to push me away.

Now I don't know what to do next. Part of me wants to take her back to my little church, but it's not nice enough for her yet.

"I'll take the head," I tell her. "You don't gotta worry about that."

For a moment, she looks confused. Then her eyes go wide with understanding. A flash of fear. My cock stirs even though I just came.

"Don't bother calling the cops," I say. "They won't find me."

She blinks, but I turn away before I do something stupid, like knock her head against the counter so I can drag her back through the woods to my church. I stalk out of the cabin, my heart hammering, and grab the head by its blood-stiff hair as I leave. Fucking blood on the porch, too. I'll need to take care of that. But not right now.

Because I finally tasted her, my perfect prey. And now that I've had a taste, I don't think I'll ever be able to stop eating.

CHAPTER NINE

EDIE

When I wake up the next morning, the lemony sunlight streaming in through the window tells me it's at least noon, probably later. For a moment, I just lay in the bed, staring up at the ceiling, trying to ignore the faint, pleasant ache between my legs, evidence that what happened last night was real.

Sawyer Caldwell is alive.

But more than that, Sawyer Caldwell made me come four times over the course of an hour.

I sit up and reach for my cell phone on the bedside table, then remember it's not there. After Sawyer slipped out of the cabin last night, I waited until I was certain he was gone and then went outside to get my purse. I'll give him this much: He took the head. Blood still slicked across the porch, though.

I brought my purse inside and took out the phone, my hands shaking. But I did not dial 911. I did not call the police because I knew they would contact Scott, and, absurdly, I'm more afraid of him than I am of Sawyer Caldwell.

Instead, I set the phone down on the kitchen counter two feet from where Sawyer made me sob with overwhelming pleasure while he jerked himself off. I found his cum splattered across the kitchen tile after he left. It should have disgusted me, and it did. But it also sent a weird, uncomfortable curl of heat between my thighs.

Sort of like what I feel now.

I move slowly, pushing myself out of bed, and get dressed. All my movements are mechanical. Robotic. I try to keep my thoughts focused, but they keep slipping into memories of last night.

I've never even had two orgasms in one session, much less four.

When I go out into the front of the cabin, part of me expects (*hopes?*) Sawyer will be there, watching me with those dark, burning eyes. He's not, of course. Everything looks exactly as it did when I went to bed last night. My phone is even still sitting on the counter.

I pick it up, knowing I really should call the police. Scott's an entire continent away, and a serial killer is living next to me in the woods. But then I see that it's nearly 3 PM and I've missed five calls and at least a dozen text messages—all of them from Charlotte. For a moment, I'm struck with a sudden surge of panic.

How did she *know?*

But of course she didn't. Sawyer Caldwell has nothing to do with why she was texting. I skim through the messages, and my panic doesn't subside but changes. Becomes more immediate. More urgent.

CHARLOTTE

Did you eat dinner?

No response? SRSLY?

Getting worried. Call me.

Edie, call me ASAP. It's not about the eating. Im serious.

She even left a voicemail, which makes my heart jitter around in my chest because Charlotte hates voicemail. I don't even listen to it, just call her, my hand shaking as I hold the phone up to my ear. I can't handle video chat this morning.

It rings twice before she answers.

"Holy shit, Edie, are you okay?"

I lean against the counter and try not to think about how I'd leaned against it last night, an apparently undead murderer's head between my legs. I don't even know how to answer that question.

"I'm fine," I finally say, which isn't remotely true. I just hope she doesn't expect me to explain why I didn't call her back last night. Or this morning. She knows I like to get up early.

But Charlotte lets out a long, relieved breath, and my panic tightens in my chest again. "What's going on?" I say. "Charlotte?"

"Fuck, I was so worried." She takes another deep breath, the rush of air filling up my ear. "Scott's looking for you."

I freeze. Sawyer Caldwell suddenly seems very far away. Of the two of them, he's never actually tried to kill me.

I would never do something like that to you.

"How do you know?" The question comes out in a rasp.

"Two weaselly pieces of shit came by my apartment this morning. Early, too, like 7 AM." I can tell how rattled she is, which just scares me even more. "They said they were PIs, that he was worried about you, that you might have *hurt yourself.*" She spits that last part out like its venom. "Wanted to know if I knew where you might have gone."

My chest is so tight that it doesn't matter how deeply I try to breathe, I can't get enough air. The kitchen spins around in a whirl of steel appliances and sunlight.

"What'd you say?" I manage to choke out.

"Said I had no fucking idea, of course, and told them to dig up the backyard at your house."

I let out a disbelieving laugh. "You didn't!"

"Sure as shit I did. Not that they'll do it. Like I said, he definitely hired them." Charlotte pauses for a minute, and all I can hear is my heartbeat pounding in my ears. "I had an idea, though. Something to throw him off the trail."

"I'm not letting you do something dangerous."

"It's not dangerous. You left your credit cards, remember?"

I blink. I did leave my credit cards, my bank cards, all of it. The only thing I kept was the card to my private bank account, where I squirreled away money from the low-paying nonprofit work I did as Scott's pretty little trophy wife. My grandmother had her expensive lawyers set it up when I got married, saying every woman needs secret money of her own.

She was right about that.

"What about the credit cards?" I ask.

"I'll start using them," she says. "Here and there around California. Create a false trail." I can imagine her counting off on her fingers as she talks. "I can hit San Jose in a bit. Then Berkeley—I want to meet with an art gallery up there anyway."

It's not the worst idea. Anything to keep him from looking toward the East Coast. Still, my heart's still pounding up in my chest. "Just be careful," I tell her. "They're going to be watching you, too, you know."

"And I'll keep an eye on 'em. You think I can't skip a tail?" Charlotte laughs, but I just deepen my frown as I curl my fist up in my shirt.

"I'm sure you can," I tell her. "But Scott has money. Resources. He's obviously trying to keep this quiet—"

"Edie. I've got you. They're focused on you being in Cali, and we're going to keep it that way. Got it?"

"Yeah." I lift my gaze up from the counter, at the small little living room. Images from last night keep flashing through my head. Sawyer Caldwell sliding his long killer's fingers into my pussy. His eyes darkening like a thunderstorm when he saw the bruises Scott ringed around my neck.

How did I get to be so fucked up, that I married one psychopath and then nearly fucked another?

"Edie?" Charlotte's voice cuts through my thoughts.

"I'm here," I tell her. "I'm fine."

"Yeah, and we're going to keep you that way. Have you eaten yet today?"

I close my eyes. "I slept in. I'm about to fix something."

"Slept *in*?"

Part of me wants to tell her. Charlotte has an artist's dark streak. A fascination with the macabre. But my mouth won't form the words. As far as she knows, Sawyer Caldwell tried to kill me fifteen years ago in the exact same manner my husband tried to kill me last week.

And trying to explain how he's still alive... even I don't understand that.

"I was exhausted from driving out here," I finally say. "Seriously. I'm going to fix lunch right now, and then I'm going to drive into Roanoke to get real groceries."

"Text me when you're back," she says. "And I'll keep you posted, okay? Especially if Scott starts pulling out that mourning husband missing person bullshit."

"Thanks." My throat's dry as we say our goodbyes and I hang up. For a minute I just stand there in the kitchen. The last twenty-four feels like a dream, like something disconnected from reality. I escaped Scott and ran into a nightmare, who—

Who killed for me.

The porch. The blood. That feels like a dream, too, something too bizarre to be real. But that's the last fucking thing I need. No one comes out here, Sawyer said, but what the hell does he know? He said he'd been in the ground for the last fifteen years, whatever that means. Surely he wasn't being *literal*.

I suck down a gulp of air and stride over to the front door before I can stop myself. My stomach surges as I brace myself for seeing that gore in the sunlight. At least I won't have to see the head again. I don't remember the man's face. I only know who it is because of what Sawyer said to me. How he deserved it.

Did he deserve it?

But when I pull the door open, the porch is clean. Not a trace of blood anywhere.

I blink down at it, not sure what to make of it. I'm so unmoored after all the trauma of the last few weeks, of the last few years, that for the first time, it occurs to me that maybe I hallucinated Sawyer's visit last night. That it had been an exhaustion dream.

You found his cum on your kitchen floor.

I stumble back into the cabin, leaving the front door open to let in the afternoon sunlight and the cool September breeze. I barely realize what I'm doing until I'm standing over the trash can. I press the lever with my foot, and there it is. Proof.

The bundle of paper napkins I used to clean up Sawyer's mess. I lift it up, bring it to my nose for a quick sniff. There's no denying that fishy bleach smell, and I feel the same thing I did when I first found it, a surge of disgust and desire. And a relief, this time, that I hadn't imagined it after all.

I step back, tossing the napkin back in and then letting the trash can lid close with a metallic clink. Outside, the wind surges, pushing autumn into the cabin. Dead leaves, a faint scent of old soil. I wash my hands and go back out to the porch, feeling numb.

So he cleaned it.

Sawyer Caldwell, the notorious Fat Camp Killer, slaughtered another person in my defense, brought me the head like a deranged cat, and then cleaned up the mess.

Because you asked him to. I had, hadn't I? Last night comes to me in tatters, but I remember that much. Worrying about the head. The blood. And he'd taken it away.

I lean against the wooden banister, the peeling paint glossy against my palms. The forest rustles around me. The leaves haven't started to turn yet, not really, but there's a burnished quality to them. Like gilded pages in an old book.

He's out there somewhere. Lurking in those trees. Sliding like smoke through the shadows. Watching me. The thought blooms in my head and then goes straight to my clit, which aches the way it had last night as Sawyer kissed me, touched me. Worshipped me.

I squeeze my thighs together, dizzy at the memory. Dizzy—and ashamed.

The wind blows. The trees sway, slow and lazy. And I wonder if he's watching me now.

CHAPTER TEN

SAWYER

Mama would tell me I'm so fucking stupid.

She had all these rules for me growing up. Things to help me not get caught. *If they see your face, kill 'em.* Or, *Don't go hunting in the closest town.*

Two violations in twenty-four hours, right there.

I was a little tense at first. I cleaned off Edie's porch because I figured she'd call the police no matter what I said to her. Scrubbed all the blood with a big rough-bristled brush early this morning before the sun came up. The head I set out on the big dogwood tree next to the church to start rotting. It hurt a little that she didn't want it, I'll admit, but maybe she'll like it better when it's just bleached white bone.

The whole day, I'm on high alert, working outside so I can track the scents on the air. If the cops show up, I'll smell 'em, and even though I doubt they're going to hack their way through the overgrowth to find my little church, I want to be prepared.

They never arrive, though. I even hike over to the old camp-grounds and watch from the trees. Everything's quiet and still. At one point, Edie comes out and leans against the porch banister with the wind pushing her hair away from her face, and my chest gets all tight and twisted, seeing her. She's so fucking pretty. So fucking *lush*. It takes every ounce of willpower not to stalk out into the open and taste her again, but I can't let myself get too distracted. I stole the truck from the two men I killed, and I need to drive it into Roanoke and ditch it so I can buy a truck of my own, something that can't be traced to a double murder. Need to buy a generator, too. I keep daydreaming about bringing Edie back to my church, cooking up some of the venison I caught, then tying her down to the bed and fucking the shit out of her so I can feel her pussy come around my dick.

Well, maybe not the fucking. I'm still afraid I might get carried away and kill her. But everything else would be good. I can't do it if there's no electricity, though. I want things to be nice for her.

Mama would say I shouldn't worry about killing Edie. In fact, Mama would say I *should* kill her after we have our fun. I'll admit I've thought about it. I think about it after Edie goes back into her cabin, the slam of the screen door echoing out into the woods. I'd do it nice. Eat her sweet pussy, then fuck her slow and romantic, and then slide my knife into her heart so she dies quick and doesn't feel anything but there's still lots of blood, hot and red and slick as silk.

The thought gets me hard, but it also gets me sad, and that's how I know I won't do it. Probably.

I take care of my errands the next day, when I feel even more certain that my perfect prey hasn't called the police on me. I don't know why not. If it's because of me, or because of the thing with her ex—she's in hiding, I figured that much out. I accept the gift, though. Be stupid not to.

Getting the truck and generator is easy. Even after fifteen years in the dirt, all the old protocols come back to me quickly. I drive out to Roanoke and leave my latest victim's truck in a Food Lion parking lot. Then I toss the keys in a storm drain while I walk the two miles to a used car dealership, where I buy a beat-up

Chevy, the engine rumbling like an old tomcat. It's more than I expected but cheap enough I can still afford the generator at Lowe's, plus some groceries and things to make the church feel a little more welcoming.

While I'm out, I see a Halloween store, a big garish orange and black sign, and I get this prickle over my face. A mask. I need a mask if I'm going to start killing proper again. The last one I made myself, a little arts and crafts project with Mama, our hands all sticky with plaster of Paris. Buying one'll be easier.

The store's mostly empty. Just a teenager manning the register, watching me with hooded eyes. I ignore him and make my way to the back where there are rows of rubber masks hanging on the walls, a bunch of vaguely familiar movie monsters. They haven't changed much in fifteen years, it looks like.

I stand there for a long time, trying to make my decision. The mask is important. It's part of my identity. It *becomes* my identity in the moment of the kill. That's something Jaxon taught me. When I drag my victim down to the ground by their throat and press my blade into their flesh, I am, in that moment, their entire universe. I'm their god. And I don't want that god to look like something they saw at the local multiplex.

Eventually, I settle on a sleek grey mask that I think is supposed to be some kind of demon or wraith or some such. Its mouth is all twisted up and angry, but otherwise, it's simple. Effective. It costs me nearly fifty bucks, but it's worth it.

The next few days, I fall into a rhythm. First thing I do when I wake up is check on my perfect prey. Not because of the cops, just to see what she's doing. She has a rhythm, too. She likes to drink her morning coffee out on the porch, sitting on an Adirondack chair she must have dug out of somewhere, her bare feet up on the banister. Something has her nervous and worried; I can sense it. Smell it. It might be me, but honestly, I don't think so. If it was, she would've called the cops.

No, it's her ex. The one who gave her that black eye, that dark necklace of bruises. Thinking of him makes me want to kill, so I try not to think about him. I've got to wait. I've got to be patient. I can't draw attention to myself.

After Edie finishes her coffee and goes back inside, I go back to my place, too, and work on the repairs. I fix the holes in the roof so the place will stay dry when the autumn rains start up in earnest. Clean the pews of the dirt and leaves and dead things that have accumulated there over the years. Repair the window frames so I can slide them open and let in the damp, musty forest air.

After lunch, I always visit my perfect prey again. I notice that she usually leaves the cabin in the afternoons and wanders around the campground, or hikes up the trail that leads into Altarida. If I catch her when she's outside, I follow her, not saying anything. Just watching her. It's easier for me. It's how it was fifteen years ago when this seed in my chest quickened and started to grow until my whole body felt tethered to her. It's easier to watch her move through the dappled, autumn sunlight, waiting for those moments when she senses me, stops, looks out to the trees.

If she sees me, she doesn't acknowledge it. And I don't say anything, just watch her, memorizing all the new things about her. I want to go to her again, but every time I think about calling out to her, my voice lodges in my throat and I think about Mama scolding me for letting those girls she brought me go. Letting them live. *That sort of thing, it's not for people like us,* she told me, eyes firm. *We're the monsters that keep them in line.*

Even though when I made Edie come, she didn't look at me like a monster.

Still, I leave it. Most days I don't see her in the afternoon anyway. Her car will be parked outside, and the cabin windows might be open, the weather being so nice now. But I don't see her, just smell her. Just *feel* her.

It goes like this for a week or so. Then one afternoon I'm at the church, doing my cleaning, and I find a bird skeleton tucked into the book holder on the back of one of the pews, a pile of tiny hollow bones topped by a pale skull, as delicate as a flower. The meat's long gone, and it's so pretty that it immediately makes me think of her.

She didn't like the first head I brought her, but I wonder if she'll like this one.

I gather up the bones as carefully as I can and take them into my bedroom and line them up on my shelf, all except the skull. That I cradle in my palm as I walk outside. I planned to hike it over to her, but it feels so small, so light. Like it's not quite enough. Certainly not enough compared to the first head I brought her, still rotting up in the trees, the flesh falling away in long strips. I squint at it, still wondering if she'll like it better when it's clean. That'll take weeks, though.

That's when I have an idea. I know she's not like me, obsessed with death and bones. I ain't stupid. And I still want to give her the bird skull because it's so pretty. But maybe I can give her something else, something I know she'll like. Another pretty thing, like that cupcake she was admiring the day I killed for her.

So I don't walk to her cabin. Instead, I nestle the bird skull in the seat of my truck and drive into Altarida and go into the bakery and get one of those spiced apple cupcakes, watching with my hands shoved in my pockets while the lady behind the counter wraps it up in a neat white box. Not the same girl as the last time I was here; this woman's older, and I listen to her heartbeat and feel my Hunter's hunger surging. Not for the woman, necessarily. I just can't go too long without killing or else I get antsy.

That's also why I drive to Edie's place instead of back to mine and walking over. Because I intend to just leave the cupcake and the bird skull and get the hell out. I know I probably shouldn't let myself near her again until I've killed someone, until I've quieted the urges.

The campground gleams in the autumn sunlight. Her car's parked in its usual spot, and the windows are open, so I know she's home. I cut the engine and gather up the two gifts, stack them on top of each other, and my heart beats way too fast as I go up to the front porch. Faster than it did the first time I did this, gripping the head by the hair as blood dripped across the dirt. Killing makes me brave.

I put the gifts on her banister, setting the bird skull on the cupcake box, arranging it so they'll be the first thing Edie sees when she opens the door. I think about knocking but decide not to; she'll see my truck, so it's not like I can disappear for real.

So I just step off the porch, turning on my heel, and trudge back toward my truck. The wind's cool, whispering of winter, but the sun's warm against my skin.

And then I hear it. The click of the door opening. A breath of silence. And then—

"Wait!"

CHAPTER ELEVEN

EDIE

When I hear the crunch of tire wheels through my open windows, I nearly have a heart attack. I'm draped on the sofa, reading a romance novel on my phone. My tenth this week. If I don't keep myself distracted, I'll start panicking about Scott.

And thinking about Sawyer.

The tire crunch sends me into full panic mode, though. Scott is keeping his search for me private. No weepy missing person's press conferences. No announcements on his various social media accounts, no earnest videos of him begging for any information about the whereabouts of his beloved wife. He's rich enough that he's a public figure even if he's not really famous, but he's keeping this close to his chest. And that terrifies me

It terrifies me what he wants to do when he finds me.

So when I hear the tire wheels, I immediately leap to my feet and pull up Charlotte's number. If she gets any kind of weird call from me, she'll be on it.

I sidle up to the window, listening. With the windows open, I can hear everything. Heavy, steady footsteps marching across the dirt. Stepping on my porch.

I peer out, trying to hide behind the curtains. I can't see the porch from here, or who's standing on it, but I can see the beat-up pickup truck parked behind my car. It was probably red once, but now it's a kind of dusty pink color.

I hold my breath, waiting for the doorbell. For a knock. There's nothing. Just the scrape of boots across the dirt. And then—

My heart drops out of my chest as the figure moves into view. Tall, lanky, dark curly hair, a blue flannel shirt.

Sawyer.

Sawyer. I toss my phone aside, my panic subsiding a little. Not entirely, of course. Has he killed someone again? Brought me another fucking head? I have the thought, sudden and sharp, that the reason I haven't seen him for a week is that he drove that dusty red pickup truck all the way to California to collect Scott's head.

Don't be stupid. That would take longer than a week. You'd have heard about it.

Then I realize Sawyer's leaving. I also realize that, inexplicably, I don't want him to.

So before I can talk reason into myself, I drop the curtain and fling the front door open and shout, "Wait!"

He stops, head lifting, and I notice what he left for me.

A small white baker's box and a small white bird skull.

I step onto the porch, the wind fluttering the hem of my dress. "Wait," I say again, and he turns his head, eyes dark and shrouded. I pick up the bird skull.

"Did you kill this, too?"

He turns around completely to face me. God, I hate how fucking handsome he is, every part of him lean and angular. When he was stalking this camp fifteen years ago, his knife blade dripping blood, I never would have expected him to look like that under the filthy mask.

He frowns at me.

"Don't kill birds," he calls out. "Not unless I intend to eat 'em."

I blink. It's not remotely the answer I expected from him.

"I found it," he goes on. "Thought it—thought you might like it. That's for you, too." He nods toward the white box, shoves his hands into his pockets, fixes his gaze on me. It would all be normal—sweet even—if he wasn't sizing me up like the murderous predator he is.

I set the bird skull back down, careful not to break it. It's beautiful. Beautiful and strange and eerie, a memento of a creature that once twittered in the tree branches and fluttered through the forest but hasn't for a long, long time.

Footsteps scrape against the dirt. He moves closer to me, slow and cautious. I pick up the white box and pull it open, half-knowing what I'm going to find but still feeling this gut punch when I see it, piles of sugared butter and glittery marzipan leaves.

Huge huge huge huge huge huge—

Dead eyes gaping at me, old blood congealing where I now stand.

"Thank you," I say stiffly, folding the box closed, hating that I can't just accept this gift even if it is from a killer.

Sawyer stops on the other side of the banister, frowning up at me. "I thought you wanted one," he says. "Saw you looking at them in the bakery the other day." His frown deepens; his eyes darken. Fear twists in my chest. But only a little. It's not like with Scott, who brought me gifts of expensive chocolates just so he could see me toss them in the trash, my thinness—such as it was —more important than my happiness.

I swallow and look out the woods, trying to figure out the best way to answer. "I did want one," I finally say. "But... it's complicated. Thank you, though." I let myself glance over at him, and he's staring at me in that way that reminds me he's a killer. Like he wants to devour me. "I do like the bird skull."

Something flickers across his face. A flare of lust. It's the same way he looked at me the other night as I relented to his touch.

I think he can see it, that strain of darkness inside me.

"What's so complicated?" he asks. "About the cupcake?" He scowls a little. "The stupid thing cost me damn near five bucks. You really ain't gonna eat it?"

I laugh in spite of myself. "Five dollars? It'd have been eight out in California."

He tilts his head, and a curl of hair falls into his eyes. It takes every ounce of my willpower not to reach over the banister and brush it away.

He's a fucking killer, Edie.

"Is that where you've been?" he says. "California?"

"Yeah." I stack the bird skull on the cupcake box and lift them both up. Sawyer just stares at me, and I realize, with a jolt, that I don't want him to leave. When he's here, I'm not thinking about Scott. I'm not *worried* about Scott. That sick, twisting anxiety that's followed me around the last week is gone.

"Do you want to come inside?" I ask.

Sawyer's eyes go wide. For a second, I'm sure he's going to say no. But then he grins, and there's just enough cruelty in it that it's not *exactly* a heartthrob grin but Jesus Christ is it close.

"Want a repeat of the other night?"

I laugh, disbelieving.

Do you?

"I was actually just going to offer you some coffee." I had no idea I was going to say this until I do. "And tell you why I'm here, if you want to know."

The grin wavers and something in his eyes softens. "Oh. Yeah. I'd—I'd like that, actually."

I try to ignore how weird this is all is, how I'm inviting the man who terrorized me in for coffee. Terrorized me on paper, anyway. In the papers. On the podcasts.

The man who actually terrorized me—well, it's easy not to think about him. Not with Sawyer here.

I carry the cupcake and the bird skull inside, listening to his footsteps as he follows me, heavy against the cabin's wooden floor. I wouldn't say I'm scared of him, but it still feels wrong to turn my back on him. The skin on my neck prickles, and I glance over my shoulder.

He's watching me.

I put the two gifts down on the counter and go to brew some coffee, sneaking glances at him like he might attack me. He doesn't. He stands stiffly beside the counter, eyes drinking me in.

As the coffee brews, I turn toward him. This is the first time I've ever seen him in the sunlight, a thought that doesn't occur to me until now.

"Your bruises are fading," Sawyer says.

It startles me, how forthright he is. My fingers go up to my throat. "Yeah."

"Are you going to tell me about it?"

The coffee bubbles and hisses as it brews. I walk across the kitchen and stand on the other side of the counter. The sunlight flooding the cabin is bright and vaguely golden, carving out Sawyer's sharp, distinctive features. He tilts his head a little, watching. Waiting.

"My husband tried to kill me," I start.

"Ex-husband." He says it quickly, eyes flashing.

"Well, yes." I run my hand nervously over my hair. "At this point, yes, obviously. Once I feel safe enough to—" I look at him. "That's the part you're hung up on? Not the part where he tried to kill me?"

Sawyer's eyes glitter. "I already knew that he tried to kill you."

Fair enough, I suppose. I lean my elbow on the counter, eyes fixed on the bird skull. The cupcake box. "He's abusive," I say. "He's always been abusive. Emotionally, mostly." I wonder if someone like Sawyer Caldwell even understands what that means.

"But in the last few years..." I trace invisible shapes on the glossy counter. "I'm in recovery for an eating disorder," I say, and the words feel strange in my mouth, kind of knotted and twisted. "I went into recovery a few years ago. Scott—that's my husband—he didn't want me to."

A darkness passes over the counter. It's Sawyer, leaning close to me. "Why not?"

His stare is so intense that it almost feels as if he's slicing apart my skin. I lift my gaze to him, wondering if that will lessen it, but it only makes it worse, seeing his big dark eyes and his full lips and his sharp cheekbones. *He shouldn't look like that,* I think, and I know it's my eating disorder voice, singing the same song in a different key.

Evil is ugly. Goodness is beautiful.

"Because I gained weight," I say flatly.

Sawyer frowns. "You're the same size as you've always been." It's not cruel, the way he says it. Just stating a fact.

I laugh, though. "It's been fifteen years. I don't know where you—"

"I was in the ground."

I still don't know what he means by that. I'm not sure I want to know. I sigh. "After what happened... here."

He doesn't react.

"After what happened, me being the only survivor, I was in the news a lot. Lots of pictures of me on the Internet. And since Camp Head Start was a weight loss camp, well... you can imagine."

"It was?"

I look up at him, certain he's mocking me.

"I didn't pay attention." He shrugs. "You don't need to lose weight, Edie."

His words hit me like a punch. Or a knife. I'm struck silent by them, and I curl my fingers against the counter and take a slow, deep breath.

"Thank you," I finally spill out, and I mean it. Has anyone ever said that to me? That exact sentence? I don't think they have.

"Didn't then, either," he adds, and then he tilts his head like he's waiting for me to continue.

And I don't know why. Maybe it's the way he's looking at me or the fact that he seems to like me the way I am when no one ever has before. But I keep going.

"It was the stress," I say. "What started it, I mean. All that attention—it made me self-conscious. And made me feel out of control. Everything was being done to me. Not eating was something for *me* to do, you know? The only thing I could do, it felt like."

He stares at me, and I have no idea what I'm seeing in his face. In his expression. I've been through this so many times, with Dr. Valunzuela and the recovery group and even Charlotte. Never with a man, though. And certainly not with a...

Whatever Sawyer Caldwell is.

"It's my fault," he says suddenly.

"What?" I *really* don't know how to react to this. I mean, he's not wrong, but I don't particularly want to tell him that.

"I killed those counselors for you." His voice is strangely flat. "They treated you like shit, all four of them. I watched it for two damn months. I knew you probably wouldn't see it the way I did, you not being a Hunter and all, but I didn't think—" Something clouds up in his eyes. "I didn't think about the aftermath like that."

We stare at each other. My mouth is dry, my heart fluttery and tight. Everything this man does startles me. Confuses me. It's been like that since the beginning, when I faced him in the dining hall and fully expected to die, only for him to show me the kindness I'd been missing since the camp closed and I'd been trapped with the tormenters my mother hired.

He reaches between us and grabs the cupcake box and pops it open. The scent of sugar wafts into the air, nearly drowning out the scent of coffee gurgling behind us. It pulls me back into the present, out of the past.

"Coffee," I say. "I'll fix you some. How do you like it?"

It is utterly bizarre to ask him that question, like he's just an ordinary guest.

"Black," he says.

What a surprise.

It's a relief to turn away from him, to go tend to the coffee. My hands shake as I pour out two cups. One black, for him. The other with a splash of half-and-half, for me. I can hear him moving behind me, and when I turn around, he has the cupcake out of the box—

And he's clutching a knife in one hand.

CHAPTER TWELVE

EDIE

"What are you doing?"

It barely comes out a whisper. Sawyer smiles, that cold smile he has.

"Eating some of the cake," he answers. "I'm not letting you toss it in the trash."

My cheeks heat. "I'm sorry," I mumble. "I'm sorry, it was a thoughtful gift—" Weirdly thoughtful, that he even noticed me looking at the cupcakes. That he remembered. "I just—it's hard for me to eat things like that. Even now."

"Why?"

He slides the knife through the cupcake's mound of frosting, slicing it in half, and I realize it's the knife he stole from me the other night. "Have you—" I can't get the rest of the question out, and Sawyer peers up at me with an arched eyebrow. I set the two cups of coffee down on the counter and make a kind of stabbing motion with my hand.

"Have I killed someone?" He looks down at the knife buried in the cupcake. "Oh. Not with this knife, no." When his gaze meets mine again, he's grinning devilishly. "I'm sure I'll christen it soon enough, though."

Terror spikes in me, and I grip the side of the counter, head swooning. He looks at me, carving out a sliver of cupcake and balancing it on the flat side of the blade.

"You're going to eat my fucking cupcake, and then you're going to kill me." I'm oddly numb to the idea. Just like how I was numb after Scott hit me. First in the jaw and then again in the eye. Harder, that time. Then he hit me everywhere. I stared up at him, my mouth filling with blood, and I felt this numbness.

But Sawyer laughs. "I fucking told you I ain't got no interest in killing you." He lifts the cupcake. "And you said you didn't want this."

"I do want it."

I don't know why I say that so quickly. Maybe it's the relief of hearing that I'm not going to die. At least not right now.

"It's just hard for me," I say. "It messes with my head. I feel guilty and shitty afterward."

Sawyer's eyes never leave mine as his long tongue slides out to lick the frosting away. I shiver, remembering how that tongue felt between my legs.

"You don't need to feel guilty about something like this." He eats the whole cupcake sliver in one bite and then licks away the frosting still clinging to the knife's steel, long and slow and sensuous.

I grip the counter's edge again, but this time, it's not from fear.

"It's good," he tells me, and he slices off another piece of cake. Something about the way he handles the knife makes my body hot and buzzy. Like it's an extension of him. And I wonder if he looked the same way when he was killing my tormenters fifteen years ago or that piece of shit who sent me spiraling a week ago.

And I hate myself for wondering and not being disgusted by the thought.

"You didn't finish telling me about your ex," he says. "Why he got mad at you for—" He waves the knife around, and the blade reflects the kitchen light into my eyes. "For getting better, yeah?"

I sigh and pick up my coffee, more for the warmth against my hands than anything else. The wind rolling in through the open windows has taken a chilly turn. I'd forgotten what a real autumn feels like.

"My husband—"

"Ex-husband."

I look at Sawyer, and he's dead serious.

"Yeah, ex-husband. My ex-husband is Scott Henser."

Sawyer shakes his head, goes to carve out another slice of cake. "If I'm supposed to recognize that name, I don't."

"He's a venture capitalist."

"I don't know what the fuck that is, either."

I smother a smile. "He's just—a rich asshole who gives money to tech companies. Anyway, he's famous, sort of. In certain circles. And he's very image-conscious."

Sawyer licks the cake away from his knife again, the moment showy, his eyes boring into me. We're both thinking the same thing. And it's not about Scott.

Still, I swallow. "I was never really his type," I say. "Even with the anorexia. I was a little too big for his liking. But my family—they're old money, and he wanted that prestige. Me going into recovery was just a step too far."

Sawyer slices another piece of cake and holds the knife lightly between his fingers, watching me. "That's why he hurt you?"

"No," I say. "He did it because he found out I was going to leave him. He wants me sick. I want to be well. But for me to initiate—" I keep staring at the cupcake. I haven't really talked about *this* with anyone, except Charlotte, and even she only knows the broad strokes. Scott launching himself at me, squeezing his hands around my throat. *You don't get to fucking leave,* he kept screaming over and over. *I leave you, you fat fucking bitch. Not the other way around.*

Then me kneeing him in the balls, wrenching myself away, grabbing my phone and running barefoot out of the house and calling 911 all at once. That humiliated him too, I'm sure. And I'm sure he paid good money to keep it covered up, the cops rolling up to the big beachside mansion on a domestic dispute call. But I was long gone by then. In clothes I borrowed from Charlotte, the two of us plotting my escape as we drove to San Francisco.

"It embarrassed him," I finally say, "and he tried to kill me."

Rage flashes in Sawyer's expression. It's the only word for it. A black, unrelenting rage that's like a tornado tearing across his face Then it's gone.

"You don't have to worry about anyone killing you," he says. "Not anymore."

His words shouldn't bring me comfort, but they do. *He's not going to have to kill anyone for me*, I think, trying to reassure myself. *Because no one will find me here.*

Sawyer's still staring at me. "T-thank you," I say softly, because I know I should say something.

"You should try this." He holds up the knife still bearing the cupcake slice. "Don't have to eat the whole thing. Just try it."

Then he walks around the counter, coming face to face with me, the knife hovering between us. I gaze down at it, breathe in the scent of butter and sugar and cinnamon. I don't want the stupid cupcake as much as I want to be able to eat a cupcake and not feel like an abomination.

"Go on," he says, more softly. "It's good."

I look up at him, and I think of all the times I refused to eat something in front of Scott or his friends, who had become my friends by default when we married. How virtuous I felt, dressed in designer clothes, sure, but in sizes at the top of the range. Every butter-drenched appetizer or sugary macaron or slice of crusty French bread was a whispered threat that my entire life teetered on the edge of a blade. And I'd shove things aside, and people would praise me and then gossip behind closed doors that I *had* to be a binge-eater, didn't I? Because no one eats that little and stays that big.

"Eat it."

Sawyer's voice is sharp and commanding. It reminds me of how he spoke to me when his hand was between my legs, ordering me to have another orgasm.

Ordering me to experience pleasure.

"Off the knife?" I say.

He smiles, a slow creeping killer's smile, and nods.

Why does my breath catch at that?

He steps closer, lifts the knife to my lips. I catch a glimpse of my reflection, although not much: a flash of my brown eyes, a curl of my black hair.

"Lick it," he purrs, and my face heats as I imagine licking something else, something as long and hard as that knife. I lean forward, cautious, and dip my tongue into the frosting.

Flavor explodes on my tongue, an overwhelming sweetness redolent with cinnamon and cardamom. Pumpkin spice. I curl my tongue to draw the frosting into my mouth, and Sawyer watches me the whole time, his eyes burning. He holds the knife steady. It doesn't wobble at all.

Which is good, because its sharp edge is dangerously close to my throat.

"That's it," he says. "Taste the gift I brought you."

His words urge me on. I don't let myself think about why. Instead, I eat the cupcake off the knife's cold steel, licking it the same way he did, with my eyes on him. It's delicious, tender and buttery and flush with sweet autumny notes of apple, but what really sets my body to shuddering is the way Sawyer's lips part, the way his pupils flood his irises.

"Lick the knife clean."

I do, drawing my tongue along the flat silver side, lapping up every crumb, every smudge of frosting. When I'm done, I let my gaze linger on him as I pull my tongue back inside my mouth, dizzy with a confused, disorienting lust.

The next thing he does, he does as quickly as a snake.

The knife clatters against the counter, the sound reminding me a little of wind chimes, and he lunges at me, wrapping his long fingers around the back of my neck. And then he crushes his lips against mine, his kiss hard and unyielding. I melt into it, kissing him back with a fire, a hunger, I haven't felt in a long, long time. He presses his body into mine and draws his fingers around my neck so that his thumb presses into the little hollow of my throat. There's no real pressure, but there's the promise of it, and I know I should hate it, I know I should shove him away and call the police, but I don't. I just keep kissing him, moaning into his hot, eager mouth as he massages my pulse.

He breaks the kiss to trail his mouth over to my ear. His other hand is on my hip, drawing up the fabric of my dress. "You're so fucking beautiful," he rasps into my ear. "The most beautiful creature I've ever seen."

I whimper and kiss him in response, attacking him with the fervor he used on me, because those are words I've never heard in my life, and every time I'm in his presence it unlocks all the shameful desire I've felt for him since that night fifteen years ago.

I'm not surprised when his fingers slide into the waistband of my panties and rub against my clit. He laughs when I jolt against him, teeth scraping my lips. "Come for me again," he says into my mouth, slipping one finger into my pussy. I spread my legs to accommodate him, winding my arms around his shoulders for balance. He responds in kind, dropping his hand away from my throat to hook my knee up and spread my pussy wider.

I shiver at the absence of his hand around my throat.

"You're so eager," he murmurs, sliding another finger inside me. I don't bother to deny it; how can I? I know how wet I am. All those dark, deadly looks. All his dark, deadly praise.

It doesn't matter anyway; he catches my mouth with his again and pulls me close for another devouring, murderous, sugar-flavored kiss. I roll my hips against his hand, impaling myself on his long fingers. He squeezes me around the waist, stilling me, and takes control, curling his fingers against my inner walls as his thumb rolls agonizing circles over my clit.

It's not going to take long. That much is clear. All the tension and adrenaline of the past week is about to spill out over Sawyer Caldwell's dexterous hand. I break the kiss to suck down air, gasping and moaning, my fingers clinging to his hair.

"That's it," he mutters, his Appalachian drawl as sweet as honey. "That's it, my perfect prey."

My perfect prey. The words shudder through me and draw my orgasm along behind them. I scream as the tension breaks and heat pulses out from my clit and my pussy both, rolling and thunderous. Sawyer doesn't stop, just keeps touching me until I think I'm never going to stop coming.

It subsides eventually, of course, and to my surprise, Sawyer does pull his hand away and lowers my leg to the ground. I lean against him, squeezing him for support, and he wraps his hands around my waist and nuzzles his face against my neck, breathing in deep.

"Thank you," he breathes. "For letting me kill you like that."

I stiffen against him, and if he notices, he doesn't say anything, just keeps nuzzling my neck. Then he kisses me, right on my pulse, and steps away. His face is flushed.

There's a telltale bulge between his legs.

"I—I mean—" I flounder, not sure what to say. My eyes keep dropping down to his cock, and to my embarrassment, he notices, because he adjusts it in his dark jeans and says,

"Not right now."

"Oh." Disappointment curdles in my chest. An old humiliation, that all his pretty words were a lie.

"Ain't safe." He sounds sheepish. Embarrassed. He doesn't quite meet my eye. "For you, I mean. I gotta—" He swallows,

Adam's apple bobbing. "Don't want to go too far. Don't want to kill you in the wrong way."

Ice shoots down my spine. I back up, knocking against the counter. "I thought you said you didn't want to kill me," I whisper.

He fixes me with his black eyes. "I don't," he says, voice hoarse. "*Want* to."

My mouth opens, closes. I have no words. Not for any of this.

He nods at me, a curl of hair falling over his forehead. Nods at the counter, with the mostly-eaten cupcake, the two undrunk coffees, the lovely bird skull.

"You don't have to eat the rest of that if you don't want to," he says, still not looking at me. "But I hope you do."

And then he's gone. He darts out the front door and leaves me standing there in the sunlight and the wind blowing in from the forest. His truck engine starts up and fades away.

I turn toward the counter, my movement shuddery.

I eat the cupcake. Slow, luxurious bites that let me taste everything. I wash it down with my coffee. The freedom of that is almost as good as the release of orgasm.

Then I gather up the bird skull. It feels like nothing in the palm of my hand. But at the same time, it's as heavy as my memories.

I carry it into the bedroom and set it down on my bedside table, where I know it will be safe.

CHAPTER THIRTEEN

SAWYER

It takes me five strokes before hot cum spills over my fingers, my body shuddering. I groan and slide my other hand out of my mouth, where I lapped up the last of Edie's taste, and lean back in the seat of my truck. My church waits for me on the other side of the windshield.

It was torture driving away from the old campgrounds, her scent wafting around me, filling up the truck cab. I had half a mind to pull over to the side of the road, but I made it home even if I didn't bother to get out of the truck first.

I wipe the cum off my fingers using a handful of old fast food napkins that had been in the dashboard when I bought the truck, then step out into the cool forest air. I'm still buzzing from touching her again, especially since I hadn't expected to even see her at all. When she came running out of that cabin, her dress streaming out behind her like a flag, my heart nearly erupted out of my chest. I wasn't ready.

She wanted you.

I hear it in Mama's voice, her whiskeyed Texas drawl. My brain fills in the rest of what Mama would say: If I want to fuck her, I should fuck her, and then kill her so she doesn't start causing me problems. *You can't be soft with these girls. You aren't like them, Sawyer. Neither of us are.*

I stalk over to my church, thoughts drumming. It's been too long since I killed someone, that's the real problem. Both of the heads from my earlier kill are still up in the tree, the flesh soft and rotting. I need to add more to my collection. The more bones I have, the quieter the urge'll be, and then I can fuck my perfect prey without worrying that'll be the end of her.

I go into the church, the door slamming shut behind me. The mask I bought is propped up on the old altar, glaring at me as I walk down the aisle. I swipe it off and go back outside, blood pumping furiously through my veins. Then I sniff the air.

It's the usual scents: The forest. Edie. Faint whispers of other humans, hikers or campers making their way through some distant part of the woods. I'll find one of them. It doesn't matter who.

I just need a kill. I just need to feel the hot blood gush over my hands. Then she'll be safe, my Edie. Then I can touch her the way I want.

Still, it takes me the better part of an hour to find my victim. A hitchhiker, grimy from travel, a threadbare backpack on his thin shoulders. I catch his scent as I wind down the mountain, wafting off the highway where he's trudging along the side of the road. As soon as I see him, my vision goes red, and I get this hot surge of lust that isn't exactly like when I see Edie, although it's close. In the same neighborhood, as they say.

Killing him is easy. He doesn't know I'm there, doesn't see me coming. It's not like the last kill, where I had a reason for it beyond my own raging hunger, and I do it pretty quick, stabbing him in the side so I can drag him behind the tree line, where I open his throat and let the blood run hot over my hands. I like the way it looks, the blood all red and glossy, and I have this fantasy about touching Edie with my bloody hands, leaving streaks of crimson across her pale belly.

It's a nice thought, and it doesn't send a hot fire raging through me, neither, so the killing really did help. Left me satiated, you know. I leave the hitchhiker where I killed him except for the head and one of the hands. Trophies for my collection.

It's nice to have my head clear for the first time in a week. I take the long way home so I can pass by the old campgrounds, although I stay deep in the trees and shadows while I watch the house. Edie closed everything up, the windows and the front door. I don't know if it's because of me or because it's late in the day and the temperature's dropping. It is colder than when I set out, but I hardly noticed it from all the exertion.

The next day, I tell myself I'm going to work on my bones and my church. Now that I'm calmer, and she's let me finger her sweet pussy on two separate occasions, it ought to be time to ask Edie if she wants to fuck. I don't think she'll say no. But I'm still hesitant about it. Someone like her, someone I've dreamt of for so long, I don't know what it's going to do to my brain the second I'm inside her. What if fucking her with my cock isn't enough? What if I need to sink my knife into her smooth, soft flesh, over and over, while I draw in her last gasping breaths?

I can't fucking stand the thought, even if at the same time it makes me rock hard.

So I focus on my first task of the day: stripping the meat off my victim's head and hand as best I can. It's too late in the season for the bugs and heat to do the work. I might have to bury everything, at least until the frost settles, so I work on tilling up a bone garden just outside the entrance of the church. The air's cool but the sun's out, and it bears down on me, slicking my skin with sweat.

When I've buried my bones, I move on to repairing another window in the church, stripping out the old sealing and replacing it with some new strips of rubber I picked up at the hardware store in Altarida. By the time I finish that, it's noon, and my stomach is growling and my muscles are aching from all the hard work I've done.

I also successfully distracted myself from the thousands of things I want to do to my perfect prey.

I go inside and take a long shower, washing away the grime. Then I start fixing up my lunch.

That's when I notice it. A change on the air.

Hunters.

I smell two of 'em, the coppery blood scent that always marks another of my kind. I take my sandwich and cold beer outside to get a better handle on the situation. They're close, from the scent of it, but they'd been downwind when I was out working, coming up from the south. North Carolina, probably.

I eat standing up, squinting out at the forest. If it's who I think it is, they'll be coming here. But if they don't come here, then it's not who I think, and we'll have a problem.

Especially if they're here for Edie.

Is her ex-husband rich enough to hire Hunters to track her down? I know some of us sell our services, even if I personally find the thought repugnant. I doubt he's a Hunter himself, from what she said. Human men are as capable of killing as we are. They just aren't as good at it. So with Edie still being alive?

Her husband's human.

Still, I worry as I open another beer and nurse it, drawing in the Hunters' scent as they come closer. I'm halfway through the can when I hear the crunch of tires on the narrow, overgrown dirt road winding up to the church. I finger the knife in my belt. Try not to think about Edie.

The car that pulls up in front of my church is as small and dark as a bullet. The windows are tinted, hiding the occupants, but I can smell them over the gasoline and machine-metal scent of the car. By this point, though, I'm pretty sure I know who it is.

Jaxon and Ambrose.

The car's engine cuts out, but I don't move from where I'm

standing, leaning up against the column that holds up the over-hang. I wait for them to get out of the car, and sure enough, Jaxon steps out of the driver's side, laughing when he sees me. He's grown his hair out, black ribbons falling around his shoulders.

"Holy shit," he laughs. "Ambrose was right. You're back."

Ambrose follows right behind him. *He* looks identical to the last time I saw him. Brown hair, grey stubble, a perpetual scowl.

"Told you I sensed him." Ambrose slams the door shut and strides toward me in his black cowboy boots. Fifteen years and he's still wearing the same damn shoes.

"I figured I had at least another month before you boys showed up."

Jaxon grins at that, sharp and wolfish. "It's your first resurrec-tion," he says. "We weren't going to make you wait *that* long."

My cheeks heat. I'm younger than the two of them, the least experienced, but I don't necessarily want to be reminded of it.

At least they're friends. Or the closest thing to friends people like us can have.

"Brought you something," Ambrose says, nodding over at Jaxon, who reaches into the backseat of the car and pulls out a slim black box. My heartbeat quickens at the sight of it. "After you went under, I saw on the news that they found your old place. Figured you'd lost everything."

"Not everything." I take the box from Jaxon, and I know immediately what it is. I can feel the energy of it coursing right into my hands. "But they took my good knife off me at the scene."

Jaxon chuckles at that, a mirthless laugh that seems to slice through the softness of the forest. "Always take your good weapons with you. Didn't your Mama teach you?"

I ignore him. I don't feel like telling either of them why I didn't have my Bowie knife on me when I dragged myself into the dirt, that it was because I'd slammed it into the wall so Edie would let me touch her.

"You wanna come inside?" I ask them as I pull the lid of the box away. Sure enough, there's a brand new Bowie knife laid out in there, identical to the one I'd had before. I pull it out, hold it up so it gleams in the sunlight.

As much as I like Edie's kitchen knife, that's purely sentimental. This knife feels like an extension of me. A part of my body.

I get a sudden flash of an image, me sliding the knife up between Edie's perfect thighs while she arches her back in ecstasy.

I shut it out. No. *No.* It doesn't matter how sweet a picture that is, I can't do it. I want Edie to stay.

To live.

"Depends." Jaxon's voice jerks me out of my head. "How disgusting is it?"

"I've been fixing it up." I push the door open. "It's nicer than what I had before."

And then I let them in.

CHAPTER FOURTEEN

SAWYER

We go inside. I don't bother turning the generator on during the day, so everything's lit up by the candy-colored sunlight pouring in through the stained glass window. Ambrose lets out a hum of approval. He has this thing about religion. Jaxon told me once he was a preacher, a long long time ago.

"Seems you're doing all right for yourself." Ambrose strolls down the center aisle, still taking in the church. "After the revival." He stops beside the front pew and looks up at the altar, where I've laid out my mask and weapons.

"It was Ambrose's idea to check up on you." Jaxon steps up beside me, silent as a cat. "We knew your mother wouldn't do shit."

I scowl at the mention of Mama. "She knows she doesn't need to worry about me." Which is true. We're Hunters; she taught me how to hunt, the way a mountain lion does her cubs. When she knew I could hunt without getting myself caught, she went south again, to pursue her own prey. It's how things are.

But Jaxon just shrugs. "I fucking hated my first revival," he says. "And I had it easier than most."

Up at the front of the church, Ambrose chuckles darkly. "Oh, you're willing to admit it was easier for you now?"

Jaxon rolls his eyes; I've heard this argument a dozen times already. Ambrose has a habit of adopting younger Hunters. Keeping an eye on them. He did it for Jaxon, and then both of them did it for me.

"Y'all want something to eat?" I say. That was a lesson from Mama, too, something leftover from growing up in east Texas. Something I rarely need to utilize.

It turns out they do want something to eat; they flew into Raleigh-Durham and then rented a car to drive up into the mountains proper. Hadn't stopped to eat for whatever reason. I fix them the same venison sandwiches I had for lunch, and we all sit down at the little folding card table I have set up in the kitchen while they eat and I drink another beer.

The conversation flows easy, the way it always does with them. They tell me about their work: Jaxon down in the Louisiana swamp, and Ambrose out in west Texas, stomping around in the blood-soaked dust. There's a new Hunter, he tells us, somewhere on the Texas coastline, although he hasn't reached out to them yet. Jaxon's been courting the media, posing his scenes with alligator skulls and palm fronds and other artsy shit and leaving them for some innocent bystander to find. Ambrose tells him how fucking stupid that is, and they bicker about it and I lean back in my chair and listen and it's like old times, right after Mama left but when I was still finding my footing. Before Edie and the murders at the camp, of course. Long before.

Eventually, though, they start asking about me. About the murders themselves, at first, with Ambrose grilling me like he's a schoolteacher and I just failed a test. "How the hell did you get shot in the head?" he demands. "Why didn't you have your eye on the door?"

I'm cagey. "Better than getting arrested." Which is true; the last thing one of us wants is to get stuck in jail, where dying means getting dragged to a mortuary and pumped full of chemi-cals. Still, Ambrose frowns.

"You should have known better," he says. "I saw the one who shot you. He looked like a fucking infant. I know you're young, but—"

"You were distracted." Jaxon gives me his Cheshire cat grin. "Weren't you, Sawyer?"

Now, how the hell could he know that?

"No," I say, too quickly. Too defensively. Both of them smell the lie and pounce on it like the predators they are.

"Shit, that makes sense." Ambrose leans forward, dark and imposing in his long black coat. "What was it? One of 'em boys give you hell?"

"The big one," Jaxon says, nodding. "The football star, right? He was there when you were shot."

"He was already dead," I snap, irritated that they think I struggled with one of my kills. "And I handled him just fine."

It's Jaxon who picks up on it. His blue eyes go wide and then glitter devilishly, and I immediately regret saying anything. I should have let them think it was that boy.

"The girl," he says slyly. "The survivor."

"The survivor." Ambrose hisses the word like a snake. "Oh, I should have known."

They both look at me. There's no denying it. I'm caught.

"Fine," I snap, crunching my empty beer can down on the table. "I was a little distracted."

That sets both of them to laughing and hollering and slapping each other's backs like this is just the funniest thing in the world. I scowl at them and go over to the cooler to dig out another beer, crack it open, and take a long drink.

"I saw her," Ambrose says. "In the papers and such. No cuts. Did you even touch her?"

My scowl deepens as I sink down in my chair.

"What was her name?" Jaxon asks. "I remember seeing her around. She went on that one podcast, what's it called—"

"Podcasts," Ambrose scoffs. "Not doing us any favors, those things. Makes anyone think they can start investigating our killings."

I'm not in a mind to listen to Ambrose rant about new-fangled technology, although there's a part of me that wants to know what the podcast is called. Wants to listen to it. Hear my perfect prey talk about me and what I did. What lies she told about those final moments before my death.

"She said you tried to strangle her or something," Jaxon says. "If I'm remembering right." He leans over the table, that devilish glint still in his eyes. "But you aren't a strangler. I know that much about you. You wouldn't give up your knife for anything."

My face is hot, and I drink my beer to keep from answering. Not that it'll work. Both of them are staring at me, waiting for me to answer.

"The girl got you killed," Ambrose says when I swallow my beer.

"No, she didn't," I snap. "I got myself killed. Turned my back to the door. And yeah, I was distracted, like I said." I can't decide if I want to tell them about her. I'm not worried they'll kill her themselves; that's not their style. But they'll tell me I should kill her. That I could take my time and enjoy myself, sure. But ultimately, they'd say the same thing as Mama.

It's better for her to be dead.

"She was pretty," Jaxon says. "I remember that."

My face gets even hotter, and before I can stop myself I say, "She's still pretty."

Both of them go quiet. I run my thumb around the rim of my new beer can, wiping up the condensation.

Ambrose clears his throat. "You looked her up? You've been back two damn weeks, Sawyer."

My head buzzes. I can feel my blood pumping furiously

through my body. The truth is I don't want to keep her a secret. I want to tell them everything I can about her. I don't have no one to talk to except my bones and they don't talk back. And yeah, I know what Jaxon and Ambrose are gonna say. But god, it's like a final breath building inside me, waiting to exhale.

"I didn't look her up." I peer up at him. "She's here. She's at the camp."

Both of them stare at me from across the table. Jaxon's the first one to speak.

"Did you *bring* her here?"

"No. She showed up a day or two after I woke up."

They look at each other. Ambrose's expression is dark, his brow furrowed. Jaxon laughs, though, and shakes his head a little.

"Well," he says. "Then it's gotta be fate, doesn't it?"

"It absolutely is not fate," Ambrose says. "It's dangerous."

But Jaxon keeps going on, looking right at me, his blue eyes burning. "The gods picked someone for you," he says. "And you're bound together."

"Not this shit again," Ambrose mutters.

Part of me agrees with Ambrose. This is Jaxon's thing, that there are these gods in the swamp and they tell him who to kill and every murder scene he sets up is some kind of prayer to them. I don't know, I don't go in for religion much myself. But right now, with my perfect prey ten minutes away from me? Knowing she arrived at the same time I dragged myself out of the dirt?

I can see it, those connections, those lines of fate drawing us together like threads of blood.

"I'm serious," Jaxon says, excitement building up in his voice. "You were chosen, man. The gods *chose* you, and chose this girl."

"We'll see about that when she calls the cops on him," Ambrose mutters. "Which will inevitably happen when she sees him skulking around the woods."

My skin prickles. "She hasn't called the cops." It's out before I can stop it.

Ambrose jerks his head up. "*She knows you're here?*"

I nod silently, my heart thundering.

Ambrose narrows his eyes. "What else does she know?"

I glance at Jaxon, who's watching this conversation with obvious interest, his eyes gleaming. I sigh. "More than you'd say she should." More than I know she should.

Jaxon laughs with delight and says something in that made-up language he uses. Ambrose just keeps glaring at me.

"What," he says, "does she know?" He shakes his head. "What did you do that night you got killed?"

I'm not telling them about everything I've done with her, about making her come and kissing her and all that. But I do tell them the story of the night fifteen years ago, how I did it for her and how she *knows* I did it for her. How I hugged her and she never told anybody, not even the cops. And how I killed for her again, last week, and she's kept my secrets this whole time.

Jaxon's thrilled by the story, the romantic that he is. "It's the Unnamed," he says confidently, which is what he calls one of the gods. "You've been marked."

Ambrose rolls his eyes. But Jaxon pushes back from the table, brimming with excitement. "I need to mark the church with the Unnamed's sigil," he says. "It's chosen you, Sawyer. It's the least you can do."

I know exactly how Jaxon plans to mark the church. He did the same thing to his own house: killed someone and then used their blood to draw sigils on the walls. I don't want blood sigils on my church, though, not if I'm gonna bring Edie here. "Can you use paint?" I say, which makes Ambrose snicker and Jaxon scowl. "There's a bunch of buckets of it in the storage closet."

"No, I can not use *paint*—"

"Sit down," Ambrose barks. "We're not finished talking about this."

He disapproves. The deep lines on his brow are more than enough evidence.

"What's there talk about?" Jaxon doesn't sit down. I know that sigil's getting painted whether I like it or not. "Even an old asshole like you *has* to see all the coincidences, right? These two are connected."

"Coincidences, yes." Ambrose is quiet, thoughtful. I understand his concern, I do. He's older than both of us, by a lot, and that means he's survived a lot. It means he's been careful. I trust his advice. Mama never told me who my father was, just that he was another Hunter, and Ambrose stepped into that role nice and tidy.

So when he speaks, I listen. Even if my heart likes what Jaxon's saying, too.

"Maybe there's something to it," Ambrose says slowly. "You and this girl. You sure she's human?"

I know what he means. But I shake my head. "She's not one of us," I say. "Not a Hunter." She smells like prey, when I breathe in her scent. She reacts to my touch like prey.

That's why she's so fucking appealing, but I don't tell Ambrose. If she were one of us, another Hunter, then she wouldn't be my Edie. I wouldn't want her so badly. I'm not certain of much, but I'm certain of that.

Ambrose's frown deepens even more. "You're young," he says softly. "But even you have to understand our kind isn't meant to get tender about humans."

I lean back in my chair. Wrap my fingers around the beer can. "I know that," I mutter. *But she's different.*

I don't know how, exactly. Maybe those gods of Jaxon's are real after all. Maybe they did tie us together that night, my blood-coated arms wrapped around her shoulders. Maybe I'm meant to protect her.

I definitely don't say *that* to Ambrose.

Instead, I just knock back a long drink of beer. It's gone warm and flat. "Mama always said the same thing," I tell them. "But I don't know. Edie—" I look through the grimy window at the forest outside, the leaves already browning at the edges.

She's different.

"She didn't call the cops."

Ambrose scoffs. Jaxon says something about that podcast he listened to, about the story she spun out for the real world, the one about me trying to kill her. Says it proves his theory. Because what sort of human lies to protect one of us?

He has a point.

"Just be careful," Ambrose says. "That's all I'm asking."

And I know he's right.

CHAPTER FIFTEEN

EDIE

Every time I look at my phone, I get this sick feeling in my stomach, like today is going to be the day that I learn that Scott has found me, that he's sending someone to Virginia. Or worse, that it will be the day Charlotte doesn't check in. And what would I do then? I couldn't stay here. Not if I thought Scott had gotten to her.

He hasn't gotten to her, though. It's been two and half weeks since I first arrived at the campground, and every day she messages me, as reliable as an alarm clock.

CHARLOTTE

Have you eaten yet?

CHARLOTTE

Bought some more shit with your card!

CHARLOTTE

Still no word from Scott's lapdogs.

She means the PIs. That one makes me nervous, that they haven't come around again. Because I know they're still looking.

And if they aren't investigating Charlotte, they're investigating something else.

The really fucked up thing, though, the thing that sometimes keeps me wide awake at night, blinking at the ceiling, is that the only time I'm not worried about Scott is when I'm with Sawyer.

That I even *think* of him as Sawyer, just Sawyer, and not Sawyer Caldwell—that gives me a deep shivery feeling, too.

I haven't seen him for a few days, which may be why I keep checking my phone, looking to see if there's a new message from Charlotte or a new Google alert with my name—there never is. Scott's still keeping my disappearance a secret.

It's weird, being out at the cabin by myself. My marriage to Scott had been lonely even though I was always surrounded by people. The thing is they weren't *my* people, they weren't *my* friends. I didn't have friends, save for Charlotte. I had *acquaintances*, and Scott expected me from the beginning to mold my life to his, to be a reflection of him.

And I accepted it for so long because it was the sort of happiness I had seen in my own family. It was everything my mother told me would make me happy, in fact: being hungry and thin (or as close an approximation as I could manage). Being married to a rich man. Living in a glass and steel mansion by the Pacific Ocean.

It was a happiness I willingly unraveled by finally seeking treatment for the eating disorder that allowed it all to happen.

So I understand loneliness. But the loneliness in the cabin is different. I'm actually *alone*. The only company I have is Sawyer, and he shows up when he feels like it, dispenses a few mind-blowing orgasms with his hands or tongue, talks about killing me in a way that doesn't make me as frightened as it should, and then leaves.

Two and a half weeks of this. I've got another month and a half before my booking runs out and I'll have to decide what to do next.

I'm wary of driving into Roanoke, the closest thing to a city out here. Even though Scott hasn't declared me missing, I worry someone will recognize me. So I make do with Altarida and the cabin's TV and my ebooks and the walking trails winding through the forest. I walk a lot, actually, listening to music through my earbuds, willing my mind to go blank.

Unfortunately, today has turned out cold and dreary, the sky the kind of steely grey that makes the rest of the colors in the world seem more vibrant and saturated. The leaves are just starting to turn, streaks of crimson and orange veining through the woods, and I go out on my porch to have a cup of hot coffee and watch the rain.

Maybe I'm hoping for Sawyer to step out of the trees. Sometimes I imagine him wearing the mask he wore that night we— met? I suppose that's the word for it, even though it feels wrong. Kind of empty. Everything with him is so fucking confusing.

Eventually, the rain stops, and the air has turned genuinely cold. I have exactly one sweater, an oversized cardigan that either I or Charlotte shoved into my bag during the flurry of my escape from California. Whichever one of us had the foresight—well, I'm grateful for it now. I need to get out of the cabin.

I shrug on the sweater, grab my earbuds, and head out to the trailhead on the other side of the run-down cabins. I've ignored them pretty much the entire time I've been here. They remind me too much of my summers at Camp Head Start, even though they look nothing like they did, all weatherworn and peeling, the windows nailed over with boards. The forest though, that's nice. Funny how the trail feels new. Familiar from the last two weeks and not fifteen years ago.

I weave into the trees. The music starts to irritate me, tinny and repetitive, and so I switch it off and just listen to the sounds of the mountains. There's a soft rhythmic dripping everywhere from the last of the rain as it falls off the leaves. My footsteps sound slick and soft as I tread over the rotting debris of the forest floor. There's no insect sounds like when I first arrived. No frog song. Summer's dead.

I'm fine with that, honestly. All my nightmares happened in the summer: Sawyer's murders at Camp Head Start. Scott trying to kill me. My entire life in California, where it's always summer.

"Fuck summer," I whisper. I'm much more used to the sound of my own voice.

The forest responds with its own crackling and creaking. I feel a shiver pass over my skin, as if ancient Appalachian ghosts are watching me hike. And when I look out at the gloom, I almost think I see them. But no, it's just wisps of fog from the thick, choking dampness.

I keep walking, looping around the trail to head back to the cabin. It feels good to get out and move around, but I'm cold, my single sweater is damp from old rain, and water's seeping in through my shoes. I'll need to see about getting more clothes. Maybe I can risk a trip to Roanoke after all.

But as I get closer to the cabin, I know that something's wrong.

My skin prickles all over, and I think at first that it's Sawyer, that he's left me another one of his presents and he's watching to see how I react. The thought fills me with a deep revulsion but also a tiny flicker of shameful desire.

You want him to touch you again.

My body warms at the thought. Traitor.

But when I reach the tree line where I can see the camp in the clearing, that warmth turns to a gripping, terrifying coldness. Something *is* wrong. And it's not Sawyer.

There's a car parked behind mine.

I stop, falling back into the trees, my heart pounding furiously up in my chest. The car isn't Scott's white Tesla, but it looks expensive, and I know immediately that he's responsible for this. Either he found out where I am and came here himself, or he sent someone.

Both options are unthinkable.

That's when the panic seizes up in me. I have my phone and earbuds and nothing else—not my wallet, not my ID, and, most distressingly, not my car keys, which I left hanging from the hook by the front door.

Find Sawyer.

The thought flares in my head like a star, but I push it aside. I have no idea how I would even begin to do that. And he's a fucking killer anyway.

My chest is tight with anxiety as I lean against the tree, listening for whoever came to the cabin in that car. I think I hear footsteps crunching around on the packed dirt and fallen leaves.

I duck behind the tree line, switch my phone to silent, and text Charlotte.

Someone's here. Don't know who.

I stare down at the phone, willing her to respond. But the message remains marked as unread.

Shit.

I slide the phone into my pocket and consider my options:

Stay in the woods.

Try to sneak into the cabin and get my car keys.

Staying in the woods feels safer, even if it's cold and damp. This intruder won't stay here forever, right?

But then I hear footsteps for sure, plus a low, soft whistling.

And they're coming closer.

I'm paralyzed. I want to go back down the trail and hide in the woods, but when I take a step it's as loud as thunder, thanks to all the leaves and broken branches.

The whistling stops.

"Mrs. Hensner? Are you there?"

The voice is smooth and calm and masculine. It's also not

Scott's, thank god, but it's someone he sent if they're calling me by my married name.

"Your husband's worried about you, Mrs. Hensner. My name's Matt Baro. Scott sent me here to help work things out."

I can't move, afraid that any sound will give me away. But he's coming closer. I can hear him crunching and crashing through the overgrown grass behind the old camper's cabins.

I catch a glimpse of him through the trees.

"Mrs. Hensner? Edie?"

The man who steps into the path is tall and well-dressed, with tanned California skin and a slick of blond hair. When he sees me, he smiles, and there's no trace of SoCal surfer in that smile at all. It's cruel. He found what's he looking for.

"There you are," he says, like he's talking to a lost pet.

I run.

CHAPTER SIXTEEN

EDIE

It reminds me of running from Sawyer fifteen years ago.

I dive off the hiking trail, plunging into the forest's thick growth. Branches lash out at me, stinging my face and hands as I try to claw them away. Baro shouts behind me, and I can hear him following me, both of our bodies crashing through the trees.

The only difference is I've been hiking the last hour. Adrenaline pushes me forward, and for a little while, at least, I can ignore the heavy ache in my legs, the constriction in my lungs. But I don't know how long.

"You don't have to run!" His voice echoes against the mountain. "I'm just trying to help you!"

Suddenly I feel strong, firm hands around my waist, and I'm jerked sideways, dragged roughly through a patch of sharp brambles. A gloved hand clamps on my mouth; a rubber mask brushes my cheeks.

"Shhh," says Sawyer, soft as a sigh.

He pins me against the ground, his hand pressed over my mouth. When I flick my gaze up to him, I only see a grey Halloween mask, some grimacing demon, and my whole body goes rigid. It's nothing like the mask he wore fifteen years ago, but it still somehow takes him, instantly, from Sawyer to Sawyer Caldwell, the Fat Camp Killer.

I whimper against his glove, and he holds a finger up to the demon's mouth.

"Mrs. Hensner!" Baro's voice drifts through the forest, his words punctuated by crashes of underbrush. "Come on out! There's no need for you to run."

I shake my head at Sawyer, my eyes wide. He gives me one small nod, then holds his finger to his mouth again. I get the message: *Stay quiet.*

He pulls his hand away from me.

For a moment I just stare up at him, shivering in the damp. Then he slides his arm around my waist and slowly pulls me to standing. Baro cracks a branch; it's followed a second later by a sharp, whispered, "Fuck."

Sawyer gestures for me to follow him, and then he moves carefully through the thick forest, stepping in patches of rain-drenched ferns. I keep one hand against his back like I need to balance myself, and I step where he steps, my heart thundering in my chest.

"Edie!" Baro shouts, but he sounds further away.

Sawyer stops and turns toward me, catching my wrist as he does. His eyes glint behind the mask, fierce and glittering, and my head spins at the memory of the last time I'd seen him in a mask. He looked at me the same way then, although I hadn't recognized it for what it was:

Concern.

He slides the mask up to the top of his head.

"Who is that?" he says, so soft I lean in to hear him.

"S-scott," I stammer out, then shake my head. "My h-husband. Someone he sent—"

Sawyer's eyes darken. "Is he going to hurt you?"

There's an unyielding darkness in the way he asks the question, and I am suddenly, painfully aware that the way I answer will determine what happens to that man.

Your husband is worried about you.

No, he's not. My ex-husband is almost certainly not worried about me. He's worried I'll tell people what he's done.

He wants me gone.

"Not him," I whisper, my voice hoarse. "But he'll tell Scott where I am, and Scott—"

Rage flares in Sawyer's face. It's the most terrifying thing I've ever seen.

"He won't," Sawyer says, "tell *Scott* anything."

He spits out Scott's name like it's a curse, and I tremble. Because I know what Sawyer's going to do.

And, even though it makes me sick to my stomach, I know that I'm not going to stop him.

"Edie!"

Baro's voice cuts through the forest. And it's closer now.

Sawyer shoves the mask back down over his face and points to his left. When he moves, I move, snaking through the trees. He's impossibly quiet. I make noise, but not much. Even so, every crack, every rustle, makes me freeze.

And then we come to a creek, swollen from the rain. Sawyer leans down and murmurs, his voice muffled slightly from the mask.

"Do you still have your phone?"

I nod, not bothering to ask how he would know I had it in the first place. I don't need to.

"Then time yourself. Follow this creek for eight minutes. At eight minutes, you'll be near a clearing with an old church. That's where I live."

I look at him sharply. But the only expression I get is that twisted demon's face, and Sawyer's glittering black eyes.

"Edie, we don't have to fucking do this!" Baro's voice reverberates around the mountain.

"You'll be safe there," Sawyer growls. "Now go."

He doesn't wait for me to respond, only turns and disappears between the trees. I stare at the place he'd been, numb to what I just unleashed. But then flashes of Scott's assault flash through my head. My neck burns from where he tried to strangle me.

He'll do it again.

A loud crack explodes through the woods, jarring me into action. I yank out my phone to check the time; still no message from Charlotte, which only adds another layer of worry. Then I walk along the creek, moving mechanically, jumping at every snap and rustle.

I've been walking for four minutes when a soft susurration floods the forest, and then suddenly it's raining again, a steady misting rain that soaks my hair and clothes. My phone buzzes in my hand.

CHARLOTTE

Holy shit are you okay? I'm calling you.

And then her face appears on the screen, the phone vibrating in my palm. I know I should answer. But I have no idea what I would tell her.

So I let the phone keep buzzing as I trudge through the rain, every muscle in my body tense and ready to run. The phone stills, and I realize I'm waiting to hear Baro scream.

I don't hear anything but the rain.

Eight minutes.

I stop and turn in a slow circle. The creek bubbles and gurgles beside me, staticky with raindrops. All I see is trees. There's no clearing. There's—

A flash of white. Just up ahead.

I move toward it, clawing through a drooping willow tree, and then, sure enough, I step into a clearing. Cold wind drives the rain into my face, but it also flattens down the tall, yellowing grass. At the center of the meadow is a run-down white church, the steeple pointing toward the storm clouds.

I stare at it. *That's where I live*, Sawyer said, and for some reason, this moment feels far more weighted than when I didn't stop him from going after Baro. Like if I cross this grass, if I go into that church, I won't be myself anymore.

I'll belong to Sawyer Caldwell.

Lightning splits across the sky, and when the thunder comes, it's so loud I feel it in my chest. I look down at my phone, streaked with raindrops. More messages from Charlotte. I'll let her know I'm okay. The rest—

The rest I won't tell her.

I slide the phone into my jeans pocket, my whole body shivering from the cold. The church rises in front of me.

There's another crack of lightning. I think I hear a man scream, but maybe not. The thunder is too deafening to hear anything else.

Call 911, whispers a voice in my head. **End this now. You can end this now.**

The rain stings my face. My hair plasters to my head. My clothes are completely soaked.

And I walk toward the church.

I DRIP water onto the foyer, staring down the aisle at the tidy row of pews and the small altar in the empty space at the front. My family wasn't a religious one, and I can't remember the last time I've been in any kind of holy place.

Not that this place is holy.

It doesn't exactly look like a killer's lair. There aren't bodies strewn around. No blood splattered on the walls. But I can tell that it's been abandoned for a long time. Half the pews are clean, but the other half are filled with debris from the forest.

The walls are grimy and falling apart except where they've obviously been repaired, and there's something strange to me about that, Sawyer Caldwell whiling his days away repairing an old church.

Unfortunately, it's also cold in here. The light switches don't work, which I take to mean no electricity—and no heat. I strip off my damp sweater, hoping that will help, but it doesn't. At least the church is dry.

I walk down the aisle and up to the altar, where I see Sawyer has laid out an array of knives, including the kitchen knife he stole from me. There's an empty space in the row, which makes me feel kind of hollow and shuddery.

Off to the side of the altar is a small, simple door. I push it open, bracing myself for dead bodies and rotting blood. Instead, it opens into a small kitchen: a rickety card table, metal folding chairs, a couple of old coolers. Beer cans lined up neatly on the counter beside a few stacked plates and a pile of silverware.

It's all so... *normal.*

Still, I'm afraid to look in the coolers. The kitchen opens into a narrow hallway, so I keep going on my little exploration. The rain sounds louder in the hallway, like the roof is thin, and I pass a bathroom and then come to a bedroom, as tidy as the kitchen.

The bed is made up with flannel sheets, and I suddenly want to crawl in and wrap myself in them. But I can't bring myself to get in Sawyer Caldwell's bed, even if I allowed myself in his home.

But I'm freezing, my body buzzing from the cold, so I peel off the top blanket and wrap it around my shoulders.

It smells like him.

I go back into the main part of the church and curl up on one of the clean pews and stare at the stained glass window beside me. It shows a brown-haired Jesus holding a white lamb, the colors muddy from the storm.

I pull out my phone. There are half a dozen text messages from Charlotte. I finally tap out a response, my hands shaking.

> I'm in a safe place. I can't talk just yet. I'll explain later, but I'm safe.

I stare down at the message, reading it over and over. I can feel my pulse in my throat, and I honestly don't know if what I wrote is true. Is the home of a serial killer ever a safe place?

It feels like it. At least right now, in this moment, with the storm raging outside.

I hit send.

CHAPTER SEVENTEEN

SAWYER

My prey is lean and athletic. He moves with an easy grace as he lopes through the rain, even though he has no idea how to do so quietly. I can sense the irritation radiating off him that he's out here in the middle of nowhere, ruining his expensive suit. But there's excitement there, too, that he found his own quarry.

"Edie!" he calls out. "This is getting absurd! It's going to start storming any minute!"

My fingers curl around my knife.

He stops under a big tulip tree, cursing quietly beneath his breath. I move closer, never taking my eyes off him. Edie said this isn't her ex-husband, but it is someone who could tell her ex-husband where she is, and we absolutely can't have that.

Which is why, when the man pulls out his cell phone, I purposefully crack a nearby branch as I step out from behind the greenery.

The prey jerks his head up, my Edie's name on his lips, but he freezes when he sees me standing there, my new Bowie knife clutched in one hand. Jaxon and Ambrose left yesterday, leaving me with the knife, a garish sigil painted on the back of my church, and a fair amount of warnings not to do what I'm about to do. But I asked Edie, and she didn't say no, and my heart fluttered furiously in my chest that she would accept this gift from me.

"Who the hell are you?" The man's fear makes the words dance.

I say nothing.

"Early Halloween costume, huh?" He looks down at his phone, trying to play it cool, and I step toward him, making the leaves rustle.

He looks up. There's a soft pattering as the rain starts again.

"Shit," he hisses. "Look, man, whatever you're doing—" His eyes drop to my knife, back up to my mask. "I'm looking for someone. A woman in her thirties. Dark curly hair. She ran out here and..."

I take another step forward, and my prey's voice trails off. The scent of his fear lifts off his skin, pungent against the steely scent of the rain.

"This isn't fucking funny," he says, and then he laughs, nervously, like it is. "She put you up to this, didn't she?" He laughs again, a breathy, panicky sound. "You can come out now, Edie!" He shouts it out into the incoming storm. "Call off your fucking redneck!"

I'm tired of it, his bravado and the scent of his fear. I want to smell his blood.

So I launch at him, moving with a Hunter's swiftness, and plunge the knife into his belly. He makes a sharp noise of surprise, lifting his eyes to my mask, and the usual expressions flicker across his face: shock, confusion, a burst of betrayal. As if I owe him anything.

I wrench the knife sideways so his blood spills out along with a mess of glistening organs. I don't care about those as much as the blood, which is rich and salty. I've never been to the ocean, but I imagine it as smelling like blood.

"Edie," he gasps out. "Did you ki—" Blood burbles from his lips.

I stab the knife higher into his abdomen, quick sharp penetrative bursts, each one splattering more blood over my hands and arms and chest. The rain makes it runny, but every stab brings another hot spray. More. I need more. And the man is tottering on his feet. He's dying.

So I cut one of the threads of blood in his neck—the carotid artery or the jugular vein, I never bothered to learn fucking anatomy. All I know is that it erupts. Blood gushes out in a gorgeous, steaming fountain, and I gasp it as washes over me, its heat a perfect contrast to the cold rain. I hold him up a minute, relishing his gasps and gurgles. When he finally silences, I drop him.

For a minute, I stand there, breathing heavy. My cock strains again my pants, and I consider, briefly, fucking one of the holes I made in him. But then I think of Edie waiting back at my church, and I realize that I don't want to be unfaithful to her.

I do palm myself, trying to ease my fire. But it's raining and cold and I can't enjoy this moment properly, so I give up.

Maybe, *maybe*, I can fuck my perfect prey instead. I can see it, me still covered in blood, thrusting deep into her.

My blade slicing across her throat just as she starts to come—

No. I will not kill her like that. I have to focus.

I move quickly, irritated by the rain. I pick up the man's phone, turning it around in my hands. It's locked, but I try his fingers and pressing his forefinger against the back opens it up. So I saw off his finger, then shove it and my phone in my pocket.

I want more than a fingerbone to remember this one, though. I don't feel like trying to get his head, so I take his arm instead, the one with the hand intact. The rest of the body I leave where it is after I root around in his pockets for his car keys—I'll need to dispose of that once I get cleaned up. Can't leave it in front of Edie's cabin.

Fortunately, we're far enough away from the trail and the cabin that it's unlikely anyone's gonna find his body. And soon enough the leaves will cover him, and then the snow, and then he'll be gone.

And if someone comes looking for him? Well, I'll kill them, too. I'll kill anyone who comes searching for my perfect prey.

IT DOESN'T TAKE me too long to get home, and I make it just before the skies unleash the storm, the air buzzing with electricity. I race across the clearing, head ducked down. Edie's waiting for me in the church; I can smell her, that sweet honeyed scent, and it makes me feel all warm and shuddery that she came here, that she's waiting for me. I never told Jaxon and Ambrose and I *certainly* never told Mama, but I always wanted to come home after killing to find a woman waiting for me, all wide-eyed and worried about me while I was on the hunt.

Before I go in and see Edie, I go around back to turn on the generator. She's probably cold. I also drop the arm there since I figure she doesn't want to see that.

This is where Jaxon painted his stupid sigil—in *paint*, at least, but it still looks creepy as shit. Maybe I'll just keep her away from the back of the church completely.

Once everything's settled outside, I go in through the side door, stepping into my little bedroom just as fat raindrops splatter across the clearing. Inside, it's dark and cool and the cover's been stripped off the bed. Edie's doing, no doubt.

I peel off my mask and drop it on the bedside table. Its work is done.

"Edie?" I call out, relishing the way it feels, calling out to my girl as I come home. If she even is my girl.

I go down the hallway, bump up the heat, and then step out into the church proper.

She's waiting for me, just like I always imagined.

She's wrapped up in the blanket on the front pew, the light from her phone shining onto her face. Her hair's all wet and bedraggled, but she looks at me as I step into the room.

Fear shoots through her, ruining the image.

"It's done," I say, as if it's not obvious, with me still streaked with blood. I pull the phone out of my pocket. "Got this for you."

Edie swallows. "Thank you." She puts her own phone aside. "I—Did you check? To see if he had contacted my—contacted anyone?"

I just shook my head. "Brought his finger so you can open it up, though."

She blanches at that. Fuck, this isn't what I thought it'd be like. She's so fucking pretty, but she's also like this scared little rabbit, and my blood is up and my cock is hard and I keep picturing myself cutting her open while I fuck her.

"You cold?" I say, trying to be normal for once. "You can borrow some of my clothes while yours dry. I need to take a shower anyway."

I can't resist coming closer to her. I need to give her the phone. And the finger.

"I turned the generator on, too," I add. "But I only heat the back." I tilt my head. "The kitchen. And the bedroom."

We both know she went in my bedroom; she's got my bed's blanket wrapped around her shoulders. But the word feels loaded to me anyway. Puts visions in my head I shouldn't be thinking about.

"O-okay," she says slowly. "The heat—the heat will be nice."

I smile at her, trying to make this feel the way I'd always imag-ined it. And to my surprise, she smiles back. It's small and it's scared, but it's there.

"Come on," I tell her, and I wait for her to get out of the pew. As soon as her back's to me, I pull the finger out and open up the phone for her, then tap her on the shoulder so I can hand it to her. She blinks down at it.

"Don't let it lock," I say. "Unless—"

"Right," she says quickly. "The, uh, the finger."

I nod.

We go into the kitchen together and Edie sits down at the table, still shivering beneath her blanket. She swipes through the phone, her brow furrowed, her worry lifting off her. I duck into my room and dig out some clothes—fresh jeans and flannel for me, sweatpants and a sweatshirt for her. When I come back into the kitchen, she looks up at me. Does she look… relieved?

"He hasn't sent anything to Scott," she says, setting the phone down on the table. "About where I am, I mean. But it looks like he had a partner. They knew he was here."

"Don't worry about that." I put the sweatshirt and sweatpants on the table, and Edie just stares down at them. "For you," I say, worried it's not clear.

Edie looks at them, looks up at me. She seems hesitant, and I don't know why. "Thank you," she finally says. "I'll—I'll wait here while you—" She swallows. "While you clean up."

I study her for a second longer, the way she looks sitting in my kitchen, wrapped in my bed's blanket. My cock throbs a little. I'll need to take care of it in the shower so I don't do something I regret.

I gather my change of clothes up to my chest. I keep thinking about what her blood will look like against her pale skin, but I don't want to end her forever.

I hate it, this push-pull. These warring desires.

I leave her in the kitchen.

CHAPTER EIGHTEEN

EDIE

He's absolutely drenched in blood. When he found me stretched out on the pew, doomscrolling through social media while I avoided Charlotte's texts, my first thought was that he was injured and I needed to drive him to the hospital.

And then my brain caught up to me. Because it's not his blood.

He doesn't seem bothered by the blood, though. Not as he hands me Baro's phone or brings me a change of clothes. I keep staring at him, thinking back to that night at Camp Head Start. Because that was the last time I saw so much blood in one place, and it hadn't belonged to Sawyer Caldwell, either.

He gives me a short nod before he steps out of the kitchen to go to the shower, his footsteps drowned out by the rain thundering against the roof. I shiver, hating the feeling of the cold, clammy fabric against my skin, but I'm afraid to change into the sweatpants and sweatshirt he brought me. The ED voice is hissing in my head, telling me that it will be humiliating to try and put them on. Sawyer is a slight man, slighter than you would expect for someone who has killed, at least as far as I know, six people. Almost certainly more.

One he *just* killed. For me.

To protect me.

The thought makes me dizzy, and that makes the ED voice louder. It's as cold and vicious as it's ever been. *You lost control*, it says. *You lost control and look what happened. And you think you'll even be able to pull those fucking sweatpants up around your thighs?*

I brace myself against the table and breathe in and count to four. Breath out. Count to four. I try not to think about Sawyer covered in someone else's blood. Sawyer asking me if I'm cold. Sawyer bringing me his spare clothes.

The shower turns on, the water rushing on the other side of the kitchen wall.

I stare at the sweatshirt and sweatpants. Maybe it's better to just wear my wet jeans and T-shirt while I wait for my sweater to dry out. I left it draped along the back of one of the pews.

The water gurgles through the pipes, reminding me that Sawyer is on the other side of the wall. Covered in blood. Naked.

My face heats. I shove away from the table and pace around the kitchen, pulling the blanket—*his* blanket—tight around my shoulders. He protected me. He protected me at Camp Head Start, in a fucked-up sort of way. Every single one of those counselors tortured me. There's no other word for it. They denied me food and water. Screamed abuse at me. Forced me to the brink of heat exhaustion. They only relented in their cruelty when he started to kill them, picking them off one by one.

Shameful heat blooms between my thighs.

I stop just at the entrance of the hallway, squeezing the blanket tight in my fist. The storm rages outside, the lashing rain pummeling the roof. The cacophony of it matches the cacophony in my thoughts, frantic and thrashing. I'm eighteen and I'm staring down at Michelle Evans' body, her blood soaking into the dirt outside the cabin. I'm hiding in a closet, my breath tight and terrified. I'm telling Blake Foster I left my phone in the dining hall after dinner and maybe it's still there and I can call for help and he scoffs and says no. *Are you kidding, Edie? Look at you. We both know you can't fucking run. I'll go.*

And then he was dead, too, and there was only me and the killer.

They can't hurt you anymore. I won't let them hurt you ever again.

For so long, I wouldn't let myself think of that moment between Sawyer and me. Not because of the trauma—that came from elsewhere, from when I cradled Gavin Ward's body while he died and then when it happened again, when Sawyer died in my arms. But that moment, between those deaths, wasn't traumatic. I didn't let myself think of it too often because I didn't want to wear the memory away until it was nothing.

So I would only ever think about it in the dark, one hand between my thighs with the other clamped down on my mouth to stifle my moans. And it's time to confront the fact that what happened two weeks ago was not the first time Sawyer Caldwell made me come.

Thunder booms so loudly that the entire church vibrates. When I move, surging forward into the hallway, it almost feels like I'm outside my body, like something else is drawing me closer and closer to him.

I stop in front of the bathroom, my heart pounding in my chest. The shower runs on the other side of the door, nearly drowned out by the sound of rain against the roof.

My face buzzes. I should walk away right now.

But Sawyer *protected me*. He's the only person, other than Charlotte, who's ever done that.

I pull the blanket away from my shoulders and let it drop to the ground.

The ED voice hisses and snarls and tells me I'm broken.

Lightning floods the hallway with a sudden, blinding light, and the thunder that follows makes the walls shake.

I know I shouldn't do this. I know I should leave. I should go back to my cabin. I should call 911. I should get in my car and drive far, far away from here.

Instead, I push the bathroom door open.

Warm, damp air greets me, a welcome balm against the church's chill. I expected Sawyer to be in the shower already. I expected to have another moment before I could change my mind.

Instead, I find him standing naked beside the tub, his back to the door. He's testing the water with one hand, but before I can duck out into the hall, he turns around and sees me.

I'm frozen in place. I can't take my eyes off him—his lean, wiry body, his skin crossed with faint scars. Blood coats his shoulders, the top part of his torso, his arms and hands. But his face is clean.

His cock is also clean. And erect. It rises from the dark thatch of hair between his legs, thick and long. It's big. Bigger than Scott's.

"Edie." His voice is hoarse. His eyes swallow me whole.

My heart beats like a hummingbird's. I can't back out now. I don't want to back out now.

"Sawyer," I whisper, stepping over the threshold. He doesn't say anything, like he's waiting for me to speak. The shower creates hot clouds of steam.

And I know I crossed this line a long time ago.

"Can I—Can I join you?"

CHAPTER NINETEEN

SAWYER

She can't be in here. She can't be looking at me like that, her eyes sweeping down my torso and lingering on my cock. It's too dangerous. My blood is boiling.

But fuck me, she looks perfect. Her wet shirt clings to her torso and reveals the outline of her bra, the pebbles of her nipples. Her hair curls around her face. I can't stop staring at her.

"Can I—Can I join you?" she whispers.

I know I should tell her no. Send her back out to the church. I can jerk myself off while I think about biting into her hard nipples until she bleeds. It's safer that way.

But she takes a step toward me, her eyes big and scared but at the same time flooded with lust. I can't send her away. The most I can do is warn her.

"Edie, if you get in this shower with me, I'm going to fuck you whether you want me to or not."

Her breath hitches, and I know I should tell her the truth of it, that if I fuck her then I might kill her. But she answers before I can.

"I want you to."

It's like a bomb goes off in my head. She gave me permission, and there's nothing I can do to stop myself. I clear the bathroom in two steps and devour Edie's mouth in a brutal, agonizing kiss. She melts into me, her tongue lashing against mine as I twist my hand up in her hair to hold her in place against the counter. I want to consume every inch of her bite by bite.

I drop my free hand down to squeeze at her tits, and I'm reminded she's still dressed.

"Get this off," I growl into her ear. "Now."

I release her and step back as she peels the wet T-shirt away from her skin, her eyes constantly flickering over to me. I stroke my cock listlessly as I watch her undress in an agonizingly slow strip tease. I need her naked. I need her flesh.

"Hurry," I tell her, not sure how much longer I can contain myself. I try to calm down by fucking my hand as she drops her shirt aside, yanks on her jeans. It's torture. She's taking too long.

And then she fucking *stops* and looks up at me in her bra and panties. I squeeze my dick so hard it hurts. "Keep going or I'm going to cut them off of you."

Something flashes in her expression. A dangerous flirtation. "You don't have your knife."

I grin at her the way I would a victim, showing all my teeth. "Then I'll rip them off you with my bare hands."

Edie just looks at me—

And then drops her hands at her side, one eyebrow arched, like she's daring me to try.

Oh, that is *very* fucking dangerous. Lust surges through me, and I lunge at her, ripping at her panties to get at her naked body. I scrape my nails against her skin and for a moment I'm not ripping her underwear off. No, I'm rending her flesh from her bone.

Edie moans as I claw at her bra, bringing me back to reality. I tear violently at the hooks on the stupid thing until it comes undone, then I fling it aside. Edie's breath quickens against my skin, and I capture her mouth again, yanking hard on her leg to hike it up around my hip and give me access to her sweet, hot cunt. I press my cock up against her folds—not entering her, not yet. But her arousal is more than clear.

"You're wet for me." I still don't quite believe it, that I could kill for her, that I could come to her covered in another man's blood, and she still wants to fuck me. And yet the evidence is right there, soaking across my dick.

And then she confirms it completely with a whispered, throaty, "Yes."

I can't stand it anymore. I need to kill her. I need to fuck her. Right now, they're the same thing.

I grab her by the waist and drag her into the shower as if I'm dragging her into the ocean to drown. She cries out when the water hits her skin—I like it almost painfully hot. I silence her scream with another kiss, ruining her mouth before I move down to ruin her neck with my teeth. Edie moans, bucking against me, and I slide my hand up between her legs until I find her throbbing clit.

"Are you ready for me?" I growl the question into her throat. I don't know why I ask. I'm going to shove my cock into her whatever she says.

It doesn't matter, though, because she gasps out, "Yes," and that's all I need to hear. I whirl her around and press her up against the tile, knocking her legs wide until I see her pussy glistening through the haze of shower steam. Then I press my cockhead against her pretty pink flesh, bracing myself before I slide into her. Because I still don't know what's going to happen when I finally feel that wet, willing cunt clamp down on my cock.

Edie whimpers and bucks her hips backward like she's as desperate as I am. And I can't wait any longer. I thrust my full length into her, and it's like I'm thrusting my Bowie knife into her soft belly and splitting her open so I can reach in and grab the most precious parts of her.

She even fucking screams like I'm cutting her.

But I'm not cutting her. My knife is on the altar where I left it, and my cock is buried in the pussy I've dreamt about for fifteen years. For a minute, I can't move. Can't even fuck her proper. All I feel safe doing is wrapping my arms around her waist and chest and pulling her up to me so we can stand like that, interlocked beneath the hot, steaming water, the blood running down my body in ribbons. She's breathing hard against me, and I can feel her heart thudding beneath my palm.

And I know, suddenly and fervently, that I will never silence that heart or still that breath.

Because killing her means I will never feel *this* again. Being inside my perfect prey is the closest thing to Heaven that I've ever known.

"Edie." I say her name like the prayer it is—

And then I start to fuck her.

It's easy, with the way the fear of my killing her just evaporated. I pound into her pussy as hard as I can, and she welcomes me, bracing one leg up against the shower wall so I can sink my cock even deeper inside her. I press her against my chest, squeezing and slapping at her big tits until she's whimpering and gasping and matching my urgency as she fucks me back.

I don't say anything. There ain't a single word in any language that could express how it feels to finally fuck my perfect prey, and so I don't try to ruin the moment. The only sounds I need are Edie's desperate moans, the wet slapping of her ass against my hips.

She's close to coming. I can feel it, the way her thighs tremble and her breath gets fast and panty. But when she drops her hand down to her clit, I know the angle ain't quite right for her to finish. Still, I immediately knock her fingers away and press my mouth against her ear.

"*I'm* going to make you come," I tell her, and then I thumb her clit. It's like pressing a magic button. Edie howls in pleasure, her body shuddering against mine, pussy walls fluttering furiously against my cock. It takes every ounce of willpower not to spill my cum in her right then and there, but I want to keep fucking her through her orgasm. I want to drag it out as long as possible until she's gibbering and wordless and limp with pleasure.

It works. Edie slumps against me, chest heaving, and I fold her over her a little so I can grip her hips as I piston in and out of her still-spasming cunt. She reacts, bracing her hands against the shower wall, and it gives me a whole new angle, a whole new sensation, one that sends a fire racing up my belly.

I'm not gonna last long, but I'm gonna enjoy every second of this.

I run my hand along Edie's spine until I'm holding her in place by the back of her neck. Some distant part of me knows I shouldn't be doing this because it's what her piece of shit ex did, but I still curl my fingers around to the front of her throat. Maybe I'm testing myself. Maybe I just want to imagine what it would be like to kill her without actually doing it. Maybe I just want her to know that she belongs to me.

I'm shocked when she doesn't shove me away.

"Edie," I gasp, increasing the pressure on her neck just a little. She moans, her pussy quivering. "My perfect fucking prey."

I can't stand it. Squeezing her throat, being inside her—none of it's enough. I want to possess her completely. I want to devour her body and her soul. But I don't want to fucking kill her.

Instead, I yank her up to me by her throat and sink my teeth into her shoulder, deeply enough that blood blooms across my tongue, salty and coppery and delicious. Edie screams—in pain, I think at first, but then I feel her come again. Small, fluttery. But undeniable.

How the fuck did I get so lucky?

I lap up her blood, still fucking her, certain I can taste her pleasure. My muscles tighten, and I keep tasting her while I come, moaning into my orgasm. It shudders through my whole body and leaves me almost as boneless as her.

"My god," Edie breathes, and I release my bite and nuzzle against her neck, holding her close to me. The shower pours around us, the air thick with steam, and I don't ever want to stop touching her. My Edie. My perfect prey. I kiss her everywhere I can, my lips leaving trails of her blood on her skin. I touch her everywhere I can, too, like I'm trying to memorize what her body feels like. Her tits, her ass, her belly. Her heartbeat.

Because I fucked her, and she survived.

And that means I can do it over and over again.

CHAPTER TWENTY

SAWYER

An hour later, Edie and I are tucked together in bed. The storm's abated, but it's still overcast, and the room is dark enough I could almost fall asleep. Edie actually has. She's all curled up against my chest. I run my fingers through her still-damp hair, listening to her slow, steady breathing.

I can't sleep, though. I'm worried. Not about what I'll do to her, not anymore, but about what other people will. The man I killed earlier is just the beginning, I'm sure. She said he had a partner. That partner will come looking for her. One disappearance is unusual enough. Two?

The only way I know how to protect her is to kill. But what if that puts her in more danger?

Edie makes a soft noise and rolls over and flutters her eyes open. Up close, I can see the streaks of green in her golden-brown irises.

"Did I fall asleep?" she murmurs, rubbing her forehead.

"For a little while." I grin, wrapping one of her curls around my finger. "I guess I wore you out."

She blushes and ducks her head, dark hair falling over her eyes. I pull her into me, wanting to breathe in her scent and feel her soft warm body pressed against mine. She yields to me, which is something else I find I like. Prey who wants to be prey. Prey who desires her predator.

"I do think—" I stop, not sure how to say exactly what I want to say. Edie looks up at me through the long fringe of her lashes, a line of worry creasing on her brow. "I think you should stay here."

When she doesn't respond right away, I add, "With me."

Her eyes go wide and she pushes up on one elbow. "Why?"

"So I can keep you safe."

Her fingers curl against my pillow. Her lips part like she's about to say something, but she only stares at me.

"You said earlier that the man had a partner," I say. "When that partner doesn't hear back, he's going to come out here. Or send someone."

"Police?" Edie says in a small, scared voice.

I melt at that. Such a human fear. "I wouldn't worry about those idiots," I tell her. "Especially if you're with me. They won't find you."

She rolls onto her back, the blanket sliding down to reveal the tops of her lush breasts, and blinks up at the ceiling. I expect her to refuse to stay, if I'm being honest. To tell me I'm a goddamn monster and she can't live in this rotting-out old church.

Instead, she says, "I think you're right."

"Really?" I sit up and she looks over at me. God, that'll never stop making my heart squeeze up in my chest, having her look at me like that.

Especially when she's naked.

"Yeah," she says. "I mean, if you don't—if you don't *mind* me being here—" She frowns and toys with her hair. "I've got another month left in the cabin, but if Scott's PIs know I'm there, I can't stay. I feel like if I leave Virginia, if I keep running—"

"They'll find you." I can't stop myself from touching her, running my fingers along the side of her neck, smoothing my hand over her chest, where I can feel her heart beating. I love it, the sensation of her blood pumping through her body.

"I can't believe they found me," she says softly. "I used a fake name. I've had a secret bank account for years, that's how I'm paying for everything. My friend Charlotte has been using my old credit cards in California so they'd think I'm still there—"

I grin at her deviousness. She's not a Hunter, but it seems she can think like one when she needs to.

"It wasn't me who ratted you out," I say, acting like I'm serious.

She laughs. It's such a soft, twinkling sound, a *normal* sound. I'm used to silencing laughter. To cause it?

I can't help myself. I roll on top of her, catching her mouth in a kiss.

She melts into me immediately, her arms wrapping around my back. The blanket's still between us, thin cotton separating me from her, and I hate it but I also don't want to stop kissing her because she's making these small, desperate noises in the back of her throat.

I do slide my thigh between her legs, giving her something to create a little friction on. That's immediate, too, the way she starts rolling her hips against my leg, chasing release.

"You want to come again?" I break the kiss so I can rasp into her ear. So I can hear her say yes.

She obliges, the word breathy and soft. "Yes."

"I'll see what I can do." I sit up and whip the blanket away. Edie lays spread out on my mattress, her body gorgeous in the grey-filtered light spilling in through my window. Her legs are spread, giving me a full view of the dark hair curling around her glistening pussy, and her tits seem to pool on her chest, each one tipped by a hard, pink nipple.

I pull one of those nipples into my mouth, sucking and licking at it. Edie moans, squirming beneath me. My cock's already up for the job, but I don't want to fuck her again just yet.

"Sawyer," she gasps, threading her fingers through my hair. "Are you—are you going to bite me again?"

I pull up just enough so that I can look at her, at the lust flooding through her eyes. "Did you like it?" *Me making you bleed?* I don't say that last part.

She nods, very sightly.

"So did I." Then I attack her tits, sucking and licking at them, and then, when she's moaning and thrusting beneath me, when she's good and desperate, I bite her left breast on its side. Not as hard as I did earlier. Not hard enough to draw blood But hard enough that Edie gasps and jerks beneath me.

"Fuck me," she whispers.

"No." I move over to her other tit, pulling as much of it into my mouth as I can. She arches her back like she's trying to force even more of her tit into my mouth. I respond by scraping my teeth against her nipple.

"Please!" she screams, legs quaking.

I release her from my mouth, feeling a little regretful. "I'm going to make you come first," I tell her.

And then I drop down between her legs

CHAPTER TWENTY-ONE

EDIE

Sawyer's tongue is a miracle. He drags it over the length of my slit, slow and teasing, and then he curls it inside me and I lose track of what he's doing because all I feel is a hot, wet pleasure.

I grab at his hair, soft and silky from the shower, and grind down on his face. He responds by wrenching my thighs open wider and sucking on something—my labia, my clit, I have no fucking idea. It makes me howl, loud enough to nearly drown out the wet, eager sounds Sawyer's making between my legs. *Nearly.*

I gasp out one shuddery breath, and then I come, my whole body vibrating as Sawyer never slows his pace, his tongue and mouth guiding me through one aftershock after another. It's almost like he wants me to keep coming forever, to be locked in an endless avalanche of pleasure.

Of course, it does subside, and I'm not surprised that Sawyer keeps going, his fingers digging deep into my outer thighs. Part of me wants to lie back and let him continue like he did that first night. Part of me, though—

I want to return the favor.

"Sawyer," I whisper, and he makes no sign that he's heard me. I try again, louder. "Sawyer."

His mouth pulls away from me, leaving a cool dampness against my pussy. When I peer down at him, he's gazing up between the mountain of my thighs, his eyes black and glittering.

"Don't want to stop," he says gruffly.

I sit up and press my back against the headboard. He frowns and moves to grab me, to force me back down. And although I won't deny the thrill that gives me, I blurt out, "I want to take a turn."

"What?" He's risen up between my legs, hair tousled and mouth flushed red.

"I want to—" I've never been good at dirty talk. Never been good at asking for what I want. It's hard to ask for sex when your entire life people have told you that you don't deserve it.

"Want what, baby?" He hoists himself over me, his cock grazing against my thigh. "Want me to fuck you?" He grins. "Not yet."

"I want to suck your cock." I blurt it out, the words bleeding together. I have to resist the urge to cover my face with my hands.

Sawyer's expression changes instantly. The coy flirtatiousness drains away, replaced with something dark and hungry and dangerous. "I don't know if that's a good idea."

Old humiliations slam through me. Every rejection rings in my ear. But Sawyer cups my face like a lover and presses his forehead against mine.

"I don't know if I can be gentle," he says softly, his breath blooming against my lips. "Even with your mouth."

It doesn't matter that I just had an absolutely earth-shattering orgasm. My pussy clenches. "Rough is fine," I whisper.

Sawyer's eyes widen a little. "You sure about that?"

"You were rough earlier. You *bit* me."

He grins at that, teeth gleaming. "And I made you bleed, my perfect prey."

That little nickname should be so unnerving, but it just makes heat flood through my clit. Honestly, the same could be said for the fact that he bit me hard enough to draw blood.

I swallow my nervousness. "I trust you."

Sawyer's face darkens, and I see in him the killer that he is. "I don't trust myself." His voice is very small.

Fear shoots through my chest. But it's a fear that's indistinguishable from desire. I lean forward and kiss him, hard, tasting myself on his mouth. There's the slightest hesitation from him before he returns it, his hands twisting up in my hair, pulling hard enough that my scalp stings.

"Please." I kiss away from his mouth and along his roughly stubbled jaw. "Please. I want to."

There's a second's pause, like the world is holding its breath. Or like Sawyer is holding his.

Then he slides off the bed and stands beside it, staring down at me. His cock is enormous and glistening at the tip. The sight of it makes my jaw ache.

I get on my hands and knees and crawl across the bed to him, licking my lips, eager to taste him the way he's tasted me so many times. He doesn't move as I wrap my lips around his cockhead. As I draw his length deeper into my mouth.

That's when I get a reaction. A long, exhaled breath, shuddery with pleasure. He ghosts his hand over my hair, frizzy from the shower and the humidity, and I clutch at his lean thighs. I want to swallow all of him, but I don't know if I can. Still, I do my best, pushing my mouth over his erection, pulling him deeper along my tongue. He tastes clean from the shower.

"Edie," he breathes, his voice coming from overhead. Hearing my name on his lips like that, like it's a prayer, sends liquid heat gushing between my legs.

I bob my head on his cock, bracing myself against his thighs, my pussy exposed to the cool air. He rocks his hips a little, thrusting deeper into my mouth, a motion that just makes me suck him harder.

His ghost-touch solidifies, and he grips my head, stilling my movement. I know now that he had been showing restraint, and I brace myself just as he begins to thrust more forcefully into my mouth. All I can do is try to be an open hole for him, jaw spread wide, tongue soft. He grunts, rutting against my face, his balls slapping against my chin, as spit drips out of the corners of my lips.

I fucking love it.

I roll my hips in time with his thrusts, desperate to be filled. I try to reach down and touch my clit but it throws me off balance, and his cock slams sideways in my mouth.

Immediately, he pulls out of me with a gasp.

"I'm s-sorry," I sputter. "I just—"

"On your back."

When he says it, he doesn't sound like Sawyer. He sounds like Sawyer Caldwell, the infamous spree killer.

And I have no choice but to obey.

I fall backward on the bed, instinctively spreading my legs. But Sawyer doesn't mount me like I expect him to. Instead, he walks around the perimeter of the bed, eyes roving over my body, his cock bobbing with each step. I watch him, my breath shuddery, not sure what's coming next. My body's prepared for anything, though, given the arousal already slicking my thighs.

He stops by my head, then slides his hands under my arms and drags me backward over the bed until my head dangles off the side. He steps over me, his cock eclipsing the room's dim light.

"I want to watch you touch yourself." It's an order, not a request.

I do as he asks and slide my hand between my thighs to run softly against my clit.

"Now open your mouth and let me fuck you."

My jaw drops open so quickly it's like I'm not even the one in control. Sawyer grunts as he slides his cock into my mouth, filling it completely. I'm overwhelmed by him: by his smokey, woodsy scent, by his hardness, by the sharp thrusts as he uses me for his pleasure. I'm so overwhelmed that I brace both hands on the bed like I need to hold myself in place.

"I told you to touch yourself." His voice sounds far away. "I want you to come with my dick in your mouth."

I moan around him, my response muffled, and then begin to work my clit with my fingers in earnest, rolling it in quick, urgent circles. Heat blooms through my core—I still can't believe how easy it is to come over and over again with him.

It's not long before we've picked up our previous rhythm, and I buck against the bed, arching my back so that Sawyer can slide even more of his length into my mouth. I'm hardly aware of anything but the building pressure between my legs and his hard, choking cock.

It's hard for me to breathe.

It's hard for me to breathe, but I desperately do not want him to stop. His roughness courses with desperation, like he's on the verge of shooting his cum down my throat, and I want that so badly. I want to taste him. I want to swallow him whole. With every short thrust, my own climax builds, and even though my chest feels tight and I feel dizzy and blood-rushed I'm afraid that if I take my hand away I'll lose my pleasure.

"Edie," he rasps, his hand pressing against either side of my head. "Fuck, Edie, you take me so well."

His hand slides around and rubs the front of my neck. I wonder if he can feel the bulge of himself as he thrusts into me. It certainly feels like he's that deep inside my throat.

I start to convulse, just on the burning edge of my orgasm. I rub my clit harder. I fuck the air. My thoughts blur. I need air. I'm choking. He's choking me. I need air.

I need—

My ecstasy swallows me in a rushing ocean wave, and then everything goes dark.

CHAPTER TWENTY-TWO

SAWYER

I am a monster. A killer. And when Edie stills beneath me, her body going slack and heavy, I come. I come fucking *hard*, harder even than when I fucked her in the shower. I roar like the goddamn animal that I am, but I also, somehow, yank my cock out of her mouth. My cum splatters across her face. Her parted lips. Her closed eyes. Her slack jaw.

You killed her.

The thought hits me with startling, painful clarity, and I fall to my knees, choking out, "No, no, no," as I grope around her pale, soft neck.

I find her pulse.

It's strong and sure, fluttering wildly against my fingers, and I sigh and slump down on the bed. I never should have done that. Abusing her cunt is one thing. She can clearly handle it. But abusing her mouth?

Too dangerous. *Far* too fucking dangerous.

I murmur her name and brush her hair away from her face. She stirs a little, eyes rippling beneath her lids. I hate to admit it, but my cum looks gorgeous on her skin, pale and pearly. A pretty picture that I snapshot for when I'm alone and need release.

She moans a little, her body stirring. I push myself up and grab one of my clean T-shirts out of the little closet. Then I sit down next to her on the bed, lift her head into my lap, and wipe my cum away.

Her eyelids flutter open and her eyes settle on me, her gaze soft and unfocused.

"I'm sorry about that, baby," I say softly, wiping off the cum that had spilled down the side of her neck. "I worried—I get carried away. I ain't—" I swallow, don't look her in the eye. "I ain't normal. But I guess you knew that."

"Sawyer." Her hand reaches up and trails along my jaw. Her touch is weak, but it's enough to get me to look at her. Fuck, she's beautiful right now. Her skin flushed, her lips swollen. A tear trail streaking down the side of her right temple.

Wrecked. Destroyed. *Murdered.*

"I liked it." The words barely came out a whisper. "I—I don't think I've ever—you choking me and me touching myself. It was—"

Her words dissolve into a sigh as she settles down in my lap, and I stroke her hair like I'm trying to smooth it down.

"I'm glad," I say, honestly. "But don't give me a scare like that. I don't want you dying on me."

She laughs, and it's kind of delirious, the way people will laugh right before I kill them. "This whole situation is so fucked."

I don't want her talking like that. I scoop her up so we're both sitting properly, then I pull her into my chest. She falls into me, sighing almost happily, and I wonder if this is what it's like to have a girl who doesn't care what you are. That just loves you.

She doesn't love you.

It's Mama's voice. I hold Edie tighter like that'll drive it away.

She burrows into me, pressing her nose into my throat. When she speaks, I can feel the warmth of her breath, and it's reassuring, knowing that I didn't just kill her.

"Sawyer? What—*are* you exactly?"

I feel myself go still. Edie shifts around and pulls back to look up at me, blinking her big brown eyes.

"I told you," I finally say.

She frowns. "You told me you can't die," she says. "And clearly —" She gestures at me. "But why? And why do you—" She stops and swallows, her pretty throat bobbing. "What *are* you?"

The question kind of hangs in the air, as heavy as the lingering humidity from the storm. I sigh and pull her into me again, then draw both of us down to stretch out on the bed. It's so perfect right now, everything dark and cool and the sweat drying on our skin and my body all loose from coming twice, that I don't want to ruin it. But I can feel her worrying the question beside me. She's not going to give it up.

"My mama called us Hunters." I say it to the ceiling, not to her, the tiles stained with old water. "I have this friend, Ambrose, he calls us boogeymen. Even though we're not all men."

I force myself to glance over at Edie. She just looks confused.

"Your mother?" she says.

I laugh. "Yeah, I've got a mother. She's like me. A Hunter, or whatever." I stroke my hand over the soft cloud of Edie's hair. "You won't be meeting her."

I mean it as a joke, and I'm relieved when Edie laughs. "You will not be meeting my mother either." She pauses for a second. "I guarantee she's worse than yours."

I chuckle at that, and Edie rolls over on her side, peering up at me. I can't stop myself from running my hand down the dip of her waist, her flesh soft and grabbable.

"Yeah? Why's that?"

"Oh, no." She shakes her head. "No, no. This isn't *Silence of the Lambs.* We're not going back and forth on questions until you finish explaining what you are. Hunter doesn't cut it."

I roll my eyes.

"Boogeyman, though..." She frowns thoughtfully. "So you're... supernatural?"

I shrug. "I guess." I settle down on my side, too, facing her, still running my hand over her hip and waist. She doesn't shy away from my touch, and I love that. "My people, people like me, I mean—We kill. That's what we do. We hunt. Different people have different theories as to why."

"What's yours?"

She doesn't sound scared. Just curious.

"It's a compulsion," I say after thinking on it for a moment. "Kind of like eating or—" Heat floods into my face, and I wonder if I should tell her. "Fucking."

Fear flickers through her eyes. But she still doesn't pull away. "Oh."

"It's not exactly like fucking," I say, even though, honestly, it kind of is, at least in how good it feels. "I could go without fucking, you know? But I can't go without eating. And killing's the same way."

"Have you tried?"

The question comes out small, almost like she's afraid of asking it. And when I hear it, something hardens in my heart. I almost want to spit out, *Have you tried not eating?* but I already know the damn answer to that, don't I?

"No," I finally say. "But my mama told me her father did. My grandpa. He—" I hesitate, the story flickering through my head. Mama told it to me every damn chance she got. "He tried to stop himself from killing. Went cold turkey." I pause, studying Edie's face. She doesn't look too scared. "But the longer he suppressed being a Hunter, the more he wanted to kill, and he wound up—he wound up killing his wife. My grandmother. Didn't matter that he loved her."

There's the fear, pooling through her her widening eyes. "Oh."

"Yeah. I'd rather not do that, so when I start to feel the itch I take care of it." I squeeze her thigh. "If I didn't, I'd risk hurting someone I don't want to hurt."

Like you.

I don't say it aloud, but from the way Edie drinks me in I know she knows anyway. Her lips curl up into a little hint of a smile. Just a little.

"I guess that makes sense," she finally says. Then, quickly: "So why can't you die?"

"That, I don't know. Mama says that's just how it is. My friend Jaxon thinks we're blessed by these old pagan gods, but he's crazy."

Edie smiles at that. "Your friends," she says. "Do they—they live here? I'm assuming they're, um, like you."

"Hunters? Yeah, of course." I move my hand a little higher to rub her arm. Her skin's soft as silk and I don't ever want to stop touching it. "But they don't live here. Jaxon's in Louisiana. Ambrose is in Texas. Mama's—I don't know. She travels around. Last I heard she was in Tennessee."

"How many of you are there?"

I give her a sharp grin. "Maybe we should play *Silence of the Lambs*. Feel like I'm getting the third degree here."

"That's because you already know everything important about me." She's serious when she says it. Dead serious, I think. "Almost all the terrible things that happened in my life, you were there."

I feel myself blanch. I don't know how to take that.

"Except for one," she adds, very very softly. "The worst one. But you—you were there after." She hesitates. "And I'm glad you were."

She looks up at me like I'm her whole world, like I'm the fucking moon and stars, and for a moment I've had that thing I've wanted my whole damn life.

I kiss her. Soft and slow and sweet, curling my fingers up along the side of her neck.

"There's something wrong with me," she whispers against my lips.

"There's not a goddamn thing wrong with you," I whisper

back, tightening my fingers against her pulse. It's quickened, like a rabbit's.

"I should be horrified by you."

She's not wrong, even if it hurts to hear her say it.

"I am what I am," I finally say. "I ain't human, like you. I've got different needs." I brush my thumb over her lips and try not to think about how glossy they looked as she choked on my cock. "And maybe you just need what I can offer."

She grabs my wrist and pulls my hand away and kisses me. And it ain't soft and slow and sweet, neither.

I roll on top of her, not breaking the kiss, and she parts her legs for me. I don't slide in just yet, though. Instead, I keep kissing her, on her mouth and her neck and her tits, and telling her all these things that are true. Like how I'm going to protect her. And how I won't let her ex-husband hurt her. And how fucking beautiful she is. And how she's my perfect prey.

And it's not long at all before I can feel the moisture between her thighs.

I settle myself between her, rubbing my cockhead against her clit until she's squirming and gasping, her eyes glassy with pleasure. I want it to be nice this time, not rough and violent, so I go slow, easing myself into her tight, sweet cunt. But I'm only about an inch in when she puts her hand on my arm and says, "Do you think I'm a good person?"

I go still, blinking down at her. She looks kind of sheepish but also kind of hopeful.

Then I push all the way in, making her whimper with pleasure.

"Edie," I say, "You're the only good thing that's ever happened to me."

Her lips part, but she doesn't say anything. I don't need her to. And honestly, I don't need to say anything else, either. I want to show her what it means to me, her being here even though she's a human woman who worries about shit like that, being a good person, and I'm the monster that girls like her are supposed to fear.

I roll my hips against her, pulling my cock out real slow and then guiding it back in, relishing the way her pussy walls flutter against my hardness. Edie sinks back on the pillow, giving herself over to the pleasure the way she does. Her hips move with mine, and I push up so I'm on my knees, her ankles propped on my shoulder. I want to see her while I fuck her. I want to watch her body move and her skin flush. And I want to reach down and play with her clit.

"Sawyer," she whispers, pushing herself down on my cock, her hands coming up to squeeze her tits. It drives me wild.

"Say my name again," I tell her, maybe a little more harshly than I intend.

Her eyes flutter open, and she looks right at me. "Sawyer," she says, louder, and I fuck her a little faster, rubbing my thumb over her clit. "Sawyer," she gasps. "Fuck, Sawyer, right there..."

She arches into me, her words dissolving into a low, throaty groan. I can tell from the way she's shaking that she's close, but she's not there yet. I close my own eyes and just keep rolling into her, letting my thoughts go blank. I don't think about killing—not her, not anybody. All that matters is how good she feels on my cock. All that matters are those desperate noises she makes as she comes closer and closer to finishing.

When she comes, she groans, her rolling hips going still even as her pussy clamps down hard on me. I fuck her through it, the way I discovered I like to, drawing everything out for her. Then I fold myself down so I can kiss over her tits and neck and mouth. She wraps her arms around me, pulling me into her, clinging to me the way she did that night I killed all her tormenters.

And just as long as we're like this, me buried to the hilt in her perfect body, her squeezing me in close, I can pretend she loves me.

CHAPTER TWENTY-THREE

EDIE

Sawyer goes with me to the cabin so I can pack up my things. He doesn't say much as we walk through the woods together, although I keep catching him when he glances over at me, his dark eyes unreadable, even as a smile curves on his lips. Every now and then his knuckles brush against mine, and I don't know if it's intentional or not. It's weird to imagine a serial killer—or a Hunter, or a boogeyman, or whatever he is because he clearly doesn't see himself as human—wanting to hold hands.

When we get to the cabin, though, anything as sweet and innocent as holding hands evaporates, because Baro's car is still parked behind mine.

"Fuck," I say, but Sawyer just tucks my hair behind my ear and smiles down at me.

"Don't worry about it, baby," he says, and then he reaches into his pocket and pulls out a key fob and winks at me. *Winks*, like we're in on some joke together.

What the fuck am I doing? Am I seriously going to *move in* with him?

You're just staying with him, I tell myself. *Until you know it's safe. He can obviously protect you.*

"I should have taken care of this earlier," he says. "When it was storming. But I—" He pauses. "I was eager to get back. Make sure you were okay."

He always does this. Says something that makes all my reservations melt away.

"What are you going to do with it?" I try to ignore the cold feeling in my chest.

"Take it to another trailhead," he says smoothly. "Leave it there. Walk back. Throw the keys in the woods." He smiles at me. It's oddly reassuring. "I'll help you load up your car first, though."

He comes with me into the cabin. Everything's exactly how I left it, which is unnerving because *I* feel like a completely different person. I have Sawyer Caldwell's teeth marks on my shoulder. My pussy and throat are both sore. I gave myself over to him, and I fucking liked it.

Focus. "I'll get my suitcase packed," I tell him. "I don't have a whole lot."

"How about your food?" He nods toward the kitchen. "We can bring that back to my place. We can try to use up anything that'll spoil tonight."

Part of me wants to leave the food behind. That's the ED voice, and I know it, trying to claw its way back into my life just like Scott is. I shouldn't eat. Not eating will purify me.

"That sounds nice," I tell him.

He grins wolfishly and ducks around the counter and starts flinging open cabinets. I leave him to it before the ED voice makes me change my mind.

My bedroom also looks how I left it, with the comforter half-heartedly tossed over the mattress and my pile of dirty clothes in the corner. I gather those up first and toss them in the washing machine. I want as many clean clothes as possible before I go to Sawyer's.

I've just started the cycle when I feel my phone buzzing in my pocket. It's Charlotte.

I hesitate before swiping to answer.

"Oh thank god," she says, before I've even gotten out a full *hello*. "Tell me you're okay. Where are you? Are you still at the cabin?"

I peer around the edge of the hallway so I can see Sawyer rummage around in the fridge. He's already pulled out the few pantry items I bought, canned soup and a bag of brown rice. He glances over at me, smiling—although it turns to a frown when he sees me on the phone.

"I'm fine," I tell Charlotte and Sawyer both, my eyes locked onto his. He nods, and I duck back into the hallway and scurry into my room. "And yes, I'm at the cabin now."

"You can't stay there," she says, breathless.

I freeze. "Why not?"

"Scott's looking for you," she says. "Those PIs that came by? They know where you are. They came to visit me and asked how long you'd been in Virginia. I told him you weren't in Virginia, I had no idea where you—"

"I'm leaving." I blurt it out, the first thing I can think to say. Charlotte still doesn't know that one of those PIs actually came *here*, and I don't want to tell her, because then it's one more path for a cop to trace between me and his death. Sawyer said I don't need to worry about cops, but I don't believe him.

"You're what?"

"Leaving. I—" I hate lying to Charlotte, but I can't very well tell her the truth, can I? "I ran into an old friend from high school." *Is that how you're describing the Fat Camp Killer now?* "I went into Roanoke and he had moved there from DC. It was such a fluke—"

"Right."

"Anyway, he invited me to stay with him for a little while. That'll get me out of the cabin, at least."

"It's better than nothing. But Edie, you need to be careful, okay? Scott, he—" Her voice wavers, and I squeeze the phone tighter.

"He what, Charlotte?"

"He came to see me, too."

Ice pours through my body.

"He was with the two PIs. He didn't—didn't say much. Just sat there and stared at me. And he—"

The floorboards creak, and I look up to see Sawyer step into the doorway, his face a mask of concern.

"He scared the fuck out of me," Charlotte finishes.

"What do you mean?" I force myself to look away from Sawyer. To focus on Charlotte. "Did he try to hurt you?"

"No. But he—he threatened me, I think? He sent the two PIs out after they finished asking me questions and then told me that he knew I was helping you and that once he found you, he would —" She takes a deep breath. "That he wouldn't 'let us embarrass him.' Exact words."

I can barely move. I just stare at the wall, my breath tight and fast. When Sawyer touches me, I jump, nearly dropping my phone.

He turns me around and gives me a questioning look.

"Edie, you know I don't want to freak you out, but it really sounded like—like he doesn't want a divorce, if you know what I mean? Like he'd rather keep you trapped?"

Of course Scott doesn't want a divorce. A divorce would make him a failure, and it would grant me freedom, and he couldn't have that. Me, as a divorcee, can tell people what he did. What he tried to do.

What he's going to do if he finds me.

"Edie?" Charlotte's voice is quick and panicky. "Shit, did the call drop?"

"I'm here," I say quickly, letting myself lean into Sawyer. He wraps his arms around me without a word. "I—I know what you mean, about Scott. I'll—"

"You should get out of that cabin before the PIs find you and go to the police."

Too late for that.

"Really?" I make my voice light and joking. "I thought you were all about ACAB?"

"I don't trust him, Edie."

I sigh. "I don't have any proof for the police," I say. "But I'm going to leave, okay? I'm going to stay with my friend."

"You don't need proof!" Charlotte cries. "You're a rich white lady! They'll actually fucking listen to you! At least have them come check on you or something!"

I press my forehead into Sawyer's chest, breathing him in, wishing I could tell Charlotte everything that has happened. "Fine," I say. "I will."

And then you'll lie to Charlotte about what they say, too.

"You should leave," I say, pulling away from Sawyer and walking over to the window on the other side of the room. The view of the forest is still tangled and wet after the rain. "Get out of town. Don't let Scott see you again."

"He's not worried about me, Edie. He wants *you*."

"I know he does." My reflection ghosts over the forest outside. I look strange with my tousled hair and wrinkled, mostly-dry sweater. "And I'll be safe, okay? I'll go to the police. I promise."

In the reflection, Sawyer comes up behind me, dark and imposing. He wraps his arm around my shoulders and presses his mouth to the top of my head.

"No police," he whispers, so faintly I almost think I imagine it.

"I'll let you know when I'm settled," I tell Charlotte. Then I hang up and set the phone on the sill.

"No police," Sawyer says, louder this time. Forceful.

"Of course not." I turn to face him, to see his real face and not the transparent reflection in the window. "That was my friend Charlotte. The one who helped me get away from Scott. He's—" I'm shaking as I draw my arms around my chest. "He's coming for me."

Sawyer's frown deepens. His eyes turn black as night.

"He wants to kill me," I whisper hoarsely.

Sawyer grabs my chin, tilting my head up to meet his gaze. In this moment, I see the monster of him.

"He will not kill you," Sawyer says.

I let out a choking sob and fall into him, burying my nose in his neck. He holds me tight—almost too tight. I don't care.

"Finish packing," Sawyer says. "I'm not letting you out of my sight until this is over."

CHAPTER TWENTY-FOUR

EDIE

It's dark by the time we get back to Sawyer's place. He takes my suitcase for me and sets it down in his room with a finality that won't be argued with. "You can sleep here with me."

"Do you even sleep?" I ask, because I'm still not totally sure what he is, if he has the same needs as a human man. He just gives me a slightly irritated look.

"Yeah, I sleep. Same as I eat. Speaking of which—" He nods toward the kitchen. "How about you bring in the rest of those groceries, and I'll make us dinner?"

I hesitate, just for a half-second, but he notices. "I know you're hungry, after all that fucking we were doing."

My face heats red hot. "Of course I'm hungry." I'm starving, actually, but the hollowness in my stomach has a seductive quality, a *calming* quality, after everything that's happened. It would be so easy to just... let it linger for a few hours more. Through the night. Until tomorrow morning.

"Then I'll make you something. You eat meat? You didn't have any."

"Oh. Yeah, I do."

"Venison stew, then." He loops his arm around my waist and tugs me toward the back door, out to where my car's parked in the grass. "I'll use up those vegetables you got."

"And what? Go kill a deer?"

He looks over at me before pulling open the car door. "I did that already. Salted and dried the meat since I can only run the refrigerator at night."

"Good lord." We start pulling out the groceries. "It's like *Little House on the Prairie* or something."

He laughs. "What? I gotta eat."

It doesn't take us long to unload everything. The church kitchen has a little pantry half-stocked with things I recognize from the grocery store in Altarida, rice and salt and canned vegetables. There's plenty of space for my meager additions: brown rice, pancake mix, my collection of soups. When I'm done, I find Sawyer chopping up the potatoes and onions and garlic we brought back from my place.

"Let me help," I say, an impulse born out of the days when my ED was at its height, and I used to cook lavish meals for Scott and his friends only to wrap my own plate up and slide it into the refrigerator, uneaten. It's scary how just being near a man spurs that impulse out again.

But Sawyer shakes his head. "No. Absolutely not. I said I'd cook. You sit your pretty ass right there—" He points with this knife at one of the folding chairs beside the card table. "—And keep me company."

I recognize the knife. It's the one he stole from the cabin. "We should take that back."

"Nope," he says, turning back to the potatoes. "It's been christened."

A cold, shuddery feeling sweeps through me, and I stumble back until I bump up against the table. "*Christened?*" I squeak out. "You mean you've—"

He looks at me over his shoulder, eyes glittering. "I cleaned it."

"You can't be serious!" My mouth has gone dry, and I feel the weight of what I'm doing wash over me. He's a *killer*.

He's my killer.

"You think I didn't clean it?" He glances at me again, smiling a little. Teasing me. "Would you like that better?"

"No! Gross." I sink down in the chair and watch him work, his movements neat and methodical. Is this what he looks like when he kills someone?

It occurs to me, suddenly and sharply, that I've never actually seen him kill a person. I've seen the aftermath. Never the deed.

His shoulders move rhythmically. The knife sings out with each slice.

I should be much more frightened of him than I am. Instead, it's everything else that has me scared: Scott. Charlotte. How much I want to cling to my hunger.

Sawyer dumps the vegetables in a big crockpot, the kind you use when you go camping, and sets it on the stove.

"You never answered one of my questions from earlier," I say, wanting to break the silence. Wanting to get out of my head, too, with its swirl of anxiety.

"Oh, yeah? Which one is that?" He sets the knife down and goes over to the pantry and pulls out a big ceramic cookie jar, which, when he opens it, does not contain cookies but chunks of dried meat.

"How many of you there are. Hunters, I mean."

He pulls out long, leathery strips of venison and starts cutting them, too. These movements make my skin feel strange, kind of hot and itchy. It wasn't the vegetables, I realize. *This* is what he looks like when he kills someone.

I shouldn't have asked about the Hunters.

"Hmmm, that's a good question." He pauses and looks up, like he's thinking. "Not that many. There's four that I know of for sure. No—five." He goes back to slicing the venison. "There's me, Mama, my two buddies. Plus one more in Texas that Ambrose mentioned. Don't know their name." He dumps the venison into the pot, then fills it with water from the tap. "But I know there have got to be others. I can sense them, sometimes. Moving around."

That makes my skin prickle. "Sense them? What do you mean?"

Sawyer stirs the soup, then goes over to the pantry and pulls out some jars—seasoning, chicken bouillon. He looks over at me. "I've got heightened senses. I can smell things. Hear things. That's how I knew you were in trouble earlier."

And just like that, I feel this deep, strange warmth for him. I stand up, go over to where he's working at the stove. He glances over at me, a lock of hair curling into one eye.

"I said I didn't need any help." He's playful about it, though.

"I wasn't going to help." I look down at the pot of stew, already starting to steam. "I just—I wanted to thank you, I guess."

Sawyer lays the soup ladle down and turns to me and I feel very much like a prey animal, a rabbit or a squirrel, caught in a wolf's gaze.

But at the same time—I like it.

"I'll be here to protect you as long as you let me," he says softly. Then he runs his fingers over my jawline, tilts his head, leans down to kiss me.

I melt instantly. Melt into his lips, his chest. He makes a low murmuring sound and then buries his nose in my hair. "That scent, though," he says, so soft it's almost like he's not speaking to me. "That's my favorite one." Then he breathes in deep, and I turn wobbly, and I'm suddenly remembering everything we've done today. In the shower. In his bed. How I gave myself over to him so completely.

How I know I'm going to do it again.

Sawyer steps away, taking a shuddery breath. "Sit," he says. "Stop distracting me."

"I wasn't doing anything!"

"Yes, you were." He grins at me. "Sit. And now it's my turn to ask you some fucking questions."

I roll my eyes. "Why? There's nothing interesting about me."

"That," Sawyer says, "ain't true at all." He points the ladle at the chair. "Now, sit."

I cross my arms over my chest, arch an eyebrow.

He growls a little. Playfully. "Don't make me make you."

"And how would you do that, exactly?"

He moves so fast I barely see him. One second I'm standing there, taunting him; the next, he has me pressed up against the card table, his thigh between my legs, his hands squeezing into my waist.

"Like that," he rasps into my ear. He saws his leg back and forth, and I gasp a little, trailing my hand over his shoulder. I've never fucked this much in one day. Scott, for all his talk about physical optimization, treated sex like an item to check off his to-do list. Step 7 in his 15-step ideal life program.

Sawyer, in contrast, seems driven by his hunger, his lust. He bites gently at my throat as I grind down against his thigh, hating that there are layers of cloth between my clit and his skin.

Then, abruptly, he pulls away, smirking. I moan in frustration and lean back against the table.

"Sit," he orders. "And I'll make you come real good after dinner."

"You're such a tease."

"No, you're the one that's been teasing me." He gives me an admonishing wag of his finger. "Can barely keep my hands off you. Now keep your distance so we can talk."

"About what?" I do relent, especially as he turns back to the stove. "I really don't want to talk about—"

"I just want to know more about you." His voice is kind of quiet. "You asked about me. It's only fair."

"I asked what you were," I say. "You already know what I am."

"Then ask about *me*." He stirs the stew one last time, then turns to face me, steam rising up behind him. "And I'll ask about you. It's been fifteen years, Edie. Give me something."

I tilt my head at him, settling back on my chair. My body pulses, still yearning for more of his touches. I do my best to ignore it. "We didn't exactly know each other fifteen years ago, you know."

He shrugs, although he has the decency to look a little sheepish. "I wanted to," he says quietly. "Get to know you. Just didn't know how. That's why I—" He hesitates. "I wanted you to notice me," he finally says. "And I hated how they treated you."

"I hated how they treated me, too," I say quietly, pulling my sweater sleeves over my hands. "But I don't want to talk about that."

"Then tell me what you do want to talk about," he says. "Tell me where you were born, to start."

And, somewhat to my surprise, I do. I tell him about growing up rich in the DC suburbs and how I never felt like I fit in. How I went to school out in California because I wanted to get as far away from here—not *here*, not *him,* but from my family, from all their expectations. I tell him how I love the Pacific Ocean, how it's dark and cold even on the hottest days, and how Charlotte and I used to go swimming every chance we got. I tell him how I learned to surf. I tell him about Charlotte, how I met her at an art gallery opening and we became best friends because she was the only person in my life who let me feel like myself. And I tell him, shyly, that he makes me feel the same way, stunning myself by the truth of those words—a truth I've been avoiding since he stepped into my cabin nearly a month ago.

"That means a lot," he says softly. "Something like that." By this point, the soup is ready, and he scoops us up two big bowls and brings it over to the table along with two bottles of beer that he fishes out of the ice chest, the glass dripping with melting ice.

And while we eat, we talk. It shocks me how easy the conversation flows, between me and the killer who haunted my nightmares—or who was supposed to, anyway. He tells me he's never actually seen the ocean, not even the Gulf of Mexico. He tells me how his mom had left him a few years before my final summer at Camp Head Start, how he roamed around the South and that was how he met his two friends, Jaxon and Ambrose. He tells me how he missed the mountains and the winter snow and that was why he came back, just a few months before I started my last season at camp. He doesn't talk about killing, not directly, but it's always there, simmering under the surface—his mother's training, his time with his friends.

It should bother me.

It doesn't bother me.

It's just who he *is*.

We keep talking well after we finish eating. I help him clean up, laughing as we wash the dishes together, the water hot and soapy. Afterward, he takes me out to the front steps of the church. The clouds have all cleared away and the air is frigid, but that coldness sharpens the stars hanging over the clearing. I lean into his arms, staring up at them, trying to find the constellations I learned a long time ago, when I was a child, before my mother and Scott and my sickness and the world had done all their damage.

Being there, in Sawyer's arms, it's almost like I can find that wholeness again.

CHAPTER TWENTY-FIVE

SAWYER

Edie's scared.

She hides it well enough, at least in the way she acts around me. That first night—me cooking her dinner and talking with her until my voice got hoarse—she didn't act scared at all. It's 'cause she ain't scared of *me*, and I can't tell you how good that makes me feel.

But she's still scared.

It's a little lighter now, two days after she came to stay. And don't get me wrong: it's not unpleasant. In fact, it's the opposite. A fucking aphrodisiac. I have to conjure up every ounce of willpower to stop myself from throwing her over my furniture and fucking her every time she's nearby. I can barely stop myself from touching her—grabbing her hand, pulling her up to me, running my teeth across her collarbone. It makes it hard to get any work done.

I do try, though. The cold weather's coming in fast—faster than usual, it feels like, with the nights coating the graveyard grass in frost. Thank god for the generator. And for Edie. We fucked both nights since she got here, and both nights we fell asleep naked, our bodies warming up the space beneath the blankets.

But the early cold has me worried since I haven't finished sealing up the church windows and patching the gaps in the slats. I need to get everything sealed up tight before the cold comes, and that's on top of knowing I'll have to handle Edie's ex.

"Do you think your ex-husband's gonna come out here himself?" I ask her one afternoon. I'm fixing the rotting sideboards and Edie's helping, handing me tools and holding up the plywood I nicked off a construction site back when I was in Roanoke. It's sunny but cold, and Edie shivers beneath the flannel I lent her. We're gonna need to take care of that, too, the way she doesn't have any winter clothes, but I don't much like the idea of her going into town alone for shopping. She won't let me go with her, either. Says she's worried about the cops connecting us to the PI's disappearance.

"I don't know." Her voice gets kind of small, the way it does whenever I bring him up. I know she doesn't want to talk about him. But I need to be prepared if I'm gonna keep her safe. "He's the kind of man to have other people do his dirty work, you know?"

I snort at that. "He tried to kill you with his bare hands."

As soon as the words are out of my mouth, I feel bad for being so blunt about it. But Edie just sighs and says, "That's because I was right in front of him. Now—he's probably going to send people."

I had a feeling that might be the case. "Good to know. I'll get ready for them." I tap the nail into place, then step off my ladder to admire my handiwork. The plywood looks good enough. It'll keep the cold out, at least. I move down to the next rotting patch, and Edie follows behind me, her fear piqued. It stirs up my senses.

"What about the police?"

"What did I tell you? You don't gotta worry about them."

"One of them shot you."

I turn away from the ladder, vaguely irritated. Edie gives me a devilish grin.

"It's true," she says.

"That was fifteen years ago," I say. "And I was distracted. What I'm talking about now is a plan to keep you safe."

The devilish grin disappears, replaced by that wide-eyed look she gets when I talk about protecting her.

"Maybe I can just disappear for a while," she says. "And he'll give up."

I settle the ladder down in the dirt. This patch of sideboard isn't in as bad a shape as the others.

"Give me the hammer," I say.

She hands it to me. "What? Don't like that idea?"

"You know him better than me." I use the clawed end of the hammer to scrape away the rot, half-imagining that I'm digging out the brains of Edie's ex instead of old wood. "Do you think he'll give up?"

Her silence tells me everything I need to know. Edie's explained a little about her ex, and I'll say one thing about the piece of shit—he sounds focused. Determined.

"Shit," she says softly.

I cover up the hole in the wood with a piece of plywood, Edie handing me the nails one by one, and then hop off the ladder and cart it around the side of the church while Edie follows with the little wagon of plywood and hardware supplies. But then I immediately stop short. It's been long enough and enough has happened that I'd forgotten about Jaxon's handiwork from a few weeks ago. I never painted over it, and its spidery, crawling lines are emblazoned across the grimy walls. That stupid fucking sigil. The thing looks demonic at the best of times, and seeing it on the side of the church is almost embarrassing, how cliched it is.

"What *is* that?" Edie squints up at it. "Did you do that?"

This is *really* goddamn embarrassing.

"No." I plant the ladder down. "Jaxon did it. Him and

Ambrose visited me right after I woke up. It's a symbol of one of his gods."

Edie frowns. I don't tell her Jaxon's theory, about those gods drawing us together.

"I want to paint over it," I say quickly. "It's just not as much of a priority as patching up the sideboards."

"I could do that for you," she says brightly. "I can't do much, but I can paint."

"You can do plenty."

Edie rolls her eyes, spins the hammer around. "Let's be real. I'm a glorified toolbox."

"Not true," I say. "You're much prettier."

She blinks like she's taken by surprise. I love doing that to her, especially when her cheeks turn all pink like they're doing now.

"Speaking of which," I say. "I'll take that hammer again, please."

She hands it to me, but I can tell by her frown she's going to suggest something I don't like.

"I could run into town for you. There's that hardware store on Main Street. If I drive, it won't take me long."

I sigh and turn toward the window. "It ain't safe. You've got people looking for you, Edie."

"Yeah," she says. "At the cabin. I haven't checked out. As far as they know, I'm still staying there."

I pause, looking at my reflection in the window's glass. She has a point.

"Please?" she says. "I've spent the last few weeks just doing nothing. Let me be useful."

I twist around to look at her, her eyes big and pleading. "Besides," she says. "I don't want to look suspicious. It would be weird if I don't go into town, and—"

"Stop worrying about cops. They're fucking idiots, and I know what I'm doing."

She rolls her eyes again. It's cute, not that I'm gonna tell her that.

"If I get in my car right now, are you really going to stop me?"

Her question thrums through me. My first inclination is to tell her yes, absolutely. She's my perfect prey, and I'd truss her up and lock her in the church's basement if I thought it would keep her safe. And while the idea does make my cock stir, I know damn well I'm not going to do it. I ain't that kind of killer, first of all, and second of all, I want to make her happy.

"Get the paint," I say. "Nothing else. Don't go poking around in the shops."

"Not even to grab myself a sweater?"

I point the hammer at her. "You can wear my flannels, and you can like it."

She grins at that. It always gives me a thrill, when something I say makes her smile.

"I'll be back in half an hour," she says. "Forty-five minutes tops."

"I'll be timing you." And I will. It's almost half after ten now. The second the clock hits 11:15, I'll be heading to Altarida, knife and mask in hand. I don't tell her that, though.

She hugs my legs, nearly knocking me off the ladder. I pretend to shoo her away, but really I like it, this back and forth, her silly hugs.

It almost makes me feel normal.

CHAPTER TWENTY-SIX

EDIE

I don't want to say it's a relief to go into town. Being at Sawyer's place isn't exactly unpleasant. *Sawyer* certainly isn't unpleasant. But it's isolating, and sometimes it feels like the woods are squeezing in around me. The leaves are peaking and all the reds and oranges and golds make the clearing feel like it's at the center of a circle of fire.

It doesn't help, either, that every now and then I come across these little reminders about what Sawyer is. What he does. Every time I think I've become okay with it, him being a killer, I stumble across something that makes my stomach twist up tight and I think that I should call the police and get the hell out. Like his big hunting knife that he polishes each night before bed, tucking it away in its leather pouch before he slides into the sheets beside me.

Or the body parts I found sitting up in a tree a few meters away from the church, the flesh decaying away and perfuming the air with a curdled sweetness.

Little reminders. Not big enough for me to run away, although they should be. But whenever I see them, whenever I think about them, Sawyer's own sweetness suddenly seems as dark as rot.

I shake my head, turn the music up. For all my doubts, I still can't bring myself to leave. And I think that's what really scares me.

I just need some normalcy, that's all.

The drive is perfect in that regard. My car is familiar compared to Sawyer's church, and I feel like I can appreciate the autumn colors better while I'm driving in them; the dappled, golden light reminds me of pumpkin spice lattes and cozy sweaters and the miniature pumpkins I'd buy every year to put on the kitchen table. It doesn't remind me of fire. Of trees blooming rotting skulls.

When I pull into Altarida, it looks like a postcard. The shops have their Halloween decorations up, cutesy skeletons and big-eyed witches. The hardware store has strung fake cobwebs in their window. Normal. It's all so fucking normal.

It doesn't take me long to get the supplies. I keep an eye on the time; I don't want to know what Sawyer will do if I'm so as much as a minute late. Not to *me*, of course. But just... in general.

Leaves skitter down the street as I load up the car. It's the middle of the week, and no one's out. The emptiness is both reas-suring and unnerving, like the world is holding its breath for something. A moment of stillness before the cops descend on us. On *me*. Sawyer tells me not to worry, but he can just die again. I'm an accessory, a thought that bothers me more for the potential consequences than its actual moral weight.

Leaves billow up around the car as I drive out of town and onto the little farm-to-market road that winds deep into the mountain. I'm good on time; I'll make it back to Sawyer's with at least twenty minutes to spare, and then maybe I can start painting over the sigil. Sawyer seemed embarrassed by it, but I actually think it's kind of beautiful. It's primal and intricate: something Charlotte would like. I ought to take a picture for her, although I have no idea if it would be a safe thing to send. A god, Sawyer said, although clearly one he doesn't believe in.

I'm on the farm-to-market, driving through the golden-dappled sunlight, when I see the car behind me.

It's nondescript, dark blue, and it's a least two cars' length back from me. But something about it sends a siege of panic coursing through my chest. No one drives on these roads. No one *lives* out here.

I keep going, telling myself I'm being paranoid. Maybe people *do* live out here. Or, more likely, maybe it's someone driving to one of the trailheads.

The trailhead where Sawyer dumped Baro's body.

The road curves; I curve with it. For a moment, the car is gone. I'm no longer being followed.

It reappears.

My face feels hot. I want to turn off the road and see if the car follows, but there are no turnoffs, not until the dirt road that leads to the church.

Go to the church. Go to Sawyer.

The car drops back a little, enough that it disappears and reappears as I twine through the road's sinuous turns. But it's there. If I hadn't noticed it, maybe I wouldn't think anything. But I did notice it.

And now I'm sure it's following me.

Maybe it's a lost traveler. Maybe they think I'm leading them to civilization.

If it's just a traveler, you can send them on their way. I squeeze the steering wheel. Yes, that does seem like the best idea. Just lead them to the church. If it's nothing, I'll give them directions.

If it *is* something—Sawyer's there. Balancing on that ladder, a whole bouquet of power tools and blunt objects and sharp blades arranged at his feet. A million possibilities flash behind my eyes, all of them bloody, all of them terrible. I hate that I'm not disturbed the way I think I should be.

The road narrows; I'm almost to the turnoff. I tap on the

brakes, slowing slightly. My skin is damp with nervous sweat, and I fiddle with the AC. It makes me too cold, too clammy.

The car slows, too.

Of course it would fucking slow down. Do you think it would just rear-end you?

The turnoff to Sawyer's church materializes up ahead. I don't slow anymore. I just grip the wheel, and breathe through my teeth, and then, at the very last moment, swerve onto the dirt road in a swirl of dust and dead leaves.

The car flashes by.

I let out a long, shuddery breath as I bump over the rutted dirt. It's only another five minutes and I'll be back at the church. I'll be safe. I can tell Sawyer about this and laugh and—

The car appears behind me.

I shrieked and slam my foot on the gas so hard my car jumps forward, suspension creaking. I can barely breathe. I don't know what I'm going to do when I get to the church. Jump out, scream? No, it could still just be a traveler, and I don't want someone innocent to get hurt. Sawyer doesn't have a phone. I can't call ahead to warn him.

The trees part; the golden grass of the clearing appears. Sawyer's church is a flash of white like a dot of sunlight. I roar up to it and sit with the engine idling as the blue car pulls behind me and slows to a stop.

I don't move, just stare at my rearview mirror, waiting. The car has dark-tinted windows. I have no idea who's inside, but they aren't getting out, like they're waiting for me to do it first. Someone lost would get out. Wave. Make themselves look friendly.

I peer through the windshield, but there's no sign of Sawyer. That concerns me, too. Shouldn't he... smell that I'm in danger? Or sense it? Whatever he does?

I kill the car's engine. I know I can't just sit here all day. I clutch the car key in my hand the way I learned in college, a dull metal blade jutting out from between my fingers. Then I step into the cool wind.

Immediately, the other car's door swings open. I squeeze my key tighter, my breath fast and panting, as a man steps out. It's not Scott, which is a relief. But it's not someone vacationing in the mountains, either. He wears a neat dark suit, his brown hair cut close to his scalp. If this is Baro's partner—and I can only assume it is—he looks meaner. More dangerous.

"Mrs. Hensner," he says brightly, flashing me with a blinding smile. I step backward, heart hammering. "So you are alive and well."

"Who are you?" I glance sideways at the church. Where the fuck is Sawyer?

Waiting. He's waiting to strike.

"Logan Greer," the man says. "Your husband hired my partner and me to find you."

The way he says *partner* bubbles with menace.

I swallow. Despite the cool autumn wind, my skin slicks with sweat beneath Sawyer's flannel. The key is slippery in my palm.

"Tell my *ex-husband*," I stress the word, "that I don't want to be found."

Greer tilts his head. His eyes have a flatness to them that makes my skin go cold.

"I'm not sure you completely understand." He steps toward me, his movements smooth and easy. I step backward and will Sawyer to come around the corner of the church. Why isn't he here? What is he *doing?*

"Your husband doesn't want you to *be found*," Greer continues. "He wanted us to *find you*. And then—" He takes a deep breath, gives me another one of those blinding smiles. "And then take care of you."

He lunges at me, tearing across the grass. I dive sideways, swinging my clenched fist—and my car key—up just in time to slice across his face. The victory's short-lived, though; Greer howls and latches out, grabbing my wrist. The key disappears in the yellow grass. He wrenches me up to him and presses his ear into my mouth.

It's nothing like when Sawyer does it.

"I know my partner was squeamish about this," he snarls, wrenching my arm painfully back along my spine. "Is that what happened to him? He actually found you out here, and then he hesitated?" His breath is hot and humid, and he squeezes my arm tighter. "I'm not going to hesitate."

Something sharp and cold presses into my waist, and I finally find the will to scream, my voice echoing across the mountain.

"Shut the fu—"

A dark blur slams into him, yanking him away from me. I stumble forward and land hard on my hands and knees, panic and terror slicing through my body.

Scott really is going to kill you.

I don't have time to dwell on the thought, a confirmation of what I already knew. Greer shouts behind me, but it's cut off with a heavy, metallic thud. I flip around and am not remotely surprised by what I see:

Sawyer in his grey Halloween mask, one hand clutching his hunting knife, the other clutching Greer's brown hair.

"Who the fuck are—" Greer sputters out most of the question before Sawyer slams his head against the frame of my car. Greer lets out a wet choking sound.

Sawyer glances over at me.

I can't see his eyes, only that twisted, snarling demon face. But I know what he's doing.

He's giving me the opportunity to leave. To not see him do what he does.

I should take it. I know I should take it. But I can't move. My body feels weighted in place, my fingers digging into the cold damp earth. I'm too scared, and I don't know who I'm scared of:

the ex-husband who nearly strangled me, the man he sent to kill me, or my boyfriend.

Sawyer turns away from me and slams Greer's head against the car again. Then he flings him down and steps over him. His knife catches the sunlight.

"I wasn't gonna touch her!" Greer shouts. "I don't know who you think I am, but I was just lost, man! I was just—"

Sawyer bends down and picks a knife out of the grass. It's smaller than his. A switchblade.

He slams it into Greer's left eye.

Greer screams, a horrible and inhuman sound, his hand scrambling frantically at his face. His blood is bright red, so bright it doesn't look real.

Sawyer looks at me again. That bright red blood splatters across his mask. I wish, suddenly, that I could see his face.

I still can't pull myself up to standing. I'm petrified by fear.

Sawyer's shoulders hitch, ever so slightly, and then he draws back his hunting knife and slams it down into the still-screaming Greer. I jolt at the suddenness of it, and then feel dizzy when Sawyer yanks the knife back out with a spray of blood and does it again, and again, stabbing and slicing. Greer's screams turn to gurgles and then fall silent, but Sawyer's still slashing at him, bathing himself in Greer's blood. I can smell it, a wet coppery scent that makes my eyes water.

It reminds me of that night at Camp Head Start, cradling Gavin's head in my lap as he died, offering him a kindness he never once showed me.

It reminds me of Blake's body in the food hall, the way Sawyer turned me around so I couldn't see it.

It reminds me of my own blood when Sawyer sank his teeth into my shoulder as he fucked me.

Sawyer straightens up. He's drenched in blood, and I know, seeing him like that, how I should react. I should be frightened. I should be disgusted. I should be retching into the grass.

Instead, I just feel a strange, terrifying calm. It's the same feeling I had that night fifteen years ago when I found Michelle Evan's body. A hollowness. An absence of emotion.

That's what scares me. *That's* what drives me up to standing, my legs wobbly and weak. The knowledge that I am okay with this, this bloody, mangled corpse, because I'm in love with the monster who did it.

And *that* is why, when Sawyer reaches out to me, I run.

CHAPTER TWENTY-SEVEN

EDIE

I burst into the church, tears streaming down my cheeks. I'm not sure if I want Sawyer to follow me or not. But it was too much, being out there with Greer's corpse, the scent of blood drowning out the autumn scent of the forest. I was afraid that scent would follow me if I ran into the woods.

I stumble down the aisle, my thoughts cottony and numb. Tears drip off my chin. I'm hardly even aware that I'm crying. I just feel this crush of guilt and fear and confusion. How many times have I thought I should call the police but didn't? They were all building to this moment of understanding.

Before I know it, I'm at the front of the church. The altar. Sawyer has his knives lined up, as always, and I stare down at them and sob.

Why did it have to happen like this? Why is it that the man who makes me feel safe and beautiful and *loved* has to be unhinged?

Emotion surges up in me, sudden and terrifying. I screech out my frustrations and swipe my arm across the altar, knocking the blades to the floor with a clatter. One of them cuts me, a thin sting that blooms red. My blood's the same color as Logan Greer's.

I slump down against the altar, choking back my tears. My whole body shakes, and I curl into myself as best I can, my breaths shuddery and thin.

There's a creak and a scrape as the church doors open, the sound filling the space.

I look up, still weeping, and Sawyer steps into the doorway, silhouetted by the autumn sun.

He's still wearing his mask. Still carrying his knife. He almost looks as if he means to kill me, especially as he walks down the church aisle, his steps slow and deliberate, his clothes dark with blood. I watch him, trembling, as he comes closer and closer.

He steps beside the front pew.

"You're bleeding." His voice is dark and raspy. A killer's voice. "Did he do that to you?"

I tear my gaze away from him to look down at my arm. The blood vines around my wrist like a bracelet.

"N-no," I say softly. "I—" I look up at him again. He hasn't moved. He hasn't put down his knife, either. "I cut myself on your knives."

His head moves a little, looking toward the altar. "You're afraid." He steps closer. "Of me?"

He's still speaking in his killer's voice, but with that one question, I hear an undercurrent of—

Sadness. Disappointment.

It twists my heart into ribbons.

"I've never—" The words barely come out a whisper, but I think Sawyer can still hear me, the way he tilts his head a little, the way he comes another step closer. "I've never actually *seen* you—"

I can't say it. I can't say *kill*. Instead, I choke on my own words.

"I will never kill you," Sawyer says.

He says it harshly, and I jerk my head up at him in surprise.

"I was afraid I would," he goes on. "At first. That I would—I'd be overcome. But not anymore."

And then, as if to prove it, he marches up to where I'm sitting on the aisle and lowers himself down beside me. I can smell the blood on him. I can see the flash of his eyes behind the mask.

"But I won't stop killing for you."

My breath catches, and my tears bloom again. But it's not for the reason he's thinking. It's because it never even occurred to me to ask him to.

And what does that say about me?

"If you want to leave," he continues. "You can go. I won't follow. Won't send anyone to kill you or hurt you or even fucking scare you, do you understand?" He rises back up to standing and points at the church door with his still-bloody knife. "You can go right now."

The sobs wrack through me, and I stare up at him through the veil of my tears.

"Go," he says, and there's something pleading in his voice. Something desperate. "Please. I can't fucking stand to see you cry. Not over this."

"I don't want to!"

The words erupt. Sawyer looks back at me, but it's not Sawyer. It's that mask. It's a *killer*.

Except they're the same, aren't they?

"I don't want to," I say again, more calmly, and I push myself up, bracing myself against the altar. "And that's the problem." My voice cracks. "Because I should. Because I shouldn't—" I look at the church doors. He didn't shut them all the way, and sunlight sneaks in. And the truth of things is right there beneath the surface of my tongue, and I know if I say it out loud, if he hears it, there'll be no going back.

"Because what, Edie?" He steps closer to me. Bloody. Masked. Violent. He still says my name like it's a prayer.

"Because I shouldn't like watching what you did."

He freezes, staring at me through the mask. I choke out another sob, the shame flooding through me. That sick feeling that I'm broken for wanting this. For wanting *him*.

And then Sawyer moves.

He attacks, although not to kill. Instead, he pins me up against the altar, one blood-sticky hand curled gently around my neck, holding me in place. He slams the knife down into the altar, the sound making me jump against him.

Against his erection.

"You liked watching that?" I can hear the excitement in his voice. The lust.

"He was going to kill me," I say in a tiny, tiny voice, as if that in any way justifies it.

Sawyer slides his hand up to cup my cheek, leaving streaks of blood on my skin. "I liked doing it." The mask leers at me. "And I liked having you watch me while I did it."

Then he pushes me back onto the altar.

I relent under his touch, spreading my legs wide as he wedges between me. When my thigh brushes against the knife, it doesn't cut me, but the cold of its steel makes me gasp.

Sawyer unzips my jeans and then slides his hand into my panties, pressing one finger into my pussy. He groans at what he finds there, and I know he feels it, the thing I'm afraid to admit to myself.

I'm turned on, my cunt swollen and soaking. Not just by what he did but by *him*, by the way he looms over me with the blood and the mask and the knife.

"Fuck," he breathes. "You're so fucking perfect."

I moan softly—at his words, at the friction as he pulls his hand away from me.

Then he grips his knife and pulls it free of the altar. Fear shivers through me, but only for a second. I trust him.

I trust him.

He rubs Lamar Greer's blood off the blade, polishing it with his shirt until it's a shining silver mirror. I stare up at him, breath shuddery, growing wetter by the minute. I keep imagining him sliding the knife into my skin, as gentle as a kiss.

He doesn't cut me, though. Instead, he slices my jeans away, shredding them to ribbons. I ought to protest—it's not like I have a ton of clothes out here—but at this moment, I don't care. I just drop my head back and moan, my hands curling and uncurling into fists. I don't feel the blade until he presses the flat side against my thigh. It's breathtakingly cold, and sensation prickles along my skin.

"I'm not going to kill you," he says, although he sounds like a killer when he says it.

Then he swings the knife up and out, cutting my panties away. He grabs the fabric, balls it up, throws it aside.

"My perfect prey," he growls, yanking down his fly, pulling out his cock. It looks almost painfully hard, the head swollen and leaking precum. He fists it at the base, squeezing it with a grunt, and then slams it up between my legs.

There's no gentleness, no preparation. Not that I need it, not right now. He just shoves his full, rigid length into my cunt, and I scream at the sudden fullness, arching my back into him. He leans over me, the cool rubber of his mask brushing against my face as he thrusts into me. I match his rhythm, hooking my legs around his thin hips to pull into me. The blood covering him is tacky, half dried, and it sticks to me, sealing us together into one monstrous figure.

"I think your cunt was made for me," he rasps, each word punctuated by a sharp, shuddery breath. "The way it wraps around my cock."

"Of course it was," I pant out, digging my nails into his back. "I'm your perfect prey."

Sawyer groans when I say that, slamming inside me so hard

and so deep that my pleasure sparks, briefly, into pain. And I want more of it. More pain. More desperation.

"Cut me," I gasp, and it's like I'm not the one saying the words. But I am. I feel them sharp on my tongue. And I mean them. "Cut me open. I'm your prey. Your prey."

Sawyer makes a shocked, strangled noise inside his mask and fucks me harder.

"You are perfect." He sounds faintly awed. I'm aware of his arm moving beside me, and then he pulls back, jerking me closer to the edge of the altar. He's holding the knife. He's been holding the knife this entire time.

"Cut me!" I scream. "I want to bleed for you!"

He slices my shirt away and then my bra, cutting it clean down the middle so the cups fall on either side of my torso. Then he presses the flat side of the knife just at the swell of my left breast, where my heart pounds furiously. Although his thrusts never slow, I can sense a hesitation in him, like he's worried he'll go too far.

I know he won't. He's a killer. But he won't kill me.

"Sawyer," I whisper, cupping his mask. It doesn't feel separate from him anymore, all that blood-splattered rubber. "Please. I want to bleed for you, just like I want to come for you."

He groans at that, bottoming out in me again. I grunt at the burst of pain as he bumps against my cervix. Squeeze him in tight. I won't let him move. Not until he cuts me.

"Do it," I whisper, never taking my eyes off him. "Do it. Please." My whole body's thrumming with pleasure, but it needs the pain from his knife to offset it. To release it. "Please, Sawyer, I'm your perfect fucking prey and I want you to—"

He flips the knife and runs the blade over my chest. The pain isn't that sharp or intense, but everything is amplified by the heat of his cock thrusting gently inside my pussy, and the angle of his body pressing against my inflamed clit. I scream as my hot blood spills over my skin, warm and wet and perfect.

"Again," I gasp, and he does, silently, the way he was silent when he brutalized Logan Greer. He cuts across the top of my other breast, then moves lower, trailing the tip of the knife over my belly. Then he tosses the knife aside with a clatter and smears the blood over my skin with his rough palms, sliding his bloodied hands over my tits to mark them, too. I roll my hips, desperately chasing my release. I'm right on the verge of it. I'm so close—

And then Sawyer roars, and grunts, his hips shuddering against me.

"Fuck!" he shouts, yanking his cock out of me. "Fuck, it was too much, seeing you like that—"

He runs his fingers through my blood again, and his cum oozes down my thigh, hot and thick as that blood.

"It's okay," I gasp at him, delirious with pleasure. "You can finish me off with your hands. It's fine." I roll my hips, trying to rut against his leg. "Or your mouth. I don't care. Just do *something*."

He looks down at me, his eyes black behind his mask. I squirm, desperate to feel him inside of me again. Fingers, tongue, anything.

But then he reaches over and grabs his knife, the blade still marked with my blood.

CHAPTER TWENTY-EIGHT

SAWYER

I can't believe I did that to her, my Edie, my fucking treasure. Can't believe I came before she did. But *fuck* she looks so goddamned beautiful right now, her clothes in tatters and her skin smeared with both old blood and new, the three cuts I made still oozing, glistening, and wet.

"It's okay," she keens, her words slurred with lust. She squirms on the altar, her body writhing with desperation. "You can finish me off with your hands. It's fine. Or your mouth. I don't care. Just do *something*."

I don't want to use my hands or my mouth, though. I want to make her come with my cock. I want to make her come with something that fucking matters.

And then it sparks in my head, what I want to do.

I grab my Bowie knife. Edie's eyes go wide, and I make a little shushing sound, trying to calm her. The knife feels good in my hand. Heavy as the erection she gave me when she begged me to cut her.

"I'm not going to kill you," I tell her, and it's true. But I am going to fuck her with the one thing that's an extension of me.

I flip the knife, catching it by the blade. I don't care when it slices into my hand; I could use a bit of pain, to ground me. The handle is nearly black with sticky blood. But I know just how wet she is, my perfect prey, and I shot a heavy load inside her.

I know she can take this.

"Spread your legs for me, baby." I don't want to force this. I want her to take my knife as willingly as she does my dick.

And Edie, perfect, precious Edie, does exactly as I say.

"It's just the handle," I murmur to her as I spread her pussy wide, admiring the glossy pink of her. She gives a nervous laugh and I look at her as best I can through my mask. Part of me wants to take it off so I can drink her in. But I leave it. She's my prey, and I want her to see what my victims see.

I want her to see who I am.

"It better be," she says, voice breathy and nervous.

I run my thumb over her clit in response. She cries out, hips jerking.

"Hold still, baby." I press the flat edge of the knife handle against her sopping-wet opening. "The blade's still here."

I don't tell her I'm blocking the worst of it with my palm, that my blood is dropping down on the handle as another lubricant, the pain from the cut as bright as sunlight. Instead, I nudge the handle inside her cunt, going slow. She moans, hands pressing down on the altar. Her blood-streaked stomach and tits rise and fall with her quickened breaths.

"That's it," I tell her, sliding another inch of the handle inside her. It's smaller than my cock and not nearly as long, but she moans like it is me, especially when I work it around in little circles, trying to hit the places inside her I know she likes.

"Sawyer," she whimpers, and I get that warm melting feeling in my chest. I don't let it distract me from my work, though, which is to kill her. To make her come.

"You like that?" I looked at her through my mask. She's wrecked, the way I like her. Sprawled brazen on the altar, sweat gleaming on her brow, completely covered in death.

"Yes." Her answer sounds like a sigh.

The handle's in as deep as it can go, and I twist it so the handguard will rub against her clit. Then I start to pump it, slow and sensual, making sure to get steady pressure on her clit. She's making all these wonderful tortured noises, little animalistic grunts and groans, and I want to listen to them for the rest of my life. Her leg muscles tremble. Her feet brace down into the altar. She lifts her hips, ever so slightly, and I move with her, still working her with my knife.

"Sawyer," she gasps out. "Sawyer, don't stop. Please. It feels so good—"

"Course it does." I squeeze the blade a little tighter, drawing out more of my blood. My hand is slick with it, and the pain electrifies me. "If anyone could take my knife and survive, it's you."

I don't know if it's what I said or if it's just because the knife's handguard is grinding up against her clit, but Edie comes. She lets out a perfect, bloodcurdling scream and arches her back into my knife, working her hips in fast, frantic circles. I fuck her through it just like I would with my cock, drawing out her pleasure until her whole body goes limp. And then I fuck her a few more times for good measure before I pull the knife out and set it reverently aside.

My hand is screaming from where the blade bit into my flesh, but I still press my cut hand against her cunt, marking her with my blood. She gasps when I touch her, and I massage her pussy for a few minutes, making sure it's completely covered and she's shivered through the last of her aftershocks.

It's only then that I take my mask off: when my perfect prey is stretched on the altar, sated. I peel the rubber away and toss the mask down on the ground and study her, running my still-bleeding hand up her thigh and over her hip, admiring the way my blood looks on her skin. She turns her head toward me, eyes unfocused, and lifts one of her hands, although there's no real strength in it. I killed her too well.

I catch her hand, though, and gently pull her up to sitting. We made a mess, me and her. There's blood everywhere, and I don't know how much is hers, how much is mine, and how much belongs to that corpse currently stiffening in my front yard. There's so much cleanup I'll need to do. Got to get rid of the body. Clean the blood and brain matter off Edie's car. Scrub the blood out of the altar carpet.

But all that can wait. Edie snuggles up against me, her breath soft against my throat. She needs a good cleaning, too.

"Come on," I murmur into her hair. "Let's get you into the shower."

She nods, her movements slow and lazy. I help her up to her feet and walk her into the hallway. Her steps are shaky, and she clings to me like I'm her whole damn world.

"Thank you," she whispers.

I stroke her hair with my good hand. "You know I like making you come."

She laughs a little. "Not that. I mean—saving me."

The warm melty feeling she gives me? It immediately calcifies into something cold and hard and black. "I told you I would. But we got to talk about what he said to you."

I guide her into the bathroom and turn the water on so it can heat up. She leans up against the counter, hair falling into her eyes. "You mean about how he was here to kill me," she says softly.

"Yeah." I strip out of my clothes one-handed, never taking my eyes off her. "I won't let that piece of shit keep sending men to hurt you."

Her eyes flit around like she's considering what to say, and then land on the cut on my hand. "You're bleeding!" she cries, as if the two of us aren't drenched in blood, as if there isn't a trail of blood leading from the front of the church to this bathroom. Before I can respond, she darts over and grabs my hand, lifting it to examine the cut. I can't deny it's an ugly one, slicing diagonally across the full length of my hand, the skin red and inflamed.

"You did this," she says softly. "While you were—"

"You're changing the subject." I tilt her head up by her chin so I can look down into her soft golden-brown eyes. The water's hot and steamy, making her hair curl in the humidity.

"I don't want to talk about Scott," she says firmly. "Not right now."

"Fine." I step into the shower, sighing as it hits my back, then hold out my good hand to help her in, too. "But later."

She nods as she steps over the edge of the bathtub and pulls the curtain closed. She picks up my injured hand again. She frowns down at it, then guides it over to the stream of water, washing the blood away. That blood joins all the other blood streaming off our bodies.

"Come here," I say softly, pulling her up to me so I can kiss her under the showerfall. That fucking we just did, it wasn't the sort that lends itself to kissing, but she's so beautiful right now, flushed and breathless and sweet, in the way she's so worried about my hand. I don't give a shit about it. Making her come on my knife handle was more than worth any pain.

Edie winds her arms around my shoulders, melting into me. I nuzzle the top of her head, and it kind of reminds me of the moment before that cop shot me. But better. Because no one's gonna shoot me now.

"I don't know what I'm going to do," Edie whispers, breaking the spell. "All these people you've—" The slightest beat of a pause "—killed, they can all be traced to me. I'm an *accomplice*, and—"

"And I'm a Hunter." I pull away so I can gaze down at her, the fear in her eyes gorgeous and tantalizing even if I don't necessarily want her to *feel* scared. I just like what I like, that's all. "The cops aren't gonna do shit to you. To either of us." I run my thumb along her cheek, over her lips. "And I know you don't want to talk about him, but neither is that ex-husband. We'll figure something out."

Edie's eyes are glossy. "I'm scared."

I smile. "I know. I can smell it on you." I kiss her before she can say something about that, and then I taste her fear, too, a spiced sweetness that reminds me of Christmas. "But I'm here, baby." I ghost her lips with my lips, breathe in the steam that smells entirely of her. "And I'm not leaving you to the wolves."

She shudders against me and then kisses my neck.

We don't talk much after that. I wash the blood off her, rubbing my thin little washcloth over her skin until all the blood is gone. She does the same to me, her movements slow and measured. When we get out of the shower, I pick her up, still wet, and sit her on the edge of the tile counter so I can tend to the cuts I made across her chest.

"Your hand is worse," she starts, but I shush her. I dig out the witch hazel Mama taught me to always keep on hand and rub it over her cuts to clean them. Then I pat them dry and dress them with some thin bandages, kissing the tape into place. I won't lie that it feels fucking odd to dress someone else's wounds. I'll dress my own, sure, but I'm more interested in splitting flesh than putting it back together. But Edie's different. Of course she is.

Only when I'm finished do I let her look at my hand. It's still oozing blood a little, and it burns like hell, although I'm numb to that kind of mild pain most of the time. It gets worse when Edie looks at it, somehow. I spread her knees so I can settle between her thighs as she rubs cotton pads of witch hazel over the cut, dropping them aside as they fill up with my blood. Then she winds my hand up with a bandage with this determined look on her face, like she doesn't want to mess up.

"Feel better?" I say when she finishes.

She looks at me. "You were bleeding everywhere."

"Yeah, well, there's a lot more than just *my* blood to clean up." I grin at her, and she blushes and looks away.

"I can't believe I asked you to do that."

I'm not sure if she means me cutting her or me killing that asshole who attacked her. But when I make her look at me, my response is true in either case. "And I hope you ask me to do it again."

Her lips part; her pupils expand. I'm sure she's leaving a streak of wetness on my bathroom tiles that has nothing to do with the lingering humidity from the shower.

"I think," she whispers, trembling. "I think I will."

Lust courses through me. I get down on my knees for her, hoisting her thighs onto my shoulders, and press my mouth to her cunt. It's somehow wetter than I was expecting. Edie slides back, tilting her hips to give me access, and I eat her like I'm starving to death, plunging my tongue up inside her pussy and flicking it over her clit. She grabs at my still-wet hair, pressing my head into her cunt and holding it there. I like it, that forcefulness. How different it is from that first night I made her come, when she was still scared of me. When we both still thought I might kill her for real.

She comes on my tongue, her moans echoing through the bathroom. I barely let her come down before I slide my cock inside her, fucking her one more time before I have to go out of this steamy bathroom that smells like my perfect prey and face the mess and the body and whatever comes next.

CHAPTER TWENTY-NINE

EDIE

I run the sponge over the altar, leaving a trail of pink, soapy water in its wake. Sawyer told me to leave it, that he'd take care of it after he disposed of Logan Greer's body out in the deep part of the woods. But I couldn't stand seeing the mess every time I walked through the church—which was often, considering how I kept pacing around, my heart thrumming nervously in my chest.

Who the hell have I become?

I dip the sponge into the bucket. I found both stashed in the little hall closet across from the bathroom—along with a pair of yellow dishwashing gloves. Whenever I think of what happened earlier, I'm shocked by what I *don't* feel.

I don't feel disgust.

I don't feel horror.

I don't feel frightened—at least, not of Sawyer. Everything else, though? The risk of getting caught? The revelation that Scott *is* actively trying to kill me? The fact that I have no idea what my future could possibly look like now?

That leaves me cold and quaking.

Cleaning up the mess of the altar helps push it aside, though, and here I can at least pretend that the blood only belongs to me and Sawyer. Because *that* part of earlier—

Well, let's just say I keep finding myself pressing my thighs together at the memory, squeezing them against my clit.

I slop more water on the altar and run the sponge over it in broad strokes. The water seems to rehydrate the blood, and it feels like I'm just pushing it around, making more of a mess. Clearly, I'm not cut out for cleaning up a crime scene.

I squeeze out the sponge and grab the towel I've been using to blot up the bloody water. *Finally*. It looks like I'm starting to make some progress.

"What the hell are you doing?"

I jump at Sawyer's voice and look up to see him standing in the church entrance—looking like Sawyer this time, my Sawyer, who wrapped up the cuts on my chest so tenderly. He strides in, letting the door slam shut behind him, and crosses his arms over his chest. "I told you I'd take care of that."

"I needed the distraction." I stand up as he stalks down the aisle. Looking at him, you wouldn't think he'd been ditching a mutilated corpse out in the mountain, although he does look like he's been hiking. His hair's wind-tossed and tangled with a few flame-colored leaves, and his cheeks are pink from the cold.

He looks... *handsome*.

He's also appraising my handiwork with a furrowed brow. "You gotta blot the blood up first," he tells me. "And work in patches." When he sees the blood-mottled towel, he groans. "Oh, come on! You used the good towel?"

"That's your good towel?" It's actually pretty ratty and threadbare.

"One of 'em." He picks it up and slaps it down on the altar, then looks at me. "You don't need to do this," he says quietly.

"I need to do *something*. Otherwise, I just start thinking, and—"

"Stop it." He points at me. "I told you not to worry. We'll

figure something out, okay? I'm not gonna let anything happen to you." He nods down at the bucket of water. "Now give me those gloves and get your cute butt out of here. I'll finish up."

"Are you sure?" I frown. "I really don't mind."

"Yeah, you do." He grins at me, eyes glinting. "You ain't never cleaned up spilled blood before, and I don't know why you'd start now. Go outside, take a walk. It'll clear your head."

I'm not so sure about that, but the truth is I *am* making a mess of the altar, and Sawyer clearly knows what he's doing when it comes to... all of this.

Sawyer strolls around the altar and smacks me on the ass. I let out a disbelieving laugh and turn on him, but he grabs my wrists. He's not wearing his bandage anymore.

"What about your hand?" I squeal as he peels one of my gloves away.

He holds it up to me. The cut has been replaced by a smooth, pink scar. "My kind heals fast."

I'm so dumbfounded that I just stand there like an idiot while Sawyer peels off my other glove.

"Is that why you didn't want me to wrap your hand?"

Sawyer stops and looks over at me, his eyes softening. "I didn't need you to," he says gently. "But I wouldn't say I didn't want you to."

I feel a sudden surge of affection for him, my serial killer who insists on doing the cleaning.

"I'm serious about you going for a walk, though," he says. "It'll be getting dark soon, and it really will be good for you to get some fresh air." Then he kisses me on the top of my head, turns me around by the shoulders, and swats my ass again.

I don't protest this time, just leave him to do his work. I go out through the back entrance so I can grab my phone. I want to call Charlotte. I'm not sure exactly how Sawyer would feel about that, although I don't intend on telling her anything. I just want to see her face, know that she's okay.

Stepping outside feels like stepping into another world. The late afternoon sun floods the clearing with gilded sunlight and the surrounding forest burns in reds and oranges. The air is cold, smelling of metal and distant smoke, and I breathe in deep four times.

I go around to the back of the church, away from my car—away from the scene of Sawyer's earlier crime—and call up Charlotte on video chat. She answers on the second ring, her hair blowing across her face. It's platinum blonde.

"You bleached your hair."

"Yeah." The camera tilts and for a half second, I see her background: a flash of a swimming pool, a pastel-colored wall. She's out on her apartment balcony. "I was just about to call you, actually. This shit with Scott really has me freaked."

Hearing Scott's name makes my stomach twist up into knots. "Is that why you bleached your hair?"

She shrugs. "Maybe. Probably. It's my favorite defense tactic, after all." She laughs, but there's no joy in it. "He really did creep me out the other day." She squints into the phone camera. "Everything okay with you?"

I nod, my throat dry. Part of me wishes I could tell her everything. Instead, I just say, "Yeah, I'm still with my friend. No sign of Scott."

"Your friend, huh?" She arches an eyebrow, and I hate myself for blushing because even over the phone's video, she notices.

"I'm not even thinking about that right now." I hate myself for lying to her.

"Yeah, I get that." She shakes her head. "I just want you to be safe. I get why you don't want to go to the police. I do. But I just think—maybe it's worth trying?"

My stomach twists into knots. "Nothing will come of it," I say, and that actually *is* true, even if I can't go to the police now for other reasons. "They might try to help at first. But he'll pay them off to get what he wants." Especially since what he wants is to kill me. He'll do whatever he can to protect himself. But I can't tell Charlotte any of that, because then I'll have to explain that I'm safe because Sawyer Caldwell is alive and well and promised to protect me.

Charlottes sighs, brushes her hand through her hair. On my phone screen, it nearly looks white. "Yeah, I know. Just—be careful, okay? He's got to get bored of this eventually, right?"

"Yeah." I force myself to smile. To sound hopeful as I lie to my best friend. "He just doesn't want the embarrassment of a divorce. He needs to meet some hot model. Then he won't give a shit anymore."

Charlotte's tinny laughter floods through the clearing. I wish it were true. Maybe it was, a few months ago. But now he's got the idea of my death planted in his head. He's got plenty of money, but if we divorce, he'll lose some of it, even with the prenup. This way, he gets richer: The life insurance payout. The inheritance that'll go straight to him because when I signed that prenup I was so dazzled that a man like him would want a woman like me.

Back then, I thought I'd overcome the worst thing that could happen to me. What a story it was, too: the fat survivor of the Fat Camp Killer who glimpsed death and lost weight for it, who turned her life around after a madman tried to slice it out of her. And then I reaped the rewards of that weight loss, too, with a handsome, rich husband and a glass house by the Pacific Ocean.

It was the story glossy profiles in high-profile magazines are made of. And it was all made of rot.

"—the hell is that?" Charlotte's voice drags me out of my past. "What?"

"That thing behind you." She squints into the camera, brow wrinkled. "Is it street art or something?"

I realize with a cold, sick shudder that she's talking about the sigil that Sawyer's friend painted on the church wall. I'd wandered over to it without thinking.

"Oh. Um—" I fumble around for an explanation. "Yeah. Street art."

"Let me see it," she says. "I want to take a screenshot."

I want to tell her no, but I can't think of a single reason that doesn't involve telling her my "friend" is Sawyer Caldwell and that sigil was painted by another murderer. So I hold up my phone to the wall, the wind cold against my skin.

"Got it!" she chirps out. I pull the phone back around. "Do you know who the artist is?"

"No clue," I say. "It's not signed."

"Too bad." Charlotte swipes her hand through her hair. "Look, thanks for checking in. You're eating okay and everything?"

I breathe out, relieved I don't have to lie about *that,* at least. "Yeah. My friend's a great cook, actually."

Charlotte grins. "Look at you. Once you can shake off Scott, you'll be all set."

I roll my eyes. Ignore the sick coil of dread in my stomach. I want so badly to tell her. But she wouldn't understand all that's happened with Sawyer, and I can't blame her. So it's better to just say nothing.

"Yeah," I say. "I'll be all set."

CHAPTER THIRTY

EDIE

Sawyer takes me for a walk after a dinner I make for him, the least I could do since he bleached the entire church spotless: an autumn salad with beets and rutabagas he picked up at my request in Altarida a few days ago, goat cheese I keep in a plastic baggie in the ice chest with his beer, a healthy sprinkling of mystery nuts he gathered from somewhere in the woods. Plus bread and butter. I ate two slices without even thinking about it.

It's dark out by the time we finish eating, but Sawyer lights our path with a hurricane lamp, the little gas flame casting a wide circle of yellow light. It shines through the pale, wispy fog curling through the mountains, making all the shadows long and crawling. With the constant rustle of dead leaves, it feels like Halloween's tonight, not a week away.

"I like walking at night," Sawyer tells me. "And today was, ah, a long day."

"That's one way of putting it." I bump up against him as we pick our way through the dark, and he reacts immediately, snaking his arm down to grab my hand and braid our fingers together. I glance over at him, touched by his sweetness, but he's just looking straight ahead, brow heavy.

"I want to show you something," he says.

My chest tightens up. "I really don't need to see—"

He barks out a laugh. "Jesus Christ, Edie, I ain't gonna show the body." He squeezes my hand. "I wanted to show you the old pier. It's my favorite place out here."

"A pier?" I frown. There's a swimming hole near Camp Head Start, a pinched-off alcove of cold water from some nameless creek. But it never had a pier.

"Yeah, it's ancient. Nobody uses it anymore." He glances down at me, his real face carved up like his killer's mask by the light from the hurricane lamp. "Except me."

He tugs me forward, out of the clearing and into the woods. I press up close to him, and he shifts his arm accordingly, wrapping it around my waist so he can guide me along the path with a firm, protective air. "City girl," he mutters, his breath blowing across my hair.

"Never denied it."

He laughs. "It's what I like about you." He pauses. "One of the things."

I smile at that, small and happy in a way I know I shouldn't feel. And yet I do. It's becoming so much easier to just give myself over to it.

He ducks us through the tangle of tree branches, his movements quick and agile, like he can see in the dark. Maybe he can. Maybe the hurricane lamp is for my benefit. All I know is that I never once trip on a wayward branch or step into a puddle of mud. It's too cold for snakes and insects. Maybe it's too cold for wolves, too.

"We're almost there," he says softly. "Can you hear the water?"

I stop and listen. All I hear is wind and dead leaves. "No. Just the forest."

"Well, it's there. C'mon."

He pushes aside a low-hanging tree branch and holds out the lamp. I duck through, stepping into darkness—

And then take a deep gasping breath at what I see.

Stars. Thousands and thousands of stars, so many that they bleed together into a puddle of light. They hang above a vast spread of darkness that catches their glow in fits and starts. The New River, I realize.

"It's beautiful," I breathe.

"We're near the top of the mountain." Sawyer comes up behind me, his hand pressing into my upper back. I'm distantly aware that he's extinguished the hurricane lamp so all we have is the light of the stars. "And tonight's a dark moon, so we'd have a good view of the Milky Way."

"The Milky Way?" I squeak, turning to look at him in the dark. He has his head tilted back, his eyes on the stars.

"Yeah, figured you hadn't seen it, city girl." He points at a bright band of light arching across the sky. "That's it right there. Mama used to always point it out to me. She said we were safest in places where you can see it."

Isolated places, he means. Places where no one lives, where two killers can go into hiding. I shiver a little. But I also draw closer to him. And he accepts, pulling his arm around my shoulders.

"The pier's down there." He gestures toward the water. I can't really see anything in the dark. Only the light, and the absence of it. "I've got a boat tied up. You know." His body shrugs against mine. "Just in case."

I don't say anything. It would ruin it, anything I could say right now. So I lean into him, breathing in the cedary forest scent of his skin. He nuzzles the top of my head, rubs his hand along my arm.

"I thought it might be easier," he says in a low voice. "To be someplace beautiful when we talk about your ex-husband."

I stiffen against him, even though I understand where he's coming from. I do. "About killing him, you mean."

Sawyer keeps running his hand over my arm, over and over. "Killing him before he kills you."

I take a deep breath. Another. Another. Another. Sawyer doesn't say anything about it, and I'm grateful for that.

"I've been thinking about it," he says. "I got an idea. Thought I'd see what you think of it, though."

He's talking about premeditated murder. But I'm not sure what else I expected.

"An idea?" I say softly, letting my gaze fall on the stars' reflection in the river.

"Yeah. You think you can get him out here?"

"To Virginia?" I realize I half-expected Sawyer to suggest some kind of murder road trip. I look up at him in the darkness. He's watching me, his eyes guarded.

"Yeah," he says. "To the camp."

I consider it. "Maybe," I say. "He'd rather send someone else, I think, but—but maybe if I pretend to apologize and tell him he's right and I'm going to lose weight—"

Sawyer scoffs.

"That's what started this all," I say. "But if I tell him I'm going to go back to being his perfect little wife—maybe. He might come himself."

Sawyer nods. "You've still got access to that cabin, right?"

"Yeah. It's booked through the middle of November. But—" I turn toward him, peeling out of his arms. "But why? Won't that just link me to the—" My throat's still dry when I say the word, although not nearly as much as it used to be. "The killing?"

A smile flickers across Sawyer's face. But there's something uncertain about it. Something... nervous.

"Yes." Sawyer takes a deep breath of his own, and his hand creeps up to touch the back of my neck in that dark, possessive gesture that unravels me so much. He tugs me in front of him, his other hand wrapping tightly around my waist so he can pull me up to him, my back pressing against his firm chest. He presses his face against my temple. "Baby, all I want is to protect you. To make sure you're happy. Do you understand that?"

I look out at the river. At the stars. "Yes," I breathe, and I know it's true, even if Sawyer's methods are a little... unusual.

"And one thing I can do is make all this go away." His voice is rough against my hair, and his hand keeps massaging the back of my neck, fingers grazing along my quickening pulse. "But you won't—you won't be able to go back to your old life in California. You'd have to stay with me."

"Have to," I whisper, the blood pounding in my ears. "Or get to?"

Sawyer's hand stills against my neck. Against my throat. "Is that what you'd want?" he asks. "To stay with me?"

I'm breathless. He was the worst thing that ever happened to me. Now, he's the best.

"What are you getting at, Sawyer?"

He doesn't answer right away. He just holds me, his breath slow and steady. The wind picks up, blowing cold air across the river's surface. I breathe it in and shiver.

"Sawyer?" I say nervously.

"The mountains are dangerous." He speaks so softly his words feel like kisses. "People disappear all the time. Especially pretty women from the city who like to go for long hikes in the woods."

Every muscle in my body freezes in place.

"Especially when there's a copycat killer hanging around," he continues. "Killing people with a hunting knife like that boy who attacked that camp fifteen years ago—"

"Killing people?" I whisper, barely daring to breathe. "Like her husband?"

Sawyer brushes my hair away from my neck so he can tease my sensitive skin with his words. "Like her husband," he growls. "The Altarida sheriff won't think much of it, will he, if he finds her husband in pieces on the cabin lawn? If her car's still there, too, and all her clothes folded up in the chest of drawers?"

I stare at the river, shivering in Sawyer's arms.

"They'll do a missing person's search, no doubt. They'll find that pretty city girl's cell phone cracked in the woods. Maybe some strands of her hair." His hand drops down to trail along the cuts he made on my breasts this afternoon. "Some blood."

I exhale, and my breath is white in the cold.

"But they won't find her body," he says. "They'll never find her fucking body."

I whip around to face him, the wind blowing my hair into my eyes. He brushes it away and fixes me with his black, killer's gaze.

"This is the best gift I can give you," he says roughly. "But if you don't want it—"

"I want it." Each word is a puff of steam. Each word is a magic spell. "I want you."

For a moment, Sawyer looks faintly stunned.

Then he takes my face in both hands and kisses me like I'm the only thing in this world that matters.

And I don't ever want him to stop.

CHAPTER THIRTY-ONE

EDIE

Two days later, I'm back in the cabin on the old campgrounds, with its electricity and central heating and designer furniture. This time, though, Sawyer's with me.

I lean up against the counter, squeezing my phone in one hand. My heart pounds in my chest. It took two days for me to work up the courage to call Scott, and I decided that if I was going to go through with this then I needed to do it here in the cabin. Who knows what Silicon Valley tech bro bullshit he has that can track my phone. I don't want him showing up at Sawyer's church with a SWAT team.

I take a long, deep breath. Sawyer is beside me, watching me, not saying anything. I asked him to be here with me while I do this. Even though it's just a phone call. Even though there's a chance Scott won't even pick up.

He'll pick up. He wants this resolved. I know him. If there's anything I know about him, it's how controlling he is. How focused.

It never occurred to me before, but it does now—I'm probably not the first person he's tried to kill.

"You need to call him," Sawyer says softly. "Get him out here as quick as you can."

"I know." I've already gone through all the arguments in my head, and I know this is the best way. Scott wants me dead or controlled. He'll pay off any authorities he needs to see that happens.

"The weather's turning," Sawyer says. "A nor'easter's gonna come through soon. If we can time it to the storm, that'll work in our favor."

"A nor'easter—" I shake my head. "How can you possibly know that?"

Sawyer shrugs. "Same way I know when you're in trouble, perfect prey." He cups the side of my neck so he can pull me toward him, an embrace I happily accept. He kisses my forehead. "I just sense things. Now call this piece of shit and say what you need to say to get him out here."

I nod against his head, then swipe open my phone. Unblock Scott's number. My hands shake the whole time, but Sawyer keeps massaging my neck, his touch reassuring.

I take one more deep breath.

And then I call up Scott on the speaker phone.

It rings twice. My heart feels like it's going to burst out of my chest, and I stare down at his name on my phone, *Scott Hensner,* how I put it in when I first met him at a gala just after college. Like he's a business contact.

On the third ring, he answers.

"Edie." His voice is flat, emotionless. "There you are."

I look over at Sawyer. He doesn't look like my Sawyer. He looks like a killer.

"Scott." I clear my throat and hold the phone close to my lips. "I wasn't sure you'd answer."

"Don't give me that bullshit. You know I've been looking for you." His voice tilts somewhat and takes on a faked layer of concern. "I was worried about what had happened to you."

"Is that why you hired that PI?"

A pause on the other end. I decided, and Sawyer agreed, that it was best to pretend that I had seen the first PI but not the second. And Scott's pause lasts long enough I suspect he's formulating his own lie.

"Of course, Edie. Although I'm curious why you didn't listen to what he had to say."

Does Scott know that I know he wants to kill me? I can't overthink this. Scott is cruel and shallow, but he isn't stupid. It's that combination that made him his millions.

"He said you wanted me to come home."

"I do."

He answered too quickly. Trying to cover his tracks.

"I'm not ready for that."

Sawyer watches me as I speak. His expression is unreadable. He almost doesn't even look human.

"Then why are you calling me?"

"I'm willing to talk. But you did try to kill me, and you can't do that over the phone."

Another long pause. I almost think I've miscalculated until Scott says, "I wasn't going to kill you that night. Not really. You know that. Otherwise, you would have gone to the police."

I tighten my grip on the phone. This is the in I need. "You scared me, Scott. But no, I didn't want you arrested. You're my husband."

I nearly choke on the word *husband*. I certainly can't bring myself to look at Sawyer when I say it, although I feel him looming beside me, his presence predatory.

"I actually do want us to talk face-to-face," I say. "But on my territory, not yours. I think that's only fair."

Scott sighs. "And what territory is that? The camp in Virginia? Because my boys went out there and didn't come back."

I freeze. Sawyer puts his hand on my arm, steadying me. I had planned for this. "Boys?"

"Men, whatever."

"No." I pray he doesn't hear the tremor in my voice. "I only met one man. Blond. I don't remember his name. I spoke to him for a few minutes before I asked him to leave."

The line crackles. There's a long, agonizing moment of silence. "What are you playing at, Edie?"

"Nothing." Maybe I answer too fast. I can hardly breathe. "I would ask the same of you, but I already know the answer. Here's what I will tell you, Scott. I'm willing to forgive you for what you did. Because—" I take a deep breath. "Because you're right. I'm not healthy. I let myself go. I realize that now." I swallow back a surge of bile, as if speaking those words will undo two years of recovery. "I'll lose the weight. I'll move home. But not without some ground rules."

Sawyer stares at the phone with a violent intensity that both terrifies me and flushes my body with heat.

"And that's what you want to discuss *on your territory?*" Scott's words drip with sarcasm.

"Of course it is, Scott. I won't be some battered wife. But I can spare you the financial hit of a divorce."

This time, Scott makes a sort of *hmm* sound that fills the silence. "You signed a prenup."

"And my family has better lawyers than you, Scott. Old money lawyers."

He laughs, and the bitterness in it tells me I've won. I relax against the counter a little. Even though the cabin is cold, with the heat turned down low, sweat slicks across my skin.

"Maybe I want the divorce," he says coolly—a lie and both of us know it. I roll my eyes.

"Then you wouldn't have sent a PI to find me."

The silence on his end is telling; he knows, and thinks I don't, that the PI was really an assassin. And what is there to say to that? I can feel him thinking, cold and calculating. This is his one chance to do me in. He just needs a push.

"I've kept quiet about what you did," I tell him. "But if you won't talk to me like a goddamn adult, then I'm taking the whole story to the *New York Times*. You know I've got the connections."

Sawyer's eyes flick up to me in surprise.

"I'm serious, Scott. You trying to fucking murder me with your bare hands will be *everywhere* in twenty-four hours if you don't come here so we can work this out."

I hold my breath, waiting for his response. The truth is that if I did do that, Scott would pay an exorbitant amount of money to bury the story and make me look like a fool in the process. He would humiliate me worse than I've already experienced—and I've experienced a lot.

But it would be costly. And time-consuming.

And deep down, I know he wants me dead.

Just like how I want him dead. A gift for my serial killer.

"Fine," Scott says. "I'll book the next flight out. Tomorrow, at the earliest."

I look over at Sawyer. He has a hunger in his eyes. A dark smile on his lips.

He nods.

"That's Halloween," I tell him.

"Well, then I'll wear a fucking costume. What do you want from me, Edie?"

"You don't need to wear a costume."

"Are you still at that old fat camp?"

"Yeah."

He laughs, cold and bitter. "What were you thinking with that, by the way?"

I look at Sawyer, who stands a few feet from me, silent and still, looking very much like the monster I saw fifteen years ago. The monster who gave me comfort. I thought I was coming here to hide from Scott, but really, I wonder if I was coming to find Sawyer.

"It just felt right," I say, and then I hang up the phone.

CHAPTER THIRTY-TWO

SAWYER

We don't have much time to get everything ready, but I'm glad Edie's ex is coming out sooner rather than later. I can smell the nor'easter on the horizon, the metallic scent of frost and snow. Every time I go outside, my skin prickles with it. An early snowstorm is just what we need. It'll blanket everything in silence, cover our tracks for at least a week. By then we'll be long gone.

She collapses into my arms after the phone call with her ex, and I hold her and stroke her hair and kiss her neck, but really my thoughts are on the upcoming kill. Taking care of the PI the other day quieted the bloodlust, a bit like an appetizer before a big meal. It means when Edie's ex shows up, I won't get so overwhelmed with need that I end it too quickly.

I'm gonna take my time with him.

I'm gonna cut him open and remove his organs one by one and leave them stacked like a box of jewels.

And I'm gonna make sure he knows it's Edie who sent me.

Watching her talk to him, I saw all the ways he hurt her. She thinks she hid it from me, playing it cool, but I felt the way her pulse changed whenever he spoke. I saw the way that pretty light in her eyes dimmed every time he opened his mouth. He took a girl who already felt worthless and told her it was true, all so he could control her, shape her into something else.

The thought floods me with rage, even as I'm holding Edie now, running my hand over her thick curls, squeezing her soft, strong body in tight. It reminds me of how I felt fifteen years ago, seeing how those counselors treated her. This ex is the same way. Just richer. More powerful.

But he'll fall under my blade just like they did.

"Is this really happening?" Edie pulls away from me and rubs her arms like she's cold. "Is this really going to *work?*"

"Of course it is," I tell her. "But we've got to get everything ready. We need to be able to run after it's finished."

I see flashes of *it*. Blood and viscera. A man's screaming face. The gleam of my knife blade. My cock stiffens.

Edie nods. Part of me wants to bend her over the counter and slide between her thighs, just to quiet the lust. But I don't want either of us getting distracted.

"Right," she says, a nervous chatter in her voice. "I need to close my bank account. That way we'll have money. We'll need supplies, right? Food? Clothes? We won't want to have to stop after we—after you..."

Her voice kind of trails off, and she gets this worried line between her brows. For the first time, I feel a tickle of doubt.

What if she doesn't let me go through with it?

What if my perfect prey ruins my gift for her?

"You're right," I say. "We'll go into town. Together, just in case there are any more surprises from your ex."

The lines in Edie's brow deepen. "Is that a good idea? For us to be seen—"

"Baby, nobody knows who I am." I grab her chin and tilt it up so she can look me in the eye and know I'm telling the truth. "I've got a fake ID. They think Sawyer Caldwell's dead. It's fine, okay?"

She nods, eyes glimmering

"We'll go into town," I continue. "Get what we need. Then you can get everything set up here, and I'll get everything set up there." I tilt my head toward the woods.

"Okay." Her voice is shaky, and I can't help myself; I cup her face, kind of pin her in place. The scent of her fear is strong, and that just excites me further. It's going to be so hard to keep my hands off her between now and the kill.

"We'll get everything ready together." Anticipation thrums through me, and when I speak, I can hear the lust in my voice. "And then we'll wait."

HUNTERS DON'T SLEEP MUCH, but in the last week, I've found I like sitting in bed while Edie's curled up next to me, her breaths slow and measured. I usually read, flipping through the stack of old paperbacks I bought the last time I was in town. I brought one with me tonight, one of those trippy science fiction novels that Jaxon's always going on about, but I can't concentrate on the words. My brain keeps going to the kill.

I haven't been this excited for a kill—well, for fifteen years. Since I decided once and for all I was going to wipe out Edie's tormentors. And now I get to do it again. Only this time, it'll be better. Because she'll be by my side.

So I don't bother to read. I just lay back and go over my plan in my head, figuring out everything I need to do to make it perfect.

But then Edie's voice rises up, small and trembling. "Sawyer?"

I look over at her, tucked on her side, her hair spilling in dark rivers across her pillow. "I thought you were asleep."

She stirs, pushing up on her arm. "I can't."

I don't smell her fear, particularly—not any more than I did earlier when she was talking to her ex. He scares her, that much is clear. But I can sense a knot of anxiety in her, in the small trembling way she shoves herself up to sitting, pressing her back against the headboard. She worries the bedsheet in one fist.

And I sense an unfamiliar surge of panic.

This is why Mama said our kind shouldn't get romantic with humans. This vulnerability, this weakness. I think of a kill and my cock gets hard and the back of my jaw aches.

Edie thinks of a kill and she strangles the bedsheet, her eyes dark.

I'm not sure what to say so I kiss her instead, soft and gentle. She returns it, smiling a little against my lips, and nuzzles my neck. I take that as an invitation to pull her into me. I can do that much, at least.

"You're not scared," I finally say. She's so quiet, and I've got to say something.

"No," she whispers. "Not really." She shifts against me, her breath warm on my skin. "You—I feel safe with you. I know you won't let anything happen to me."

That fucking floors me, hearing her say that. And that's how I know Mama's wrong about us and humans. Because it makes me feel all warm and proud and satisfied, like how I feel after I finish up one of my projects at the church or clean up a particularly messy murder scene. And I wouldn't get that feeling with another Hunter. Another Hunter wouldn't want me to *protect* them.

"I will," I say, after fumbling around for my voice. I bury my face into her hair, breathing her in. "So why can't you sleep?"

"I don't think you'll understand."

All that pride I felt a moment ago drains away. "Why not?"

Edie tilts her head up to me. My night vision's good, and it makes her skin seem to glow a little in the darkness, like she's suffused with moonlight. "Because you—you're a killer."

She says it like it's something to be ashamed of, but I'm not ashamed. I brush her hair behind her ear.

"And you think you're about to become one, too?" I'm taking

my best guess, but from the way her face flickers with darkness, I know I've landed on it.

"I just keep thinking there's something wrong with me," she says. "That I'm okay with all this. That I love—"

She freezes. I freeze, too, going as still as I do when I'm stalking my prey.

"That I love you." She barely says the words. If I weren't a Hunter, with a Hunter's hearing, I don't think I'd have heard them.

I ought to be celebrating. Ain't no one ever told me they loved me before except for Mama, and she usually only did it to make a point about why I should listen to her. But it's all spoiled because I know this love Edie feels for me, it makes her upset.

"And you wish you didn't," I finally say.

It takes her a while to answer, but I'm patient. "I wouldn't put it like that," she says. "I wish—I wish I could be like you. And not have any of this bother me."

I shift my body around so I'm facing her. So I can look her straight on. I'm still figuring out how to respond when she says, "Why did you choose me?"

"What?"

"Fifteen years ago," she says. "When I was at camp. Why me?" Her eyes glitter in the darkness. "Why am I your perfect prey?"

The easy answer is that I thought she was beautiful, but I know that's not the answer she's looking for. It's also not the full truth of things, is it?

"You're my perfect prey because I want to hunt you over and over." I hope I'm explaining this right, that I don't scare her away. "I saw you and I wanted to hunt you but I didn't want to kill you, not really."

Her eyes bore into mine, almost challenging me. It makes me feel stripped bare. Vulnerable.

It makes me feel almost like I'm prey myself.

"There's something in you," I say. "Some strength that tells me you're the one I chase but let go. I felt it the first time I saw you. And I feel it every time I look at you."

It feels good saying that out loud. Feels good to see the effect it has on her, the subtle shift in temperature as her cheeks warm, as her heart rate picks up. I can't stop myself from pressing my hand against her frantic pulse.

"I love you," I say simply. "But I love you the way a hunter loves prey. And there's nothing I can change about that, Edie." I let my hand slide up to her face. I don't want her looking away from me while I talk. "But I will protect you. That man, your ex, he caused you so much pain. And I'm going to take it away. Do you understand that? I'm going to take it away and do my best to keep you happy. But I am what I am, and nothing is going to cha—"

She lunges at me so fast I almost think she's attacking me. But then her lips press to mine and her tongue slides into my mouth, and then I'm attacking her, devouring her, nipping and biting at her sweet, pulsing flesh.

"Why do I want this?" she gasps between kisses, and I press her down onto her back and crawl on top of her. Not so much to fuck her but because I want to feel her body beneath me, pinned in place.

"Does it matter?"

She gazes up at me, lips swollen from my kisses. Her nightgown's neckline is pushed down, and I can see the dark crescent of her areolas peeking out from behind the lace.

"I think I'm a bad person," she says.

"You think you're a killer."

Something flickers across her face. That's it. That's what's bothering her.

"You're not going to kill anyone," I tell her, pressing her legs open with my knee. "I'm going to do it. Because I like it. And because that's what it'll take to give you the life you deserve."

Edie shivers a little. But she never turns away from me. Her eyes blaze with something as hot and bright as the sun. It's not lust.

"Say it again," I order, rubbing my thigh up against her pussy.

"Say what?"

"That you love me."

Her lips curl into a faint, delicate smile. "You say it first."

I press my head down so our foreheads touch. Grab at her wrists so I can pin her arms above her head, holding her in my Hunter's trap.

"I love you, my perfect prey."

Her eyes gleam. She hooks a leg around my hip, pulling me into her. I hope she knows my cock is hard from the thought of killing her ex. I hope she knows I think of death every time I fuck her. Because that's who loves her. And I love her because she isn't those things. I love her because she's the moonlight in the shadows, the porch light flickering in the dark woods.

She's the Milky Way, a band of celestial light that marks a place as safe.

"Now say it back," I order.

And she does.

But I still don't know if she understands.

CHAPTER THIRTY-THREE

EDIE

Sawyer was right about the weather turning.

I sit on the sofa in the cabin, the TV turned on low to the local station. A *Blood Raisers* marathon, since it's Halloween, all eight of those stupid horror movies. I've had it on all day, ever since Sawyer gave me a long, lingering kiss on the front porch, cold winds sweeping across us. Then he was gone. He has to set everything up for tonight, and I have to be the bait that draws Scott into Sawyer's trap.

I'm not watching TV, though. I'm staring out the window at the fuzzy grey sky. It's been years since I've watched clouds fill with snow. Years since I've seen a real snowfall. Scott prefers warmer weather.

It's getting darker, too, the sun dropping behind those storm clouds. Scott should have landed in Roanoke already. He should be driving along those windy mountain roads, underneath the heavy snow clouds.

I stand up, jittery with anticipation. I want so badly to call Charlotte and tell her what I'm doing. I know when she hears I've disappeared she'll be devastated. But I can't. I trust her to keep the secret, but I don't want to put that burden on her.

She's not like me, willing to fall into the darkness.

I look out the window, chewing on a hangnail. The driveway in front of the camp is still empty. Part of me hates the idea of Scott coming to this place, the ammunition it would give him to see the fat camp where I failed over and over to lose weight. He'll probably make some joke about it when he gets here. Look me up and down, his lip curled in disgust. Assuming he doesn't try to kill me right away.

No. I can't worry about that. Sawyer is out there in the cold. *That* I'm sure of. Especially after last night, the way his eyes burned black as he told me he loved me. It almost felt like a threat, the way he said it. But everything he says, everything he does, is edged in violence—

And I love it. I *burn* for it. And maybe that's the real reason why I can't call Charlotte. I don't want her to know what I truly am. I'm not like Sawyer, but I can accept him. I can stand here in this cabin, a lure for his next victim, and know that the next time he fucks me, I'll come at least in part because of what I'm doing right now. Because of what he's about to do.

Tires crunch outside. My whole body goes cold, and I take a long, deep breath.

This is it.

Time to burn my life down so I can start it anew.

I sidle up to the window and peer out through the sheer curtain. Headlights sweep across the driveway and then come to a stop, flooding the little patch of dead grass in front of the cabin with yellow light. I drop the curtain, knowing Scott can see me.

Maybe it's from being with Sawyer, but I sweep my eyes around the room and settle my gaze on the rack of knives beside the refrigerator. One's still missing, of course.

Footsteps outside. A thump on the porch. Three heavy knocks.

I take a deep breath, and then I go to answer it.

Seeing Scott is startling. I thought I'd memorized his face, but it's astonishing how much his features have faded from my mind after only a month. Funny how long Sawyer's eyes lingered even after fifteen years.

"Edie." Scott pushes inside, his gaze sweeping cautiously around the room. He's on guard, I realize, a thought that makes my shoulders knot up with anxiety.

He knows.

Scott turns around slowly, eyes still flitting around like he's waiting to be attacked. I dig my nails into my palm, trying to steady myself.

"What's wrong?" I hope my voice sounds light.

Scott settles his gaze on me. His eyes are blue and very pale. When I first met him, I found them striking, but now they seem flat and dead.

Just the way they did the night he nearly killed me.

"You tell me." He looks me over, up and down, the judgment clear on his face. "You wanted to come out here. To *talk.*"

His voice drips with condescension. I wish Sawyer had stayed here with me, wish he was hiding in the closet like the villain in one of the *Blood Raisers* movies still playing softly in the background. But he insisted on leaving. Said he needed to do some final prep before Scott arrived.

I can sense everything that's happening here, he told me, his arms around wrapped around me on the porch. *You won't see me, but I'm here. You're safe.*

I'm still not sure about that.

Scott stares at me, waiting for a response. I choke one out.

"Yes," I tell him. "And can you blame me? You attacked me. If I'm going to come back, then we need to lay some ground rules."

"Yeah, we certainly do." Scott's eyes narrow. "You're fatter than when you left. Did you know that?"

I squeeze my hands into fists. But the ED voice stays silent. Because it's not true. My weight hasn't changed at all. I know it. Scott knows it.

"I mean, this can't keep going." He gestures at me. "I'm just worried about your health."

He's been repeating that same lie for the last two years. Undermining my recovery at every turn. But somehow, tonight, it's easy to see his words for what they are. He doesn't care about my health. He wants to control me.

"You're right," I say as sweetly as I can. The lie gives me a surge of adrenaline. "That's why you're here, isn't it? So we can talk things through. Decide what we'll do next." I step closer to him. "Maybe I can start going to the gym with you again."

He'll like the idea. Scott married me in large part because I was a story he loves to tell: the ugly duckling who put in the hard work to become a swan. He wasn't attracted to my body, even when I was thinner, but he was attracted to my eating disorder.

So I'll offer it back to him.

But then Scott replies in a flat voice: "Maybe."

With that one word, alarm twists inside me. That's not the answer I expected.

Scott walks in a half-circle, appraising me. "You know, I only agreed to this because I have some things to talk to *you* about."

I don't like this. I have to stop myself from glancing over at the window to look for Sawyer.

Where are you? I think desperately, as if he can hear my thoughts. But whatever magic he is, it's not that.

"What do you have to talk to me about?" I counter, trying to press confidence into my voice. "You *attacked* me, Scott."

"I did." He stops, still watching me. "But you lied to me."

I go very still, afraid that if I move I'll give myself away.

"About what?" My heartbeat pounds in my ears.

Scott moves a step closer. "Yesterday," he says, "when we spoke on the phone, you asked me about the PI. One." He holds up one finger.

I dig my nails so deeply into my palms that I'm sure I've drawn blood.

I hope Sawyer smells it.

"And yet, *two* of my best guys came out to visit you. Matt Baro." He holds up a second finger. "And Logan Greer."

"I only ever spoke to one," I say, but there's a shudder in my voice that I know betrays me. "Matt Baro, I think? The blond? I never met a Logan Greer."

"That, Edie, is the lie." Scott's smile stretches cruelly across his face, and when he steps toward me, I step back. My body rushes with panic. And still, there's no sign of Sawyer. No heavy footsteps outside the door.

He's abandoned you.

The thought spurns a dozen others, all cascading through my head at once. He's not really Sawyer Caldwell. Scott hired him. This has all been Scott. This has all been some trap that Scott, with his billionaire's boredom, orchestrated to humiliate me—

No, that doesn't make sense. I know it doesn't make sense. Scott wouldn't kill his own men... I don't think.

But then where the hell is Sawyer?

"I know you spoke to Logan because Logan called me while he was tailing you after he spotted you buying—" Scott pretends to pause, the same stupid trick he uses when he's talking to potential clients "—house painting supplies? That can't be right. I told him, Edie Hensner isn't doing any kind of manual labor. It would interfere with stuffing her face."

I glare at him, barely registering the insult. The panic overwhelms it. We never checked Logan's phone, did we? My mind, at least, had been elsewhere.

"The last I heard," Scott says, "you were pulling up in front of an abandoned church, and he was getting out to talk to you. And then—" He ripples his fingers. "Silence. Now, bear in mind, this is *after* Matt also went missing while here in scenic Altarida." Scott's grin widens further, and his teeth are too white, too neat, too perfect. "So why are you lying to me, Edie?"

My mind has gone blank. I'm certain Sawyer's not coming.

"What do you want from me?" I whisper, tears turning the question jagged.

In response, Scott lunges at me.

I react purely on instinct, darting sideways—toward the hallway, away from the door. Stupid. But I am stupid, aren't I? I thought I could trust Sawyer.

I ran into the hallway, tears streaking down my face. Scott is faster, and he grabs me by the arm and jerks me backward so I land hard on my ass, pain shuddering up through my spine.

"This is why you don't let yourself go." Scott jerks me across the floor, pulling so hard on my arm that it feels like it's going to wrench out of its socket. "Fatasses can't run."

I'm sobbing now, and I hate myself for it. I hate myself for everything I've done in the last month. For being such a stupid fool.

Something thin and cool wraps around my wrist, and I hear a sound like a zipper. I choke back my tears and look over to see that Scott has zip-tied both of my arms to the leg of the heavy wooden coffee table, forcing me to stretch out an awkward angle.

"There," he says, stepping back with his arms crossed over his chest. "You can stay right there while I call back the others and we can figure out what the fuck is going on here."

Others?

Scott pulls out his phone and taps against the screen. There's the *whoosh* noise of a sent text. "I figured you hired someone," he says, still looking down at his phone. "God knows you aren't exactly capable of taking out two grown men."

I stare at him, my whole body shaking with a new fear. Sawyer didn't abandon me. But if there are *others*—

I've seen him die once.

What if he dies again?

I pull desperately on the zip tie, flopping my body around. It doesn't do any good. The plastic digs painfully into my skin, and all I accomplish is jerking my arms around in their sockets.

That's when I hear it. The echoing report of two rifle blasts from deep in the woods. I scream, adrenaline bursting out of me. All I can think of is Sawyer's head exploding from a gunshot fifteen years ago.

Scott hears them, too, and he tilts his head, listening. "So you did hire someone. Sounds like one of my boys took care of him, though." He squats down and looks at me thoughtfully. I glare up at him, desperately trying to hide my fear with anger.

"I wanted to kill you," he says calmly, turning the phone around in his hand. "But I almost think I like this better."

"Kidnapping me?" I don't know how I get it out without sobbing. *Sawyer's still coming*, I tell myself. Maybe if I repeat it enough it will be true.

He laughs. "No, of course not. Having you arrested." He stands back up, shakes out the sleeves of his jacket, glances down at his phone. His face doesn't give anything away. "This whole little trip was a ruse, wasn't it? And as soon as I opened the door, you attacked me. Fortunately, I thought you might try something like that, and I was able to subdue you." He glances at his phone again, frowning, but then slides it into his pocket. "I'm sure once the cops start scouring around here, they'll find some kind of evidence to prosecute you for the murders."

I want to snap something back at him, some clever one-liner that will cut him down and put him into place. But he's right, isn't he? Sawyer's a murderer. Two of those murders he did to protect me, but not the others. Which means no one will believe me when I say Scott was trying to kill me first.

Scott gives me a slow, easy smile. "My boys are taking their time, aren't they? Let me guess—you had your man waiting in the woods to attack me." Scott laughs. "Well, I bet he can't go up against three military-trained mercenaries. This is going even better than I expected."

I scream in both rage and terror, yanking hard on the zip ties.

I keep telling myself Sawyer will be here. He hasn't been shot. He's still coming. He's still coming. He's still coming.

Scott pushes his hand through his hair and gives me one of those appraising looks. "We could kill the time—" he says, then laughs. "Kill! I didn't even mean to do that."

I thrash against the coffee table. Tears edge through my lashes, and I blink them away. Scott can see me scream, but I won't let him see me cry. Never again.

"How about a blowjob for old time's sake?" He steps toward me, his hand on his belt.

"Fuck you," I snarl.

"I don't think so," Scott says. "Not with you looking like that. But you give good head. Fat girls always do."

Enraged, I swing my body around, kicking out my legs. Scott sees it coming, but I still manage to clip his ankle. It does nothing. Doesn't even knock him down. But he lunges at me, shoving my head back against the edge of the coffee table. He does it hard enough that the world blinks black and white.

"Open your fucking mouth," he says, yanking out his belt. Unzipping his pants. Taking out his half-limp cock. I blink at him, my vision still fuzzy. It's unreal, what's happening to me. I feel like my thoughts have split apart from my body. "And if I feel even a hint of teeth—"

He reaches behind his back, under his shirt, and pulls out a small, black gun.

"I'll shoot you in self-defense."

CHAPTER THIRTY-FOUR

SAWYER

As soon as I see the dark car pull up to Edie's camp, I know something's wrong. I can smell the stranger's fancy cologne and a rippling undercurrent of malice. But that's not what worries me.

It's the other scents, too.

Men. Men who are accustomed to killing, although they ain't Hunters. At least two of 'em, although there may be more.

I slip through the trees, getting closer to the clearing. I didn't want to leave Edie alone in the cabin—I know she's scared—but I'm sure as shit glad I did now. I didn't tell her my reasoning, just said I needed to finish up the preparations. I didn't want to scare her further. But I wanted to be out here, out in my element, in case her piece of shit ex tried anything tricky.

And it certainly seems he has.

I follow him in the shadows, watching as he strolls up to the cabin, which is lit up bright in the darkness. The air's heavy with the impending snow and crystallized with cold, but the cold is good. It heightens things. Makes it easier to hunt down the others.

I just hope he doesn't do anything to Edie right away. Times like these, I wish I believed in Jaxon's gods. I know the Christian god ain't gonna listen to my prayers. But Jaxon's gods might, and I'd like knowing a god is on Edie's side.

But I don't believe in them, and so Edie just has me. I'll work fast.

Her ex is knocking at the front door. I wait until he goes inside to pull my attention away from him and spread it out through the woods. I keep Edie's presence in the background. She's scared, but it's the same fear I've been smelling all night. It seems the asshole is gonna let her talk, at least for a little while.

I pull back into the woods and stand very still, eyes closed, listening and smelling. The cold might as well be a white searchlight, the way it illuminates everything in the darkness. And there's not much out here, not with that snowstorm coming. The mountain animals are all hunkered down in their little hideaways. Only animals left are the humans.

It doesn't take long for them to announce themselves: a rustle of fallen leaves here, a broken twig there. One of 'em even coughs, a small puff of air. That one's close; the wind gusts, and I catch his scent, strong and sure. He ain't scared.

He's about to be.

I move toward the scent, working as fast as I can. I don't know how much time Edie has. Fortunately, I know these woods well, and it only takes a minute or two until I spot my prey. A gorilla of a man, with big shoulders and a huge chest. Dressed all in black. He's got a rifle, the sight of which sends a phantom pain ringing through my skull.

I can not let him shoot me in my head.

I come around behind him. I wish I could take my time, play my little games. But I'm not killing for me tonight, so I just dart up to him and wrap my arm around his thick neck and draw my blade across his throat.

The snow's almost here because the gurgle he makes as he

topples forward is as loud as a thunderclap. I grab the back of his shirt and ease him down, just in case the other is nearby.

No. *Others.* With one gone, I can sense there are two more. One's out behind the cabin, the other's across the clearing. Triangulated around my Edie. But she's *my* perfect prey. Not theirs.

She's still scared. Scared, and a little angry. I move toward the man behind the cabin.

Halfway there, the snow starts. I feel it rather than see it, little blooming bursts of cold through my clothes. The forest goes even quieter, so quiet I can't silence my footsteps proper 'cause there's nothing for me to blend them in with.

"Who's there?" The voice is sharp and commanding. A military voice. He's trying to intimidate me but all he does is draw every ounce of my attention to where he's crouched beside a big white oak tree, sweeping his gaze around through what I can only assume is some night vision scope on his rifle.

I know I shouldn't. Edie's panic is rising, and I can't fuck around. But I also can't help myself.

I let him see me. Just for a moment, through his night vision. Then I dart sideways, ducking into the shadows. Making him doubt what he saw.

And it works. His fear curls through the air, dark and intoxicating.

"Freeze!" He shouts. "I'm armed and authorized to shoot."

I somehow doubt that, but at the same time, I'm not taking any chances with a gun. I move around sideways, slow and steady. It's easier now because the snow's falling more thickly, making a staticky noise up in the half-empty tree tops.

My prey whirls around, gun flashing. I wait until he turns away from me, and then I slam my knife into the base of his spine. He screams, a sound I cut short when I jam the blade into the side of his neck. When the snowflakes hit his blood, it steams.

I let him fall. Let him make noise. There's one left, and he's on high alert, fear and adrenaline spiking. If I can get him to come to me—

But then Edie's fear erupts.

It drowns out any other scent in the forest. It drowns out any *sound* in the forest. Any sight. For a moment all I see and hear and smell and taste is her terror. My chest seizes up, and I lunge forward toward the cabin, my blood-slick fingers tight around my knife.

If that sack of shit does *anything* to her—

Footsteps to my left. I tense, glancing sideways and scanning the darkness for the final soldier—or whatever the fuck they are. The snow's falling more thickly, turning the world to static, but I see a flash of green light, the gleam of a gun.

"Freeze!" the voice shouts.

Edie's terror is the sweetest perfume I've ever smelled, but it also coils a sick knot of worry in my stomach. All I want is to stride through the snow toward her, to stop whatever her ex is doing or about to do. But that soldier will shoot. I can hear the promise of violence in his voice.

I can't fail her, my perfect prey.

So I grunt out my frustration and then do as he says, tightening my fingers around the knife. He comes closer, moving out of the shadows until I can see his outline. He watches me through the gun, the scope gleaming a little.

"Put your hands up," he orders.

I do, even though it means he sees my Bowie knife.

"Drop it," he says.

Edie's fear wafts out of the cabin and curls through the snow. Everything is sharper in the cold.

I need to get to her.

"Drop it," the soldier says again, moving closer. "And take off that fucking mask."

Everything is sharper in the cold, and that will work to my advantage.

I lunge sideways with every ounce of my Hunter's speed. He fires off two rounds, but they splinter the trees behind me, loud as explosions. I tackle him, my knife sliding into his neck over and over, hot blood gushing all over me. For a moment, it's all I can smell, that metallic coppery tang. One of my favorite fucking scents in this world.

And then I smell Edie's fear again, lifting over it, and that's even better.

I stand up and he falls over dead, his blood dark against the white of the accumulating snow. I take just one moment to check if there are any others.

There aren't. Just Edie's ex. And I have very specific plans for him.

I run as fast I can toward the cabin, drawn forward by Edie's terror. I'm manic and furious at the thought of her ex hurting her. Killing her. She's *my* prey. *My* treasure to stalk and hunt a thousand times over. I will not let some human psychopath take that away from me.

The lights from the cabin shine up ahead, as bright as a bonfire. There's about an inch of snow on the ground now, and that makes everything brighter, too.

His blood is going to look so pretty against all that white.

As I come up to the cabin, I start to hear them through the walls. He's grunting softly, and her heart's pounding violently fast. What the fuck is he doing to her?

I race around to the front, my own breath sharp and panting inside my mask.

Then I slam the door open to a flood of artificial light.

CHAPTER THIRTY-FIVE

SAWYER

The first thing I do is look for Edie. I can smell her, I can hear her. But I want to *see* her. And at first, I can't.

It's because her ex is looming over, his hips rocking. Then I realize she's on the floor in front of him. Hands bound and tied to the coffee table. He's pressing a gun to her temple.

And then I realize what he's doing to her, and my blood turns to fire.

But I wasn't quiet in my entrance, and he whirls around to face me before I launch myself at him. His dick's out, shiny from raping my Edie's mouth. Behind him, Edie retches like she's trying to spit out his poison.

"What the—" He stumbles backward, taking me in. I know what he sees. I'm drenched in the blood of his soldiers. I'm hiding my face behind a rubber mask.

I'm not what he expects at all.

He stammers out a string of frightened expletives, fumbling at his cock with one hand, so concerned about his vulnerability he forgets the gun in the other. Makes it easier for me. I clear the room in three steps and slide the knife into his side. He doesn't even know what hit him, given the way he looks up at me in surprise.

It takes every ounce of willpower not to keep going until he's dead.

I yank out the knife along with a spray of blood. The gun clatters to the ground. I leave it where it is. Let Edie's ex have that little glimmer of hope so I can snatch it away from him later.

"Edie, who the fuck is this?" He clutches at the knife wound I gave him, his eyes staring at me in confusion. "This is who you—"

I slam my foot into his knee so it cracks backward. He howls and collapses to the floor, screaming and sobbing and writhing around.

I look over at my Edie.

She's sobbing, tear tracks streaked over her cheeks, but she looks at me with pure relief. No one's ever done that before, especially not when I'm in my mask and covered with blood.

I go over to her and cut the plastic ties around her wrists. As soon as she's free, she collapses forward, grabbing at my shoulders to hug me. I take her arm, maybe a little too roughly, and pull her to her feet. Press my mask against her temple. Hold her close. She's real. She's alive.

"He forced me to— to—" She can't get the words out, but she doesn't need to.

"I know," I tell her, my rage flaring. "And he's going to pay for that."

I look over at him, my next victim, clutching at his malformed knee. He shakes his head. "She begged me for it!" he screams. "She's a fat fucking slut! You think I need to force someone like her to—"

I kick the gun so it goes skittering across the room and under the dining room table. What little hope is in his eyes dies out, and god does that make me hard.

I kick him in the chest, send him sprawling on his back. His dick's gone flaccid and it flops against his thigh. I can't help myself, having it out like that. I crouch down, grab it with one hand, and start sawing the thing off.

He screams. It's the kind of scream I like to savor, a long and miserable wail. I yank hard on his cock to detach it from his body, the tissue snapping, and stand up. Blood pours out of his crotch, and he keeps screaming in disbelief. I turn to Edie.

She stares at me, eyes glossy with tears. But she's not afraid. Not anymore.

Her ex is still screaming.

I offer his dick to her like a flower, but she just shakes her head no. I smile inside my mask. My perfect prey. She's not a sadist.

I am, though.

I throw the dick against the wall. It splats like spaghetti and slides down, leaving a snail's trail of blood behind it. Edie's ex stares at it in horror, wailing wordlessly. I glance over at Edie again. There's a part of me that expects her to ask me to stop. That this, what I do, is too much for her. And I'm prepared to reel myself in if that's what she wants.

But she doesn't.

I stalk over to her ex, my fingers flexing. He tries to scramble away from me, dragging his broken leg with him, but of course he doesn't get far. His hair's just long enough that I can grab it and jerk him around and drag him out onto the porch.

It's been a long time since I've set a proper scene, but I think Edie's worth it.

The storm is here, swirls of snow glinting in the pale boundary of the porch light. Edie's ex screams and kicks with his good leg and tries to grab at my hand. I ignore him and throw him hard against the porch railing. For a moment, I remember the first gift I gave Edie, that severed head. And the bird skull, too. That's tucked away in my truck, wrapped in a little scrap of fabric. Edie made sure I didn't forget it.

"Why are you doing this?" The ex's pained scream cuts

through my thoughts. I look over at him, and he recoils from my mask. His face is turning ashy and pale from blood loss. But I still have time to play.

I wrench one of his arms up and press his blood-soaked hand against the railing. Then I pull the knife from Edie's kitchen off my belt. We need to return it to the cabin before we leave, after all.

I slam it through her ex's hand, making him scream in agony as I pin him against the banister. He twists toward it, reaching with his other hand to try and pull it out. I stop him and slam that hand up against the railing, too. He tries to fight against me, but he's not strong enough. Even if he wasn't dying, he wouldn't be strong enough. All the gym-cultivated muscles in the world can't match a Hunter's strength.

I brace his wrist against the railing and jerk his hand back-ward, snapping the bone. When I release his arm, it flops down into his bloody lap. He screams and stares down at his shattered wrist, confusion clear on his face.

"Edie!" he screams.

I stiffen. Tighten my grip around my Bowie knife. Hearing her name on his tongue fills me with an unexpected rage.

How *dare* he call out to her? After all the hurt he did to her? After *raping* her?

"You can stop this!" he howls, looking past me, his eyes wild with panic. "I know you hired this monster. Call him off, Edie!"

Hired? He thinks she *hired* me, that I'm doing this for money?

I don't know why, but that just enrages me even more. I lunge forward and swipe my blade across his face, forging a path from his left temple through his eye and over his nose, clipping the side of his mouth. He screams and thrashes, trying to pull out his pinned hand. The flesh tears, a soft ripping noise that almost sounds like the snow.

I want to do the either side, marking his face with an X, but before I can do anything, Edie steps onto the porch. I feel my perfect prey beside me, shivering in her jeans and sweater, her hair falling into her eyes. She puts a hand on my arm.

"Yes, that's it," her ex cries, the words slurred from pain and shock. "You can stop this, Edie. Please. Just call him off. We can talk about this, okay?" He's begging for his life. I don't usually let it get this far, but I've certainly seen it before.

He ain't begging me, though. He's begging her.

I look over at her, then. Edie's face is cold and hard. She's not the prey right now. Not at all.

"Please," her ex whimpers through the blood slicking his features. "Please, Edie. Tell him to stop."

I look at her through my mask, waiting for her to tell me what to do. It doesn't matter what it is. I'll do it. For her.

She lifts her gaze to meet mine. My entire skin burns, waiting.

"Make him suffer," she says.

CHAPTER THIRTY-SIX

EDIE

It's shocking how easy it is to watch Sawyer torture Scott, especially with my mouth still sour from his assault. When Sawyer offered me Scott's severed dick, I almost took it. I almost picked it up as delicately as I had picked up the bird skull he brought me. The only reason I didn't, I think, was the blood. I didn't want to feel any more of Scott's fluids on my skin.

But now, on the porch, the blood doesn't bother me. It's dark and glossy in the porch light, and it steams in the cold, reminding me of the mountain's pale curling mist.

It's pretty, almost.

Scott's nearly unrecognizable, especially with the cut across his face. He keeps babbling at me, begging me to tell Sawyer to stop. But it's the first time in our entire relationship that I've ever felt like I had any kind of power. Because when Sawyer glances over at me, eyes gleaming behind his mask, I know he'll do whatever I ask of him. I could tell him to throw down his knife and walk away, and he would. I could tell him to kill Scott quickly, and he would.

And I know it's fucked up. I know it's wrong. But I decide to embrace that power instead.

"Make him suffer," I say, three words that feel enormous. Sawyer gives me one firm nod, then turns back to Scott and, without warning, slides the knife between Scott's ribs. Scott's pleas become screams, the sound dampened by the snow and the howling winds. I wrap my arms around my chest, but I'm really not that cold.

There's a quiver of excited heat working from between my legs.

Sawyer wrenches the knife sideways and steps back, admiring his handiwork. I'll be honest; all I see is blood, shiny and bright as red leather. Scott trembles, his knife-pinned hand shaking. The snow has melted into his hair, and it hangs wet into his eyes.

"Edie," he whispers hoarsely. "Please."

I step closer, my shoes smearing the blood pooling across the porch. Sawyer cuts Scott again, slicing the knife across his stomach so that something pink and shiny sticks out. Scott thrashes against the knife holding him in place, which just seems to open the cut more, to push more of his insides out. I watch it with a strange, delirious detachment. I wouldn't say I like it.

But what I do like is the knowledge that Sawyer is doing this for me. I felt his rage when he burst in earlier, interrupting Scott's assault. It was a heat that flooded through the room. The same heat that keeps me warm now,

The same heat that throbs between my legs.

"Edie," Scott gurgles, but it's weak. I know he's dying. And yet his taste is still in my mouth. I feel like I could scrape my tongue with Sawyer's knife and I would still taste him, sour and sordid. When Scott dies, I want every trace of him gone.

Sawyer's still cutting at Scott, making small, precise movements. And like that, I know exactly how I want to drown out Scott's taste.

"Sawyer."

He stops immediately and looks over at me. But I'm still

looking at Scott's desperate, pleading face. There's one last thing I want him to see before he dies.

"Come here," I say.

Sawyer stands and walks over to me, his knife dripping blood across the porch. His free hand hooks around my fingers, a gesture of intimacy, of sweetness, that nearly undoes me. Maybe it does. My knees buckle, and I let them fall so that I kneel in front of him. My boogeyman. My masked killer. My Hunter.

When I touch the button on Sawyer's blood-soaked jeans, his body jumps in surprise.

"What... are you..?" Scott's voice drifts through the cold. I yank down Sawyer's zipper, careful not to catch his enormous erection. He grunts a little. In surprise. Encouragement.

I peel away his underwear to pull out his cock. It's as hard as I've ever seen it: heavy in my hand, bulging with veins. The back of my throat aches to flood my mouth with *his* taste.

"Edie!" Scott's voice is shrill. Panicked. "What are you—"

I look over at him. I'm scorching with a black fire I never knew existed in me until this moment.

"How about a blowjob?" My voice is calm. Assured. "For old time's sake."

Scott's eyes widen, and I turn away from him to take Sawyer's cock into my mouth.

Sawyer softly growls out his pleasure, his free hand coming up to cup the back of my head. I moan as I pull his thickness over my tongue, my eyes fluttering closed. I can sense, vaguely, that he's surprised, but I know he's pleased as well, especially when I start bobbing my head up and down his length. He holds back, though; this isn't like before, when he shoved his cock so far down my throat that I couldn't breathe.

No, he's letting me have full control tonight.

I brace myself against Sawyer's blood-soaked thighs, swallowing him as deeply as I can. He brings his other hand up to my head and presses the flat blade of the knife against my scalp. The metal is cool but sticky, and I'm not worried about him cutting me.

"Edie?" Scott whimpers, and the confusion and fear in his voice just make me wetter.

Sawyer's grunts grow louder. More urgent. I know that what he's been doing has turned him on, and he's going to come fast. I quicken my pace, desperate to flood my mouth with his cum. I suck hard, tracing the veins of his arousal with my tongue. When he presses against my head, stilling me, I know he's close, and I let him, just for that moment, take over. He thrusts down my throat four times and then stills, his leg muscles tightening against my hands as he unleashes in my mouth. His cum is exactly what I needed, hot and salty as it spills over my tongue, washing away every trace of what Scott did to me.

I swallow it eagerly, moaning around Sawyer's cock as I clean it. After all, the last thing we want is DNA evidence at a crime scene.

I fall back on my heels, gasping, my lips wet. I can hear Scott, but I don't give a shit about him. I only care about Sawyer. His mask wears the same expression it always does. But I feel his desire.

He grabs me by the hair and hauls me to my feet, a violent and painful gesture that only makes me groan with lust. He yanks me close to him, his masked forehead pressed against mine, and twines his arm around my back, the knife pressed against my spine.

"I love you," he whispers, so soft I almost think it's the wind.

Then he roughly unzips my jeans and shoves his hand inside them, fingers finding my inflamed clit immediately. I rock my hips against him, riding his hand, one leg hoisted up around his hips, my arms hooked around his neck. Scott's sobbing and choking, but all I care about is Sawyer's eyes behind his mask as he finger-fucks me to oblivion. It's oblivion I see in his eyes: the oblivion of death, of murder. Of ecstasy.

My moans match the moans of the snowstorm, and I thrash against him as my orgasm builds, a towering column of heat surging up through the center of my body. I'm aware, distantly, of his hand moving behind my back, but I'm also on the precipice of coming.

"That's it, baby," Sawyer rasps into my ear. "That's it. You're close. Come on."

His words urge me on. I let my head drop back, my eyes close, and I thrust against his fingers with abandon as he swirls my clit in furious circles.

"Look," he growls.

I don't know what he means at first, but pushes my head to the side, away from his piercing gaze.

To Scott, dying.

I gasp out my pleasure. I'm on the verge, my legs trembling, my pussy clenching and fluttering. Sawyer keeps his thumb on my clit as he slides his fingers in and out of my cunt. He knows the exact right places to touch.

I scream into my orgasm—

And Sawyer flings the knife. There's a flash of silver and then it embeds itself in Scott's heart. Scott makes a surprised gasping sound, and as I roll through pulse after pulse of pleasure, the light in his eyes goes out.

I choke out a sound that might be a sob. My face feels wet, but I'm not sure if it's tears or snow. Or both. Sawyer pulls me into him, his palm still gently massaging my pussy. He doesn't take his hand away until the last of my aftershocks have faded.

"You're a fucking goddess," he whispers into my hair.

I cling to him, gasping, breathing in the scent of his skin beneath the steely tang of blood. For a moment, I feel as I did that night we met fifteen years ago. No longer scared. Safe in the arms of a killer.

I know now that this darkness has always been inside me, that it was inside me then, a black diamond tucked inside my heart.

And he saw it, my serial killer. My Hunter.

Sawyer reaches up and pulls his mask away, shoves it in his back pocket. Seeing his face is startling; it's strange, how he wears two faces, and how I love them both.

He cups my cheek, leaving a sticky imprint of Scott's blood. I nuzzle into it.

"We're not done yet," Sawyer says gently.

"I know." My breath condenses in the air. I'm shivering again, and Sawyer pulls me closer, wrapping me in his warmth.

"Are you ready?"

I lay my cheek against his chest, listening to his quickened heartbeat, and look over at Scott. His head has slumped sideways in death. His eyes stare sightlessly ahead.

I feel a freedom I haven't known in a long, long time. Maybe not ever.

"I'm ready," I say, and then, begrudgingly, I step backward, out of Sawyer's arms. He smiles down at me, his mouth gentle but his eyes dancing with a killer's fire. He runs his finger up and down my arm. I take a deep breath. Only one. I don't need four anymore.

Then I look at him and speak.

"I'm ready for you to kill me."

CHAPTER THIRTY-SEVEN

EDIE

I burst into the woods, arms pumping, hair streaming behind me. No coat. No phone. No car keys.

It needs to look believable.

The snow falls in thick white clumps, sticking to my hair and sweater and leaving little prickling dots of cold. At least in the woods proper, it hasn't piled up too much yet, although the ground is slick and I stumble more than once, catching myself on the nearby trees.

Sawyer's behind me. Half-following me, half-corralling me back toward the church so I don't get lost in the dark, snowy woods. When the cops show up here in a few days' time, there need to be two sets of footprints:

One from the predator, and one from the prey.

Branches snap off to my left, and when I glance over, I see Sawyer slipping through the trees, his hair falling into his eyes. He nods, points forward, and I keep moving. My breath comes out in white puffs; the cold burns in my lungs.

This one last thing, and then I'll be free.

I surge forward and come across the creek that leads to Sawyer's church, the water slushy from the cold. I follow it, listening to his footsteps thudding behind me. There's something exciting about this, about being chased by the man who just murdered my ex-husband while he made me come.

Because that's who I am, this woman running through the swirling, silvery snow. The sort of woman who gets excited by those things.

It's freeing. As freeing as running through the woods.

The trees shiver around me, reaching out with their long grasping branches to pluck at my hair and my sweater. The more evidence I can leave behind, the better.

And Sawyer, of course, is always there. Stalking me. Seeing me home.

My foot lands on a slick patch of ice, a place where the creek splashed water and froze, and my legs fly up in front of me. I shriek in panic. There's a split second when I'm flying, but I never land. Two wiry arms catch me. Pull me up.

Sawyer yanks me up against him, his breath hot against my neck.

"Careful," he purrs.

I wriggle my ass against him. He's already starting to get hard again.

"Put your mask on," I tell him.

He arches an eyebrow, eyes going bright with lust. "Is that what you want, baby?"

I nod, breathless from the cold and from the chase. He grins, steps back, and pulls his mask out from his back pocket and slides it on over his head. Seeing it, his second face, sends a jolt of lust through me.

Not that we have time for that.

"Run," he growls. "It's cold out here. You'll catch your death."

I grin. Then I turn and run, flush with a second wind. This time, Sawyer runs, too, jogging so he's just behind me, a constant threat.

"Turn!" he shouts, and I do, veering off to my left.

Two seconds later, I erupt into the clearing.

I stumble to a stop, gasping at the sight. The clouds have cleared, and the moon's out, heavy and full and high in the sky. The snow fell more thickly here and piled up in drifts against his church and the graveyard. Even though it's the witching hour, the middle of the night, everything glows.

Sawyer grabs me by the waist and yanks me up against him. "Got you," he snarls into my ear, and I moan a little, dropping back into his embrace. I'm freezing, my bare hands numb and raw, and I slide them up under his arms, trying to seek warmth.

"You're shivering like a little rabbit," he murmurs, then pulls me around to face him.

We both know I'm shivering from the cold and not fear, but I won't hide who I am anymore. I won't hide how much his darkness turns me on.

"A killer's after me," I whimper, making my eyes big and scared.

Sawyer pulls out his Bowie knife. He cleaned it of Scott's blood, and the blade is like liquid silver in the moonlight. He presses the flat side against my cheek, and I gasp at the ice of the metal.

"The killer's caught you," he says.

Then he pushes up his mask and kisses me, his mouth hot and bruising. Just as I'm melting into his warmth, he sinks his teeth into my bottom lip, hard enough to draw blood. I moan at the sting of the bite, the taste of my blood. Moan as he licks it away.

"I'm going to fuck you so good," he murmurs into my ear. "As soon as it's safe."

As soon as we're away from this place, he means. All afternoon, we've been getting ready: clearing the church of any evidence that I willingly stayed there, planting strands of hair and drops of blood for investigators to find. We packed his truck with a few crucial supplies, mostly food and money. Then he drove the truck to a landing spot downriver. Our escape car.

But first, we have a scene to stage.

I step away from him, gazing up at him in the moonlight. He still has his mask pushed up on his forehead, and his face is carved of light and shadows and speckled with blood. He's the most beautiful man I've ever seen.

"Are you ready for me to cut you?" he says softly.

I nod. Blood's dripping down my chin from his bite, but that, I know, won't be enough. And that bite wasn't for the scene anyway. It was him claiming me. Me letting myself be claimed.

Sawyer pushes his mask back down, a single movement that makes my pussy pulse. *That* isn't necessary, strictly speaking.

I just like it. And Sawyer knows how to please me.

Then I steady myself and hold up my arms, just like we talked about. Sawyer steps forward and flashes the knife out, slashing it over the front of my forearms three quick times, shredding my sweater and slicing my skin just like we discussed. The pain is blinding, as blinding as the snow in the moonlight, and I shriek and stumble backward, clutching at the cuts. Blood splatters out and forms a delicate lacy pattern in the snow.

I clutch my arm to my chest, breathing hard through the harsh, burning pain, and look up at him through my snow-wet hair. He flicks the knife out, splattering more blood.

"Almost there, my perfect prey," he says, tucking a loose lock of hair behind my ear. "I know it hurts. I know you're cold."

I nod, curling my fingers around the wounds. There's no threat of me bleeding out—Sawyer knows where to cut. But they still hurt like hell. And I am frozen solid.

"I'll make sure you don't get lost." He tilts his head across the clearing. "Now run. Make it look good." Behind his mask, his eyes catch the moon and gleam. His voice drops into a rough, dangerous growl. "Bleed for me."

And despite the cold, the pain, my aching muscles—my panties are soaked.

I stumble backward, kicking up glittering flakes of fallen snow as I cut across the clearing, leaving footsteps and trails of blood in my wake. The snow hasn't quite stopped completely; the last few flakes that drift through the air look like stars.

With the cuts on my arm and the heavier layer of snow on the ground, I can't run nearly as fast. Worse, the damp is seeping into my shoes, making my feet burn with cold. It's a relief when I make it to the tree line, where most of the snow is caught up in the tree's branches, forming a cathedral of white overhead.

I shamble along, running and stumbling, and Sawyer follows. My limping footsteps will help sell the story, which is what I tell myself as I push forward. My entire body shivers; my lip throbs where Sawyer bit me, a reminder of his kiss. And the cuts on my arm burn nearly as bad as my feet. The blood seeping through my fingers is hot and sticky, and it pours down my arm to splatter across the forest floor. A trail of deception.

Every now and then, I hear a crack in the woods, and I glance over my shoulder to see Sawyer lurking behind me in his mask, his bloody knife at his side. He urges me on, knowing what's waiting for me at the end of this chase.

The end of one life. The start of another.

It's not long before the woods clear out and the river appears up ahead, a black expanse against the brilliant white of the snow. I make it to the rickety old pier and stop, leaning against the railing. The wind here is as sharp as Sawyer's blade.

"Keep going, perfect prey." He stops just behind me, his hand on my hip. "Only a little further now."

I look over at him. At some point, he took off his mask, and Sawyer, my Sawyer, gazes down at me. He presses his forehead to mine, eyes closed. I expect him to kiss me, but he doesn't. He just breathes me in.

"What are you doing?" I ask.

"Remembering the way you look right now." He straightens up and steps back. The wind whipping off the river pushes his hair away from his forehead to show his heavy, furrowed brow. "How you looked when you gave up everything for me."

I smile through my shivers and my pain. "It was always you, Sawyer. Even when I couldn't see it."

Something flashes across his face. Happiness, I think.

Then he leans in and kisses my forehead. Presses his mouth to my ear. "Go. It's time to drown."

I laugh at that—would Sawyer Caldwell ever kill by drowning? But I turn from him, and I run the length of the pier in one burst of strength, shaking my arm so the blood splatters across the wood. At the end, waiting for me, is a small, cozy boat. He's fixed it up with a thick flannel blanket, a silver Thermos I don't remember ever seeing. A First Aid kit.

I stop and look out at the shimmering mountains. The snow like falling stars. The endless, velvet cold.

And then I jump, somehow landing on both feet in the boat, somehow not tilting the whole thing over. I grab the blanket and slump down on the little seat, wrapping it tight around my shoulders. A few seconds later, Sawyer follows, moving slowly and carefully. He hands me the Thermos.

"Hot cocoa," he says. "With marshmallows."

I laugh, delighted. "You're kidding me."

"Absolutely not." He smiles up at me, his expression almost shy. "I knew you'd be cold. I just hope you like it."

He watches me as I take my first sip. I do like it. It's dark and hot and sweet. Just like him.

As Sawyer rows us away from the pier, I sip at the hot cocoa, shivering wildly beneath the blanket. The wind is brutal on the water, but Sawyer moves quickly until we catch the current that will take us half a mile downstream, where his truck is waiting. Where our future is waiting.

"Let me see your arm." The boat pushes along on its own, and he kneels in front of me, carefully guiding my injured hand out from under the blanket. My entire body vibrates from the cold, but his hands are as warm as fire. He pushes the sleeve up, tugging gently against the cuts. Even in the dark, they look angry and cruel. I know they'll scar, but I don't mind. They mark me as his.

We don't speak as Sawyer dresses my wounds, cleaning the blood away with witch hazel and then wrapping them in bandages from the First Aid kit. When he finishes, he kisses my blood-streaked palm, then rises up enough to kiss my blood-streaked mouth.

"Is this really what you want?" he whispers.

I cup his face, trembling in the cold. It feels like the end of the world, all this darkness, all this cold, all this blood.

But all I can feel is hope.

"Yes," I whisper back.

And just like that, Edie Hensner is dead, killed at the hands of Sawyer Caldwell.

But I'm not dead, and I wrap myself in his arms instead.

EPILOGUE

EDIE

SIX MONTHS LATER

Rain pummels against the big plate glass windows that look out at the beach. I'm curled up on the sofa, trying to read a novel. The storm's too distracting, though. All that driving wind and torrential rain. I'm still not used to the thunderstorms here in Pensacola, which have all the crash and turmoil of hurricanes even though it's April and, I've been told, hurricane season hasn't started yet.

Thunder cracks overhead, making me jump, and I look up at my reflection in the windows, pale and transparent and streaked with raindrops. Sawyer's out in this somewhere. Hunting.

"Storms are good," he told me this evening, right at sunset, the light strange and glowing as the sun's last rays struggled to break through the looming storm clouds. "Give me cover. Just like that snowstorm back in Virginia."

Then he kissed me, his hand curled around my neck.

Then he was gone.

I flip another page of my book without reading any of the words on it. Look at the window again. During the day, in clear weather, I can see the Gulf of Mexico. But right now, I can't even see our little backyard, all the tropical plants that I grow in heavy terra cotta pots. I've taken up gardening since we settled here. Because Edie Hensner has been missing six months and presumed dead, I can't work; maybe someday, Sawyer will wrangle up a fake identity like the one he used to land a job on a construction site. But we don't really need the money. The house I paid for with the cash from my secret bank account, and Sawyer's work brings in enough for living expenses.

It's a carnival mirror version of my old life with Scott. A curved, distorted reflection. Maybe a little eerie at first. But the more you look at it, the more beautiful it becomes.

Thunder booms, and the thin walls of the house shake. I throw my book aside and jump up, too jittery to read. A million worried thoughts flash through my head: Sawyer plowing his pickup truck into a black pool of deep floodwater. Sawyer in glittering silver handcuff. Sawyer shot in the head again, unable to drag himself back home to me.

I pace around the cozy living room, past my spider plants with their trailing, curling vines. Smoke, the little black cat Sawyer found when we were fleeing Virginia, skitters across my feet, as unnerved by the storm as I am.

"Smokies," I call out, and she stops, looks at me with her big green eyes. Then she trots over and nudges her head up against my hand. She's Sawyer's cat, really; she sleeps curled up by his side every night. It wasn't exactly a surprise when he told me he loved cats.

Still, she'll tolerate me when he's not around.

I scoop her up and snuggle her against my chest. Soft, calming purrs vibrate against my heart, even though the howling rain drowns them out.

"I know, I miss him, too." I speak the words into her silky fur.

"But you know Sawyer. When he gets the urge, he just *has* to go hunting."

Smoke mews in agreement.

"Just like you, I know, I know. But *you* don't go hunting mice in a storm like this, do you?"

Immediately, a shattering bolt of thunder cracks the room in two, followed a second later by a searing lightning flash. Smoke leaps out of my arms, her fur standing up straight, and bolts back into the bedrooms. But I'm not worried about her.

A figure stands in the garden.

The lightning fades, and I can only see my reflection again. My pulse quickens—with fear, but with excitement, too.

"Did you make it home, my perfect Hunter?" I whisper.

I switch the overhead light off, plunging the room into darkness. The figure in the garden watches me through the glass, not moving. But he wears Sawyer's killing face.

I smile and turn the light back on, throwing myself back on display. The rain lashes against the glass, but my Hunter is unbothered by it. He just watches me, waiting.

I know which game he wants to play.

I lay back down on the couch and slide my panties off, dropping them on the floor beside me. Then I press my dress hem up around my thighs, trace my fingers along my skin. I pretend I don't know that Sawyer is out there, watching me, as I reach between my legs to massage my clit and feel the wetness already pooling in my cunt.

When I drop my head toward the window, all I can see is my reflection: my body splayed out, my legs spread. I arch my back and reach into my bra to squeeze at my breast, teasing my pebbled nipple. I can't see Sawyer out there, but I know he's watching the show I put on for him as I play at being the clueless victim in a horror movie, so intent on making herself come that she doesn't hear the killer creep inside.

I dip my fingers into my pussy, drawing out my arousal to slick against my clit. Heat builds in my core, and in the dark window, I watch myself writhe on the couch. My hips roll of their own accord, grinding down against my fingers. My legs tremble. I'm close—

Lightning floods the yard and the house both with white, hot light. In the flash, I see the garden, with all my half-drowned plants.

But my killer's gone.

As much as I want to keep going, I also want to keep playing the game. I snatch my hand away from pussy and sit up, pretending to be scared. "Who's there?" I call out, my voice breathy like an actress in a scary movie.

A thump from somewhere deep in the house. For a moment, I smile, breaking character; he left the guest bedroom window unlocked.

"I'll call the cops!" I cry out, skittering into the kitchen to grab the biggest chef's knife we have.

Footsteps, slow and heavy. He's in the hallway, but I know he likes it when I wait for him, my pussy wet and my hand clutching a knife.

I press my back up against the refrigerator door, brandishing the blade.

The footsteps draw closer.

And then he steps into the doorway. It doesn't matter how many times we play this game, the sight of him like this always sucks the air out of my lungs and floods my pussy with heat. He's wearing his leather jacket and dark jeans. And his mask, of course, stained with old blood.

He twists his Bowie knife in his gloved hand so it catches the track lighting and throws bright dots into the kitchen.

"Who are you?" I cry, holding up my own knife.

He steps into the kitchen, dripping rainwater all over the tile. *He* will be cleaning that later. But both of us have other things on our minds right now.

"I told you, I'll call the police." I put a breathy tremble into my voice, the way he likes. He steps closer to me, and I can feel him drinking me in, breathing in the scent of my skin, listening to the sound of my pulse.

"Mister, I don't—"

He doesn't let me finish. Before I fully realize what's happening, he's wrenched both of my hands over my head, his leg pressed up between my thighs. I whimper, grind my aching pussy down on his cold, rain-soaked jeans.

My knife clatters to the kitchen floor. His knife presses up against my throat.

"What are you going to do to me?" I whisper.

His eyes burn black behind his mask.

Then he shoves me down to my knees.

He holds me in place, one hand pressed against the top of my head and the other still holding the knife lazily against my throat. I know that on the surface, this looks exactly like what Scott did to me. But it's not the same. When it's Sawyer, the act transforms into something that makes me whole again.

"Put my cock in your mouth," he orders, his voice graveled and deep. Desire bursts in me like the lightning, and I fumble at the jean's fly, pulling the zipper down with excited, shaking hands. Sawyer presses the tip of the blade just a little deeper into my skin. I know what it means. *Hurry.*

His cock is rock-hard, heavy with lust—the way it always is after he kills. I wrap my lips around the head, feigning hesitation.

I'm punished with a small, delicate swipe of his knife. Blood pools and then streaks down my neck. I nearly come on the spot.

"Put my fucking cock in your fucking mouth."

This time, I do as he says, sliding him over my tongue, drawing as much of him into my throat as I can. I can't take him fully, not at this angle, but he tilts his hips a little, rocking forward until his swollen cockhead presses against the back of my throat.

"Suck," he orders.

I do. I've been waiting for this since he left, this sign that he's alive, that he made it through another kill unscathed. His cock tastes of rainwater and the salty tang of his sweat and precum, and I slide my mouth along his thick girth, trying to draw him in deeper. He holds the knife carefully, close enough that I can feel its cold steel but not so close there's any risk of him cutting me.

Sawyer groans and presses his hand more firmly against the top of my head, his fingers like a spiderweb. He rolls his hips just enough to make me whimper with need. My pussy is screaming to be filled—and with more than just my fingers.

But in this game, I can't ask for what I want. In this game, Sawyer *takes*.

He thrusts deeper into my mouth, nearly choking me. I groan, knowing the vibration of my throat drives him crazy. I'm rewarded with a sharp, rattling clatter as he drops the knife to the tile.

"Jesus, you're such a good little cocksucker." His fingers tighten against my head, gathering my hair into his fist. His praise makes me whimper even as I'm choking on his dick.

He lets out a loud, raspy sigh and yanks his cock out of my mouth, a thin, glistening string of spit connecting me to him in the process. Then he pulls me up by my hair, pressing me against the humming refrigerator. I gaze up at his blood-splattered mask, wet lips parted, my body burning for him.

"I know you want this," he growls. "With that little show you put on for me."

I whimper like it's not true—like I'm afraid, like I'm the first victim in one of those *Blood Raisers* movies. Sawyer shifts toward me, his cock digging into my thigh, and presses the rubber of his mask against the side of my face.

"You're going to come for me, aren't you?" He squeezes one of my breasts over my dress, running his thumb over my sharp nipple. "You want my big killer's cock in that tight pussy of yours?"

"No!" I cry, even though I'm currently humping his hip.

Sawyer chuckles, a raspy, ominous sound that drenches the inside of my thighs. Then he turns me around, pressing my cheek against the fridge. He knocks my legs apart and hikes my dress up around my waist, revealing my bare ass to the cool air of our house. I gasp out feigned protests, squirming my hips like I'm trying to escape. Sawyer grabs me hard, digging his fingers deep into my flesh, and forces me to go still.

He presses his cock against my entrance and laughs again.

"Oh, you are wet for me, my little victim." Then he thrusts hard, shoving his full length inside my cunt. I scream in pleasure, arching back into him.

He drops all pretense the second he's inside me. "Edie," he moans against the back of my neck, his breath warm on my skin. "Fuck, I needed this."

Then he fucks me, hard and fast and frantic. The sound of our slapping skin fills up the room. Sawyer grunts and bottoms out inside me, filling me so deeply that it's almost painful. Almost.

He shifts around behind me and then nuzzles his face against my neck, his mask gone. I tilt my head toward him, catching his mouth in a kiss, and he begins to thrust again, slamming me up against the refrigerator even as his tongue moves slow and sensual through my mouth. When he breaks the kiss, it's to bite my shoulder, notching his teeth into the scar he left the first time we fucked.

I'm desperate to come, and I reach down to touch my clit. But Sawyer knocks my hand away and takes over, rubbing it with his gloved fingers. It's always so much, having his hand on my clit and his cock in my cunt. The double sensation sends fire rising inside me, and I thrash against him, moaning and shaking.

"That's it," he rasps, quickening his pace. "That's it. I want to feel you come on my cock."

"I'm close," I gasp out. "So... close..."

"How about now?" And then he presses his thumb hard

against my clit at a very particular angle that completely unravels me. All the strength goes out of my body, and I'm wedged between Sawyer and the refrigerator, quaking with pleasure.

"Fuck me, but that feels fucking good." His thrusts sharpen, shudder, become more erratic. "God, I love making you come."

I thrust back against him, overwhelmed by the sensation of his slick, hard cock filling my overstimulated pussy. I know he's close, and I want to feel the heat of his cum inside me. "Spill in me," I gasp out. "I need your cum, Sawyer. I need it so fucking ba—"

I don't finish because he does, jittering his pelvis up against my ass and roaring out his pleasure. He sinks his fingers so deeply into my hips that I feel the delicious pinprick of his nails. I slump back against him, his wet jacket cool against my lust-heated skin.

Sawyer nuzzles me and wraps his arms around my waist. "I will never get tired of coming home to that," he murmurs.

I catch his gloved hand and braid our fingers together, then pull it up so I can brush kisses against his knuckles. He pulls me around and guides me out of the kitchen, into the hallway, and then our bedroom. I'm too boneless to protest.

He tosses me on the bed, and I giggle and I roll over to look up at him, flushed and happy. The storm's still raging outside, but it doesn't scare me anymore. Not with him here.

"I was so worried about you," I tell him. "So was Smoke."

Sawyer shrugs out of his jacket, then sits on the edge of the bed and pries off his boots, tossing them across the floor. Then he stretches out on his side, and I roll over to face him. He pulls off his gloves and brushes his fingers against my cheek.

"You don't need to worry about me," he says softly. "I'm a nightmare. Storms like this are where I belong."

Then he kisses me, the soft slow kisses he always gives me when he's happy. When I'm happy.

The mattress flutters; it's Smoke, jumping up to nudge against

Sawyer's hand. He pets her distractedly, but his eyes are fixed on mine.

"This was a perfect fucking day," he says.

I roll my eyes; only Sawyer would say that in the middle of a tropical storm. But honestly, now that he's home safe, now that he's made me come and planted his seed inside me, I can't disagree with him.

Smoke tightrope walks along Sawyer's legs and then curls herself into a ball on the ledge of his hips. Sawyer sighs like he's annoyed, but I know he likes it. I do, too, our entire family tangled together in the warmth and light of our little house by the sea.

A predator, a predator's pet, and his perfect prey.

The End

I hope you enjoyed *Bird on a Blade!* You can read an extended epilogue about Sawyer and Edie's travels to Florida by signing up for my newsletter here: rosebitterly.com/newsletter.

The Hunter's Heart series continues with Charlotte and Jaxon's story in *The Fire Went Wild.*

THE FIRE WENT WILD

COMING 12.13.24

CHARLOTTE

It's been three months since my best friend Edie disappeared.
The cops don't care, so if anyone's going to find her, it's me.

Until I make the mistake of stopping at a roadside diner in
southern Louisiana. Now, a serial killer has me chained up in his
crumbling old house in the middle of nowhere.

He says he's not allowed to kill me.

So what is he going to do to me instead?

JAXON

When I first saw her, I thought she was a victim, marked by my gods for the slaughter.

But then it becomes *very* clear that the gods have other things in mind for her. I just don't know what.

So I keep her alive.

And I try to keep my distance.

But there's more to this human woman than meets the eye—

And it might be enough to be my undoing.

Preorder Now

ABOUT THE AUTHOR

Rose Bitterly is a hopeless romantic who has been reading and writing scary stories since elementary school—imagine her excitement when she learned you could blend the two! Today, she writes dark, immersive horror romances featuring slashers and other monsters, all shot through with a hint of the occult. Visit her online at rosebitterly.com.

Never miss a new book! Sign up for Rose's mailing list and receive free bonus stories: https://www.rosebitterly.com/newsletter.